THE SIN EATER

PRAISE FOR *THE SIN EATER*

Lee McIntyre's riveting debut novel harnesses the raw emotional power of a father searching for his daughter to fuel a gripping thrill-ride through two very different worlds: a harsh and lawless biker subculture and an equally harsh and lawless state bureaucracy. The relationship at the story's heart—a male friendship forged in violence, secrecy, and honor—becomes the key to unlocking both treacherous worlds as the mystery deepens, twists, and finally explodes in a climax you won't see coming. Ingenious plot, crystal clear prose, and motorcycles blowing across the Pacific Northwest. Who could ask for more?

—**ELISABETH ELO**, author of *FINDING KATARINA M.* and *NORTH OF BOSTON*

Buckle up and prepare for a wild and unexpected ride. This unique and exciting road-trip thriller, with a twist around every corner, tests a loving father's determination and pushes family devotion to the limit. At once both gritty and heartbreaking, this page turner will surprise you — and has important things to say not only about corruption and greed, but the price of loyalty, and what it means to be a family.

—**HANK PHILLIPPI RYAN**, Nationally best selling and award-winning author of *THE MURDER LIST*

Lee McIntyre's THE SIN EATER *is compulsively readable. Think:* EASY RIDER *meets* THE FUGITIVE, *with more than a few utterly original twists and a mind-bending take on sin and culpability.*

—**HALLIE EPHRON**, *New York Times* bestselling author of *CAREFUL WHAT YOU WISH FOR*

A terrific debut! McIntyre ratchets up the suspense and takes us on a thrill ride that plumbs the depths of the human soul. How far would you *go to protect your child? A smart, sophisticated thriller that will engage your brain even as it scares the hell out of you.*

—**GARY BRAVER**, Bestselling and award-winning author of *ELIXIR* and *TUNNEL VISION.*

Lee McIntyre deftly navigates the gray areas between justice and the law. Hard-charging, harrowing, and ultimately hopeful, THE SIN EATER *is a powerful debut.*

—**JOSEPH FINDER**, *New York Times* bestselling author of *JUDGMENT*

A stunning debut. I couldn't put it down. You're going to wish you had a Tugg Morgan in your life.

—**CHRIS MOONEY**, International Bestselling Author of *THE MISSING* and the Darby McCormick series

Whip-crack pacing, an ingenious premise, and memorable characters are expertly interwoven in Lee McIntyre's propulsive debut thriller. THE SIN EATER *takes the reader on a hair-raising journey into the darkest heart of terror and mines the depths of the human condition in a way only a trained philosopher like McIntyre can bring to the page. Lee is a writer to watch!*

—**DANIEL PALMER**, USA Today bestselling author of *TRAUMA* and *THE FIRST FAMILY*

No one ever said life was fair—a lesson Adam Grammaticus and his lifelong buddy Tugg Morgan learned early and violently. In his debut novel, philosopher Lee McIntyre poses a series of questions that command our attention. If, like Adam, the powers that be maneuvered to take our good name, (legally) seize our child, jeopardize our marriage, ruin our job prospects and turn us into an outlaw, would we fight to preserve what we love? With Tugg's help, Grammaticus does and McIntyre straps us in for a wild ride. A page turner! I read it in two sittings.

—**LEN ROSEN**, Award-winning author of the Hénri Poincare novels and *THE KORTELISY ESCAPE*

THE SIN EATER *rockets us from the idyllic world of Lake Oswego suburban bliss to a rollicking fever dream of skinheads, bikers, and social workers. Lee McIntyre's unbridled storytelling is mesmerizing as is his use of the full range of Oregon's geography and culture.*

—**RAY DANIEL**, awarding-winning author of the Tucker mysteries

A high octane roller coaster ride that will keep you guessing until the very end.

—**WALT GRAGG**, Best Book Award-winning author of *THE RED LINE* and *THE CHOSEN ONE*

THE SIN EATER

Lee McIntyre

Aura Libertatis Spirat

THE SIN EATER

Braveship Books

www.braveshipbooks.com

Aura Libertatis Spirat

This is a work of fiction. Names, characters, places or incidents are either the product of the author's imagination or are used fictitiously, and any resemblance to actual persons, living or dead, business establishments, events or locales is entirely coincidental and beyond the intent of either the author or the publisher.

Cover Design by The Cover Collection

Book layout by Alexandru Diaconescu

www.steadfast-typesetting.eu

ISBN-13: 978-1-64062-088-9

Printed in the United States of America

For G.B.
Who knows why

Acknowledgements

There are so many people over the years who have helped me pursue my dream of writing fiction that I couldn't possibly name them all. Here I'd like to mention only a few without whom this particular book never would have happened.

To my friends (and beta readers) Peter Bahls and Lia Oppedisano, thank you so much for your excellent comments. I have so many friends through Mystery Writers of America that I'm afraid to begin listing them, for fear of leaving someone out; no other group has been so generous to me as a writer. Other friends, whom I met at Thrillerfest, convinced me that sometimes people who write about crime and mayhem are the nicest people in the world. Special thanks go to Leila Philip, who gave me the title for this book twenty years ago, without probably realizing it. Special thanks also to my writing teacher, Chris Mooney, whose extraordinary patience let me find my voice in an earlier manuscript. And to my friends Donna Bagdasarian, Jon Cullen, and Jess Dawson thank you for all of your wonderful support and advice over the years.

My penultimate debt for this book goes to my talented editor, Clair Lamb, who helped me in ways too numerous to mention. And to G.B. ... *above all.*

I give easement and rest now to thee, dear man.
Come not down the lanes or in our meadows.
And for thy peace I pawn my own soul.

Prayer of the last sin-eater

A social wasp will sacrifice itself when its colony is threatened.
A solitary wasp relies on its venom to hunt.

Biotropica

Portland, Oregon
August 1992

Adam Grammaticus saw the gang of teenagers coming down the sidewalk toward him and his best friend Tugg Morgan, but they were still too far away to know how much older they might be or even how many of them there were. Or if they were trouble.

"One."

"What was that?" Tugg said.

"I said 'one,' don't you remember?" Adam replied. "What's the sense of having a system if we're not going to use it?"

"There's a lot more of them than one, pal."

"*Threat* level one," Adam said. "Not one guy. Do you think I'm stupid?"

"I think you worry too much," Tugg said.

Easy for him to say. Although Adam was a year older, Tugg was built like a house and had in fact been skipped a grade because he had so completely demoralized every bully, jock and meathead in 7th grade that the school board thought he might find a little humility in high school. But after making friends with stick-thin Adam on the first day, Tugg had proceeded to cut a swath through all the assholes in 9th and 10th grade. Now sophomores, Adam had filled out only a little, but Tugg had just kept on growing. Adam supposed that there were worse things than having your own personal bodyguard at a tough school like Jefferson. But now Adam felt sick, because he counted four guys headed toward them, all at least seventeen or eighteen.

And they were skinheads.

"What's in the bag, boy?"

Tugg took the backpack from Adam and stepped out front, moving his body between Adam and the punks. He slung the pack over his shoulder and gave a neat little grin.

"I guess you'll just have to take it and find out."

The head guy's eyes flashed joyously. At least Adam thought he was the head guy. With their shaved skulls, ballpoint tattoos and uniform of black leather jackets, torn jeans, and Doc Martens steel-toed boots, they all looked the same. L.A. had Crips and Bloods, but in Portland, Oregon, they had Vietnamese gangs and skinheads. And right now he and Tugg were standing in the no-man's-land neighborhood right between them.

"I'm really going to enjoy fucking you up," said a guy in back. While the skinheads laughed at this little piece of wisdom, Adam flinched to see Tugg throw the bag at the head guy's face and follow up with a murderous punch directly under his jaw. Lights out. The guy fell like a redwood. They all stood stunned as his head bounced off the sidewalk.

"Get 'em!" one of the skinheads yelled.

Tugg grabbed the bag and tore out Adam's track spikes, which he put on each hand.

"Adam, I want you to run."

Two of the skinheads launched at Tugg, but he made them pay with a series of slashes from the hard metal cleats.

"I can't leave you."

"NOW!" Tugg screamed.

When the third skinhead moved in his direction, Adam took off.

Feet flying, hurdling over trashcans filled with branches and grass clippings, Adam saw the yards as a blur. He couldn't remember ever moving this fast, even with his coach screaming at him in the last leg of the 440. The big boots clomped behind him like a sledgehammer. Track was one thing; now he was running for his life.

The boots stopped, but Adam kept going.

Tugg is one tough shit. He'll be all right.

Adam slowed and wheeled around. Down the street, his friend straddled one of the punks on the ground, punching him in the face, with the other guy kicking Tugg in the back. The third guy hadn't reached them yet.

"Fuck him up! Fuck him up!" yelled the guy on the ground.

One of the kicks caught Tugg in the side of the head and he rolled onto the ground, just as the third skinhead arrived.

Adam's feet felt encased in cement as he watched the flurry of kicks.

He'll die if I don't go back there. And I'll die if I do. No—

Adam took off.

Back over the garbage cans, Adam grabbed a long tree branch and ran full power at the scrum.

Adam didn't remember screaming, but he must have, because all three skinheads stopped kicking and turned in his direction at the last second.

The branch didn't look that sharp. Maybe it was about speed or momentum or one of those things he'd learn in physics next year, but Adam watched the branch enter one ear and explode out the other from a perfectly shaved head.

Oh my God. It's not real. It's not real.

Adam smelled the leaves and coppery blood in the air as he snapped the branch and started whaling on the other two.

Adam....

He heard his name from somewhere far off as he swung the branch wildly, jabbing repeatedly at a bloody stomach. When the guy fell to his knees, the last skinhead ran.

"You! Wait!" Adam screamed.

Adam held the branch like a javelin and made his approach.

One, two, three, launch!

The stick wobbled a bit in the air, but sailed directly at the big white head as if it were a cue ball, bringing the guy crashing to his knees. Adam rushed over, grabbed the stick and pointed it at the guy's neck.

Adam!

He looked up the sidewalk at Tugg, who was getting up, bodies motionless all around him.

Adam! Siren!

He saw Tugg's mouth moving and heard his voice, but Adam couldn't quite put them together, like a hammer pounding a nail 100 yards away, out of sync.

Adam dropped the stick and ran back to Tugg. He picked up the gym bag.

"Adam, what the fuck did you do?" Tugg croaked. "You killed them."

"Only two." Adam's hands were shaking.

The siren grew louder.

"Only two?"

"What about the other guys?" Adam spit out.

"They're done."

"Are you sure we should leave them?"

"They're *done*!" Tugg yelled. "We've got to get out of here. Now!" Tugg grabbed Adam by the shoulder and pulled him along as they broke into a run down 15th Avenue, away from home. "Let's get to the park, then double back along Fremont," Tugg said. "We need to book."

The yards flew by again as Adam's feet fell into a rhythmic pattern. Tugg jagged right and Adam followed, down the cross street toward Irving Park.

Tugg didn't run track, but he was damn fast when he had to be. Adam breathed through his nose and exhaled from his mouth as he paced himself to keep up.

"Almost there," Tugg said over his shoulder. "What the fuck were you thinking?"

Three blocks away. The sirens had stopped. The cops must have found the bodies.

Tugg pulled Adam flat against a fence and crouched down. "Give me a second," Tugg said, wheezing. "Wind."

"One more block, shouldn't we just go?"

"I said, give me a second. We're going to make it, okay? I'm not going to let anything happen to you." Tugg's breath grew even and he nodded his head toward the park.

"I think we should just walk from here. Less suspicious," said Adam.

"Good idea." After half a block Tugg looked over. "You hurt?"

"No, I don't think so. You?"

Tugg shook his head. "Nothing I can't live with. But it sure could have been. Thanks."

"No problem."

"No, seriously man. I owe you. That was about to go sideways."

"It looked like it already had. But you'd have done the same for me. In fact, you already did. Four guys?"

No longer out of breath, Tugg still hesitated. "I was *trying*, man. You know? I thought I had it handled."

They were on the path to the park. Deep shade from the towering fir trees made it seem later than it was, but dusk was approaching.

"We'll wait by the slides. After dark we can cut through the backyards and we're home. My mom won't be home till eight."

"My stepdad probably won't be home at all," Adam said.

"Stay over again then."

"Sure," Adam said. He hesitated, then continued. "Four guys is too many, Tugg. No one could do that. Everybody needs backup."

"I sure as shit did today."

The light shifted to a silver grey. Tugg bent down under the slides and sat cross-legged on the wood chips. He looked at his watch.

Adam sat next to him. His hands had calmed somewhat, but he was still shivering.

Tugg looked at him. "Can I ask you something?"

"Sure."

"Why did you do it? What made you go apeshit?"

Adam swallowed dryly.

"I couldn't run forever," Adam said. "I didn't plan it. It's just when I saw you, I had no choice. I owe you more than that."

"You don't owe me shit. Never have."

"Not sure about that," Adam smiled. "But that goes both ways, then."

"Not hardly even close."

"Cut that shit out. We're in this together. Nobody owes anybody then. I mean it."

Tugg looked at his watch again. "It'll be dark in another ten minutes. Get ready to go."

Adam stood up in a crouch because they were still under the slides. He peeked out to make sure no one was coming.

"Before we go back, can you promise me something?" Adam said.

"Sure. Anything."

"Never tell anyone what happened here today, okay? No one. Not your mom. Not your wife if you get married someday. Not even when you get old, all right? This thing has to die with me. It's too big." Adam looked at the ground and sucked in a shuddery breath. "I can't believe I really did it."

"Yeah okay," Tugg said, "But you got something wrong there. What you just said."

"What?" Adam said, sucking in mucus.

"This thing dies with *both* of us."

Chapter 1

"Hold still, honey. We're almost done."

"The water's cold again, Daddy. Can you warm it up?"

Adam Grammaticus smiled at the sparkling face of his three-year-old daughter, Emma. She was working her mouth open and shut like a fish, in a mock attempt at teeth chattering, and had her knees pulled up to her chest in the far end of the bright yellow tub.

His wife, Kate, sat in the bathroom doorway in her wheelchair, smiling.

Adam dropped the plastic Halloween bucket and scooted on his knees over to the faucet. He turned on the tap. "Keep back from the hot water and keep your eyes closed. You've still got soap in your hair."

"I know, Dad."

Adam repositioned his towel on the lip of the tub and watched the plastic toys bob in the churning water.

"Hey Dad, BWAA HAA HAA!" Emma put her hands in front of her eyes and made an elaborate gesture of yanking them off, even though Adam could see that her eyes were still shut.

"Very funny. Almost warm again."

"You remember the time you got soap in my eyes?"

"Well, I remember the time that *you* got soap in your eyes. That's why you have to keep your eyes closed."

"I know, Dad. I'm doing it. I'm not a baby anymore."

Adam looked over his shoulder and gave Kate a quick smirk. Same beautiful hair. Same radiant smile. For a moment, Adam thought he saw the woman that Emma would become. What had he done to be so lucky?

"Yeah? Then why are we using baby shampoo?" he said, turning back to his daughter. "Again? Huh?"

Emma's cheeks were all scrunched up, in an inscrutable frown of contempt and whimsy. Apparently some questions didn't deserve an answer.

Adam wondered how many more years he still had for Daddy to be perfect. Or was it Emma who was perfect? At least they could hope. The doctor had warned them that Kate's multiple sclerosis might be passed down, but they had refused to get the test. Some things you just didn't want to know.

He turned off the tap and mixed the water together with his hands, then scooted back and filled the plastic bucket.

"Do you want it slow or fast?"

"Fast is okay."

"Hang on, then." Adam put his left hand over Emma's face and splashed the entire bucket over her head in one gesture. "Was that okay?"

"Yes," Emma sputtered, rubbing her eyes with tiny fists. When the water stopped dripping from her hair, she opened her eyes and looked around the bathroom.

"There's Mom!" Emma chirped. "There's my bucket. There's the ducks."

"What else can you see?" Kate said.

Emma gave a delighted grin. "There's the light. There's the towel. There's the heater thing I'm not supposed to touch."

"Okay," Adam said. "Stand up."

Emma stood and Adam wrapped her in a thirsty white towel, then lifted her out of the tub and grabbed a second towel, which he draped over her head.

"I can't see anything now."

Adam briskly rubbed the soft brown curls and wiped her ears, then took the towel off her head.

"Oh, there's Dad."

"Ho, last place as usual. Behind the bucket and the ducks. I guess I don't count for much around here."

Emma reached out a pudgy little hand and put it solemnly against Adam's face. "Daddy, you're so handsome you could win a boy contest."

Kate and Adam both erupted in laughter, followed, a few seconds later, by an incredulous Emma.

"Adam, can you go back in and get my sweater? The sun just went behind the trees."

Adam lowered Kate into her comfortable chair out on the deck, adjusted her pillows and hustled back through the screen door.

"It's not on your wheelchair," he called out from the living room.

"Look in the backpack."

"Found it," he said, emerging triumphantly. "Do you want it now? Half the candles are already out, and the food's going to get cold."

"Just lay it on my lap, sweetheart. Thanks."

Adam relit the candles and rearranged the plates on the little iron table. A cool breeze blew off Lake Oswego and the water danced like a thousand gold coins from the setting sun. Adam was a long way from the Cedar Shade trailer park in Northeast Portland, where he'd grown up with his stepdad after his mother died when he was twelve. After that, he'd taken off back east for college and never looked back. Twenty years later he was home, living in a house in the richest part of Portland. Not bad.

"Is it okay?" he said.

"It's perfect," Kate replied. "But the dining room would've been okay. I'm sorry about the chair."

"We'll get the door widened this summer," he said. "There are bound to be a couple of bumps in the road. The new normal, huh? At least the ramp works — sort of."

Kate gave him a smile. God, she was gorgeous. That same smile had drawn him hither at the Halloween Dance sophomore year in college and, no matter how much she changed physically, Adam knew that he would never see Kate as anything but the vibrant, kind-hearted girl he had fallen in love with. She had no patience with pity, so Adam had never shown her any, but the truth was that sometimes he felt *he* was the one who needed help. Everyone had weaknesses. And secrets. Adam saw in Kate a strength that he knew he did not possess. And he also knew a secret: he needed her more than she needed him.

"You didn't have to carry me out here," Kate said. "It's gorgeous out and you're sweet, but I would've been fine in the chair. For now."

"I told you, I'll carry you anywhere you need to go."

"If I get my way, that won't be necessary. I'm going to get back on the canes if it kills me."

"If anyone can, it's you." Adam scooted his chair back and jumped to his feet. "But for now, prepare to be served." He draped a napkin over one arm and removed the serving lid with a flourish. "Voila! No more duck, okay? I learned my lesson. This is just plain old chicken."

"It's perfect."

"Do you want me to cut it for you?"

"I'm not totally incompetent, sweetheart. I can manage. Eat your food."

Dinner at home probably wasn't what Kate had planned for their twelfth anniversary. Then again, it was nice just to have things back to normal. Or close enough. Kate had been fighting her illness ever since college. Until recently, she'd actually been pretty lucky.

"Just like it's always been, there'll be good days and bad," the doctor had said. But the bad days seemed to be accumulating at an alarming clip. Short of quitting his job, Adam didn't know what they were going to do until Emma started preschool next year.

Then they'd found Rachel.

Kate stabbed a piece of chicken and dragged it through the mushroom sauce. "Mmmm, this is good."

"Made it myself — no help!"

"Are you sure?" Kate looked at him skeptically. "Rachel didn't even help you get it started?"

"Nope." Adam shook his head. "There are some things I can do myself."

"I know. You're always taking on too much. You make me feel guilty with all you do."

"Hey, it could have been either one of us, right? For better or worse? You'd do the same for me."

"You know I would."

"And it'll be easier now that Rachel can add some hours. That's a load off, huh?"

It was. On both of them. As Chief Information Officer at Tektel, Adam was on the fast track through the "silicon forest." Even so, every perk brought a trade-off. Yes, you could take off in the middle of the day if it was an emergency. But how would it look to his staff if he kept having emergencies? Hal, the CEO, had been nothing but understanding about the clusterfuck of details Adam had to deal with when Kate had collapsed, and had given short-term family leave willingly. But now that Kate was back from the rehab hospital, Emma had a nanny, and the rest of the arrangements were in place, it went without saying that there had better be no more holes in the safety net.

Adam hoped not. Rachel was weird, that was for sure, but ultimately — in the month they'd used her so far — she'd proven to be completely reliable.

Forget the jet-black dyed hair, the Goth-girl makeup, the nose ring, and the tattoos she didn't try very hard to hide under her slim-fitting black tank tops. Rachel was so damned good with Emma that they'd looked past all that. They'd even defended her when friends asked, "Are you *sure* you can trust her?" Adam knew what they meant. Rachel was blunt to the point of rudeness when dealing with adults. But he also knew that just a few of those well-meaning questions were based on concern about the full lips, translucent skin, and hard-bodied figure that lay beneath the Goth-girl facade. That was an easy one. Kate was and always would be the only woman in his life.

But trust Rachel with Emma? Like he'd trust the protective instinct of a German Shepherd.

"Emma's got a bald spot and a scar just above her hairline over her right ear. What's up with that?" Rachel had asked on her second day of work.

"She had an accident when she was a baby," Adam had answered.

Rachel just stared at Adam and then Kate.

"She fell off the changing table," Kate said.

"Who was changing her? You?"

Kate had flushed red, but Adam knew it would be okay. They had talked about this very issue before they decided to hire Rachel and both had vowed to live with it. Rachel didn't mean any harm. She was just clueless.

"No," Kate had replied. "Actually, it was Adam. That was two years ago, just after we'd moved here. I could walk back then, but I couldn't stand up and use my hands at the same time because of the canes. I always changed her on the floor. Adam used the changing table."

Rachel was silent.

"I just looked away for a second." Adam didn't have to justify himself to the nanny, but maybe he was still trying to justify something to himself. Or to Kate. "I thought I heard Kate fall in the other room. By the time I turned back, Emma was on the floor."

Rachel continued her silence.

Kate took over the narrative. "We called the ambulance and it turned out all right. It's nothing for you to worry about, okay? She had some swelling and then she had to have an operation to relieve the pressure. Of course we were worried, but there wasn't any permanent damage. We did all the tests. More than enough tests. She's fine now."

"Bet you're glad." Rachel had turned back to Adam.

"Of course, Rachel. We're all glad. But it's nothing for you to worry about. We know about the bald spot and the scar."

"Okay, just so you know," Rachel said. "Nothing like that will ever happen when Emma's with me."

"That's great," Kate said.

Adam and Kate shared a telepathic glance across the room.

What is this girl's problem?

Kate put down her fork.

"Was that Emma? Did you hear something?" The sun was down, but Adam could still see Kate's face by the candlelight.

"It's 8:30. I put her down half an hour ago. She should be asleep."

Kate struggled in her seat and the sweater fell on the deck.

Adam bent down to pick it up and replaced it on her lap. "I'll go check on her."

As Adam walked across the living room, he heard feet scuffling on the front porch. Just as he looked through the peephole, the doorbell rang. *Now what?*

"Hello?" Adam said. "May I help you?" He flipped on the porch light and saw a small, dark-haired woman accompanied by two burly cops through the screen.

"Are you Adam Grammaticus?" the woman said, holding up an ID badge. "My name is Lisa Castro and I'm from Multnomah County, Child Protective Services. We're following up on a complaint we received from Ms. Rachel Norwood. She says she used to work for you?"

"She still does," Adam said. "What in the world is this about?"

"Are your wife and daughter home? Do you think we might come in?"

Adam looked back toward the deck and saw Kate struggling to put on her sweater.

Chapter 2

Adam settled Kate into her wheelchair in the living room, as the social worker and cops pretended not to watch. It was galling to have them standing there, and Adam was anxious to get this conversation started — and ended — as soon as possible. He couldn't just leave Kate on the deck, and he'd be damned if he'd invite them out to their private retreat. The sun was down, and the food was ruined.

Let's get this conversation over with.

"We're sorry to have intruded on your dinner, Mr. and Mrs. Grammaticus. It's protocol not to announce our visits," the social worker said.

"Is it protocol to bring the police with you, too?" Adam asked. He looked back and forth between the cops: one black, one white, both built like offensive linemen and seeming content to remain silent.

"It's at our discretion. Is your daughter home?"

"She's sleeping," Kate said. "In her bedroom. Where else would she be? Can you just tell us what this is about?"

The trio sat on the couch and Adam took a chair near his wife. She gave him a horrified look and Adam shook his head. A wave of panic passed over him as Castro began to speak.

"We received a report of parental abuse concerning your daughter Emma from Rachel Norwood, whom I understand is her nanny."

"What?" Adam said. "That's the most ridiculous thing I've ever heard. Rachel has only been with us for a month. She's mistaken."

The social worker looked back and forth between Adam and Kate. "The report was pretty specific. I'm prepared to go into detail about the allegations, but tonight is just the first visit. There are a lot of steps from here. I'll need to see Emma tonight. Then there will be a few more random visits. If necessary, things will proceed to an inquiry before a judge and, if warranted, removal of the child from the home."

"You must be kidding," Kate said. "What in the world did Rachel say?"

"I know what this is about," Adam said. "You can check the hospital records. Emma fell two years ago. We had a follow-up with a social worker when we left Doernbecher Hospital, but it was nothing. It was an accident. When Rachel saw Emma's scar, she had a lot of questions." Adam was breathing hard and fighting a familiar pull of desperation. Cops. Sirens. He was a boy again with Tugg, peeking out from under the slides.

"This isn't about a scar, Mr. Grammaticus," Castro said. She looked down at the file folder on her lap and flipped a couple of papers. "When did you say Emma had this accident?"

Kate waved her hands spastically in front of her face. "What did Rachel say we *did?*"

"Okay, let me read from the report. Ms. Norwood said that last week when she was playing with Emma, she spontaneously said, 'Daddy hurt me with a sharp tool.' Does that sound familiar to you, Mr. Grammaticus? Can you tell us what Emma might have been referring to?"

Adam's limbs went dead. "A sharp tool? What sharp tool? I never did anything like that to Emma in my whole life. Are you sure that's what she said?"

The police officers were staring at him.

Castro nodded. "Yes, that's a verbatim quote from the report. Apparently after this Ms. Norwood continued to play with Emma, to see if she would say anything else. Good instinct. According to Ms. Norwood, Emma was quite consistent in her story. She used the word 'sharp tool' more than once."

"That sounds like something somebody told her to say," Kate said.

"That's possible," Castro replied. "That's why we need to interview Emma tonight to make our own assessment. I know she's sleeping, but it's absolutely necessary that we speak to her before anyone else does. Can we see her?"

"Sharp tool," Adam said, leaning forward. "What the hell. Rachel's claiming that I attacked my daughter with a knife or something?"

The white cop leaned forward.

"We don't know what happened," Castro said. "Emma's description covers a lot of possible ground. May I ask who normally cuts her nails?"

"I do," Adam said.

"And combs her hair?"

"I do," Adam said.

"I have multiple sclerosis," Kate said. "Adam has to do all of the childcare these days. I just can't."

"For how long?" Castro said.

"The last two months."

Castro checked her notes again. "Ms. Norwood felt that the abuse was recent. Within the last few weeks or so. And Emma specifically identified Mr. Grammaticus."

Adam stood. "Rachel is a fucking liar."

"Please sit down, sir," said the black cop.

"I'll be goddamned if I'll sit." Adam glared at Castro, but kept his hands carefully at his sides. "Have you taken a good look at your witness? Does she look reliable to you? Now look at us. I've got a good job. We live in Lake Oswego, for Christ's sake. How many social service calls do you get from this zip code?" Adam was breathing hard. He knew that he was out of line, but he stood absolutely still and kept glaring at Castro.

"Abuse doesn't happen only in poor families, Mr. Grammaticus," Castro said. "But as I said, this is just the first visit. There's a lot we don't know yet. I think we're done talking for now. Can I please see Emma?"

Angry tears started to course down Kate's cheeks. "Do you think a good mother would allow you to wake her daughter and ask all these ugly questions in the middle of the night? Do you have to do this right now?"

"Yes, I'm afraid so. We have to interview Emma before her testimony is tainted by other conversations." Castro and the cops all turned their heads simultaneously toward Adam. "But I understand your concern about startling her. Maybe you and I could go in together and leave the men here in the living room? You can be present during the interview, as long as you don't interfere. Otherwise I'm going to have to ask you to wait here as well."

"I can't fit my chair through the doorway to her bedroom," Kate choked out. "It's new. We don't have everything fixed yet. Adam, can you carry me?"

Castro shook her head. "We can do the interview at another location, but I expect you'd probably want to avoid that. Perhaps you could call her from the hallway?"

"Can't I just go in?" Adam said.

"No," Castro said. "We'll try it from the hallway. Mrs. Grammaticus can watch and hear everything from there. I won't go into the room until Emma is completely awake and comprehends what's going on."

"How in the world could she comprehend what's going on?" Kate said.

Castro got up from her seat and pointed down the hallway. "Is it this way? Do you need me to push you, Mrs. Grammaticus?"

"No, I can manage," Kate sniffled. She grabbed the toggle and buzzed across the living room, cutting in front of Castro as she sped down the hallway. "Emma? Sweetie? Can you wake up for a minute?"

Adam could hear the desperation in his wife's voice. He wanted to go to her, but when he took a step forward, the white cop shook his head. When the women disappeared, Adam sat down and buried his face in his hands.

Chapter 3

Even though the cops and social worker had gone, the air hung with their presence. After half an hour of singing and soothing, Emma had finally gone back to sleep — in Adam and Kate's bed — while they huddled down the hallway in the living room, speaking in whispers.

"Is Emma all right?" Adam asked.

"I think so. But you heard her. How would you feel finding a stranger in your room in the middle of the night?"

"So what did she say?"

"Nothing really. Nothing about a tool, that's for sure. I think Rachel is making the whole thing up."

"So was Castro convinced?"

Kate let out a sniffle and rubbed her nose with the back of her hand. "Probably not. She didn't ask her directly about any cutting, but she did ask whether Daddy ever hurt her. Emma said no."

"So that's good?"

"Not really. She said no to everything. 'Do you have a nanny? Does Daddy brush your hair? Do you like your room?' She didn't get much out of her." Kate's voice broke into a sob and she slumped forward in her chair. "She'll probably be back."

Adam leaned forward and hugged Kate. He kissed the top of her head rhythmically as he held her hands and looked out at the ruined feast on the deck.

"Adam?" Kate said softly. "What should we do?"

He waited until she looked up at him. "Maybe we should take Emma and run."

Kate frowned with her mouth open. "What are you talking about? How can we do that? *Why* would we do that? I'm in a wheelchair, Adam. How far do you think we'd get? And what are we running from if nothing happened? We need to fight this."

Adam *was* prepared to fight. There was no doubt about that. *No one* was going to take his child. But this wasn't about him, it was about Emma. Yes, he needed to clear his name. But he also needed to make sure that Emma didn't go someplace where she would be surrounded by strangers and bad things could happen to her.

A terrible thought occurred to him. "Kate! Kate!"

"Quiet, Adam. You'll wake her."

"You don't suppose somebody *else* hurt Emma, do you? Could Rachel have done something? Maybe she brought her to someone's house and they hurt her. What the hell is this about a sharp tool unless there was one? Maybe Rachel hurt Emma and now she's trying to cover it up." Adam was furious. "I will fucking kill her. I will take her life with my own hands. Fucking Goth punk with all her piercings. She's probably got plenty of sharp tools around her apartment."

"Adam, calm down. Before the social worker left, she turned on the overhead light and made Emma take off her pajamas. She looked her all over. Everywhere. That's what all the crying was about. There's not a mark on her. She found the scar and the bald spot, but that's it. Emma's fine."

"So you're saying Rachel didn't do anything?"

"I don't trust her, of course not. She's definitely lying about something. *Someone* told Emma to say that thing about the sharp tool. Or maybe that's what Rachel is lying about. I don't think Rachel actually hurt Emma — physically, anyway. But she's never going to go near my child again."

Adam sat back down and took Kate's hands again. "Who can we call? Tonight? They could come back in the morning and take her. I want to know what we should do. Now."

"Maybe I can call Elaine. She's a lawyer," Kate said.

"It's two in the morning in Boston."

"So? We stayed up way later than that in college. The freshman roommate thing, remember? It lasts for life. After my parents died, she was all I had until you came along. You've got Tugg and I've got Elaine."

"Tugg was high school, but I see your point."

"Elaine does criminal defense. Maybe she'll know something about this. Help me find my cell."

* * *

The wind was cold out on the deck. Adam resisted the temptation to clear the dishes and just *do something*. He forced himself to wait. He could see Kate talking animatedly through the sliding glass door, but couldn't hear a word. Didn't want to. He welcomed the chance to be alone and think.

Adam listened to the towering fir trees rubbing against one another and the small wind-whipped waves lapping the shoreline. What made wind so much more exciting in the dark? The house was small, but perfect for them. Great view. Great schools. Great neighbors. What did any of that matter now? You could make every right decision in your life, and trouble would still find you. Kate in a wheelchair. Child Protective Services at the door. For what?

Sometimes Adam wondered if every bad thing in his life was some sort of karmic punishment for what he'd done when he was fifteen. He'd never paid for that. Maybe he was paying now. The temptation to tell Kate had been overwhelming over the years, but he'd held fast to his promise. Kate might be the love of his life, but Tugg had seniority.

Adam saw Kate waving for him to come in.

"What did she say?"

"Just what you'd expect. She said don't even think of running. They'd catch you and you'd never see Emma again. Follow the process. And get a local lawyer. She said she'll send us some names in the morning, but there's nothing more we can do tonight."

Adam paced up and down in front of the sliding glass door.

"She's asking us to trust the process, but I don't," he said. "You saw what they did to us tonight. They could come back and take Emma anytime."

"But they'd have to have a reason, wouldn't they? And if they'd had one, they would've taken her tonight. Wouldn't they need more than what Rachel's said so far?"

"What if Rachel says something else? Are you willing to wait around for that?"

"Not really, but what else can we do? We'll get a lawyer in the morning."

Adam stopped moving.

"I need another perspective on this. I need to call Tugg."

"What can he do?"

"He's my best friend, Kate. You just talked to Elaine, I need to talk to Tugg."

"You haven't talked to him in over a year. Do you even know where he is?"

"Of course I do," Adam said. "Wherever he is, he's got his cell. He has to get off the motorcycle sometime."

"Okay, but please make me a promise?"

Adam just looked at her.

"Don't do anything without checking with me first. It's not that I don't trust you, it's just that I don't want you two deciding to do something that's risky for us. For Emma. You know how Tugg gets. Once he hears you're in trouble, it'll be Defcon Three."

"He's my best friend."

"A friend will help you move. Tugg would help you move a body." A tiny smile cracked her face. "But let's hope it doesn't come to that."

"Dude, how's it going? Long time."

The sound of Tugg's voice was like coming home. No matter how long it'd been since they last talked, they always picked up right where they'd left off. With men, your best friend could be someone you hadn't seen in ten years. Why didn't women understand that?

Kate had finally settled down in their bed next to Emma, and both were fast asleep. Adam had shut the door and returned to the living room.

"Tugg, it's good to hear your voice. Where are you?"

"Oh, you know. Somewhere north of Kingman. Beautiful night. Don't even need the tent, so I'm looking at the stars."

"Sounds great. Are you alone?"

"As alone as I'll ever be, talking on a cell phone that's trackable and allegedly not monitored by the National Security Agency. How about you? Kate and Emma okay?"

Adam hesitated. "No. That's why I'm calling."

He had to steel himself for what came next. Kate was right about Tugg. Tugg had probably always had the tendencies. Maybe it had just gotten worse since what happened to them as kids. But after that whole thing in the Air Force, any tendencies were set in cement. For Tugg, there was no bright line between friendship and samurai. Loyalty took precedence over consequences. Maybe that was why he had so few friends.

When Tugg got out of military prison and got his papers, he had just started riding – moving — always alone. "Better than Zoloft and a chaser of Jack Daniel's," Tugg always said. Adam wished that he could help him, but for the last two years that had meant never asking Tugg to do anything that might set him back or set him off. The doctor had said not to push him. Now he had no choice.

"Share it, brother," Tugg said. "What do you need?"

"Nothing right now. Just some advice."

"About?"

"Well, this is where it gets complicated."

Adam held back at first, but finally poured out the whole story about Kate's recent physical deterioration, the wheelchair, the new nanny, and the visit from social services.

"Bitchy Goth girl lied, huh?" Tugg said. "Do we know why yet?"

"Not a clue. And we're worried she might keep on lying. That's the problem. We don't know what to do."

"Damn few people would."

"So, Tugg. What would *you* do?"

"You want me to come up there?"

"No, thanks. We've got our hands full right now. I'm just asking for advice."

"So who you going to have watch Emma while all this is going on? You got no nanny. You got no family."

"You're my family."

"Damn straight. Let me come up then. The 'guilty until proven innocent' crowd don't trust you, and Kate can't do it. Yours truly folds a mean diaper."

Adam laughed. "Emma's been out of diapers for a while now, Tugg. But thanks. I can just see you sitting on the floor playing Thomas the Tank Engine in all that leather."

"You're worried what CPS would think of me. I respect that. But the offer stands. I'm there if you need me."

Adam felt a catch in his throat. "You're a good man. For now, just tell me what you'd do. If you were me, how would you handle this?"

Adam heard Tugg take a drag on his cigarette. He imagined a lone figure standing on a windswept plain.

"I'd snatch her and run."

"Kate's friend is a lawyer," Adam said. "She told us not to."

Adam heard Tugg inhale, then blow out again. "She has no idea what's coming."

Chapter 4

After three days at the house, with Adam and Kate on their phones practically non-stop, even a trip downtown to the lawyer's office felt like an outing. Lisa Castro hadn't come back and Rachel had apparently made no new allegations, but they were determined to get ahead of this. Meeting with the lawyer was the next step.

"Can you swing your legs out, or should I just pull them?"

The taxi driver sat frozen in his seat, probably a little pissed that the meter wasn't still running, while Adam negotiated the complex set of arrangements. He had to get Kate turned ninety degrees so that she could get out of the back seat and into the wheelchair that was waiting on the curb of S.W. 6th Avenue. Forget parking downtown on a day like this; Adam had wanted to make it as easy as possible. *This was easy?*

Bless their neighbor Mrs. Nguyen for agreeing to watch Emma for the morning. And bless Kate for being such a good sport about the lawyer not being willing to make a home visit and insisting that they just come see him, like everyone else.

"Just let me turn a little bit. Give me a minute," Kate said.

"How about if you just lie down on the back seat and I pull you out?"

"Maybe you could give everyone on the sidewalk a camera so they could take a picture of my coochie while you're at it, Adam. Shit. Just give me a minute." Kate scooted her bottom back and forth in a dozen little movements, like a new driver trying to recover from a blown parallel parking job, but she finally got herself turned. "Now just lift me out and put me in the chair."

"Okay, sorry about that."

"We'll get this with practice. The new normal, right?" Kate clasped her hands around Adam's neck and he gently lifted her out of the cab and sat her down into the wheelchair.

After making sure that the brakes were locked and she was belted, Adam slammed the car door, paid the driver through the window, and turned back to Kate. "Welcome to our little adventure in litigation."

"We're not there yet," Kate said. "This chair's got no motor, so you're going to have to be gallant and drive me."

"I can do that, m'lady." Adam unhitched the brakes and rolled toward the building.

What a nightmare. The doctor had told them that stress would make Kate's symptoms worse, and what could be more stressful than what they'd just been through and what they had in front of them? Stress over the child abuse allegations was bad enough, but there were other factors too. Stress over the effect that all this might have on Emma. Stress over who would watch her now that Rachel was out of the picture. Adam had called work and made up a story about Kate having a relapse, so he could buy himself another week. But how long might it be before the allegations went public and they had *that* worry on their hands, too?

And of course there was the plain fact that even before any of this had happened, Kate had been upset over her recent physical deterioration. What a change from the life she'd been living when Adam first met her. Goalie of the field hockey team. Track in the spring. Kate had been determined to get as much out of her body as she could before it failed her. After college, Kate had turned her fierce intelligence and enormous heart toward helping some of the truly disadvantaged in society, even while she became progressively more disadvantaged herself. After twelve years as a Victim Witness Advocate at the DA's office in Boston, she'd jumped at the chance to become the new resource coordinator for Families in Transition when Adam got his new job in Portland. Now Kate could make even more of a difference in the lives of people who were undergoing some of the worst "transitions" that a family could make: losing a child to violence, preparing to support a family when the primary breadwinner was headed to prison, applying for social services after a catastrophic illness. Kate had seen real suffering up close for so long that Adam knew she wouldn't buckle. In fact, what had happened to them was really pretty small when compared to some of the horror stories Kate had to deal with on a daily basis. They had the resources and connections to do whatever it took. It was different, however, when it happened to you.

People whooshed by in the revolving door at the front of the building. Adam pressed the blue button and watched the adjacent glass door gently swing open in front of Kate's wheelchair. When they got to the elevator, he remembered to pull her to the side, so she wouldn't block the doors.

The change in Kate's physical condition was heartbreaking to watch. She could move her hands well enough to use the phone and take notes on the computer, but she still couldn't walk, and needed Adam's help every time she used the bathroom. That'd been fine over the last few months, while he was home, but what would they do next? *One thing at a time.* They'd both done yeoman work on the phones so far, with Kate on her cell in the bedroom and Adam on the landline in the living room, battling away at all they had before them: finding a good lawyer, looking for a new nanny for Emma, looking for a home health aide to be with Kate during the day if and when Adam went back to work, and God knows what else Kate had been preoccupied with on the Internet and phone over the last three days. Adam had heard her talking to colleagues at work, who sounded ready to move the whole office out to Lake Oswego to look after her round-the-clock. They could use the help, but how to accept it without letting everyone know that Adam had been accused of child abuse? He'd also heard her crying on the phone with Elaine a couple of times. Best not to interfere with that.

Maybe I should call Tugg again, too.

The elevator door opened on a suite of offices with floor-to-ceiling glass walls in the hallway, the reception area, and the conference room, all the way to the outside of the building, so that they could see the spectacular views of downtown Portland and the Willamette River.

"Elaine says this guy is the best in Portland. She went to law school with someone from the Governor's office in Salem who recommended him. He does a lot of work with government agencies and he's an expert on child welfare issues. Very well connected, but not many private clients. We're lucky to get him."

"Except he doesn't make house calls," Adam said. "And I can see why. He probably bills $500 an hour."

"His paralegal said $550 when she set up the appointment. But whatever it takes, right?"

"Absolutely," Adam said, tightening his jaw. "Whatever it takes."

They rolled up to the receptionist's desk.

* * *

Steve Carnap's office had an even more impressive view than the reception area. And he was pretty impressive himself. Tall and lean, he had a kind face and watery eyes, and he had already moved the chairs so that Kate would have a free path to sit next to Adam.

Carnap sat in a wing chair with his back to the view.

"I just got off the phone with CPS half an hour ago," he said. "There's been some progress on your case, but it requires a commitment on your part to cooperate. If you're willing to do that, then I think this whole matter might be cleared up relatively quickly. Within a matter of weeks."

Adam looked at Kate, who was smiling, then swung back to Carnap, who was not.

"What do they want us to do?" Adam said.

Carnap hesitated. "You're not going to be crazy about this, but it's the best path forward. I've seen it before and I think we can work with this."

"Work with what?" Adam said.

Carnap looked directly at Adam. "They want you to acknowledge the abuse."

"What?"

"They said that they would drop the investigation if you were willing to enroll in parenting classes and acknowledge the abuse. The feeling is that willingness to acknowledge past abuse is a vital part of demonstrating parental fitness, which is what they need to determine in order to protect Emma's welfare. Without that, they're worried that any abuse might continue."

Adam felt as if he'd been hit by a bomb.

"This is bullshit," Adam said. "I didn't hurt Emma. What kind of a Catch-22 is this? If I lie and say I abused her, they'll let us keep her? But if I tell them I'm innocent — which is the truth — then they'll take her away?"

"I know it's awful, but that's how it works."

Kate shook her head. "You want Adam to confess to a felony? How can that help us?"

"Well, let me be clear about something." Carnap cleared his throat. "You hired me to represent you in making sure that Emma didn't get taken into custody by CPS. Nothing else. You might want to get the opinion of a criminal defense attorney for Adam's sake if you decide to go this route. My retainer only covers the CPS matter. And I'm not a criminal attorney."

"Twenty-five thousand dollars is a lot of money," Adam said.

Kate shifted in her seat.

"Indeed it is," Carnap said, "but if you don't admit the abuse, things could get protracted. Of course, you don't want to decide such an important question on the basis of fees, but even so, on the narrow question of the custody matter alone, that would probably be the cleanest route."

Adam could feel the blood pulsing in his ears. "So I have to confess to something I didn't do, based on one allegation from a twenty-year-old kid who's a liar. With no physical evidence. Is that about it?"

"They're worried about the incident two years ago, too," Carnap added. "That came up repeatedly. It seems that you were put on a state child abuse registry at the time and may not have known about it."

"*What?*" Adam said. "How could that have happened?"

"Wouldn't they have told us?" Kate said.

"Not necessarily," Carnap answered. "This isn't like the sex offender registry. It's not on the Internet and it isn't available to the public. It's used as a screening tool for day-care centers, schools, adoption agencies, and people who want to become foster parents."

"But it's a mistake," Kate said. "They cleared us. It was just a routine assessment they did at the hospital because Emma came in with an injury. There was no investigation because no one was really worried. The social worker told us that."

"It doesn't take an investigation. Just a report. And unfortunately, the downside of it not being public is that there are a lot of mistakes on the state registry. People don't even catch it usually until something goes wrong."

"Like now," Kate said.

The lawyer nodded.

"Can we get removed from it?" Adam said.

"You could request a hearing." Carnap inhaled deeply. "But in the present circumstances I would say that this doesn't seem like a fruitful use of your time and resources."

Adam was reeling. How much more could they pile on his shoulders? They had to give him *something*. "What about Kate?" he asked. "So she's listed too?"

"No, just you," Carnap said. "As I understand it, she was in the other room when Emma fell. They said that she'd have to go through the parenting classes too, if you want to get the investigation dropped, but she isn't on the registry and she wouldn't have to admit to any abuse. Either time. They don't think she knew about it. And, in fact, there's another angle."

"Which is what?" Adam said.

Carnap drew another breath. "In the current context, they're worried that you might be a threat to Kate as well."

"You must be kidding me," Kate said.

How much worse can this get?

"Let me explain." Carnap stood and went over to his desk to retrieve a file. When he came back, he just stood there, towering over them like a prosecutor making his case. "Kate is physically unable to care for Emma by herself. So, without a caretaker for Emma, they're reluctant to leave her in your home. At this point Adam is the only caretaker. And unless he admits to past abuse, he remains under suspicion for the likelihood of future abuse. To you and to Emma."

"That's the most ludicrous thing I've ever heard," Kate said. "Adam didn't touch Emma. He's the gentlest man I've ever known. But put that aside for a moment. Can they show me any research at all that shows that failure to acknowledge past abuse leads to future abuse? I've been reading everything I can about child abuse for the last three days, and I haven't seen anything about this. They can't be serious. They're just making things up."

Adam teared up a bit, but he couldn't tell whether it was pride in Kate's logic or joy in hearing her defend him so vigorously. He felt that he should say something more on his own behalf. "More Catch-22. If we had a nanny we could keep Emma home, but our nanny is the one who's lying, so we're out of luck."

"Sorry, that's the way it is," Carnap said. Instead of sitting down, Carnap walked back to his desk and perched on its edge while he searched for something in his file drawer.

"So what are our choices?" Adam said. "I won't confess to something I didn't do and I won't let them take my little girl."

"You may have no choice," Carnap said. "Is there anyone else who might take Emma temporarily?"

"No, no family," Kate said.

"Neither of you?"

"No," said Adam.

"Any friends or co-workers who might help out?

Adam hesitated. "I don't want anyone to know what's going on. I could lose my job."

"Then you should find another nanny." The lawyer's head disappeared as he reached for the bottom drawer. "That should help things temporarily." His head reappeared. "But we don't have to wait for a hearing. We can request one. Let me see what I can do. If you don't want to admit to the abuse, I'd say your best interests are served by getting this in front of a judge right away. I just found the docket list for the next —"

The phone on his desk rang.

Adam and Kate exchanged a quick whisper about what to do next, then turned back when they realized the call was about them.

Carnap's side of the conversation consisted of a series of "uh huhs" and other cryptic interjections such that neither of them could figure out what was going on. His face told them more than words could. When he put down the phone, Carnap looked visibly shaken.

"That was CPS. I have some news about your case, but at this point I'll need some time to think about its impact. And the retainer will have to be increased to fifty thousand dollars."

"What is it?" Kate said. "Did Rachel make up another lie about us?"

"No." The lawyer shook his head. "Rachel is dead."

Chapter 5

Emma kept running back and forth in the living room between Adam and Kate to show off her newfound treasure. "It's a flower, Daddy!"

Adam held up the carefully folded tissue paper, with curled red petals on top and squished green tape on the stem, and gave it back to Emma.

"It's beautiful, honey."

"It's a rose! Mrs. Nguyen showed me how to make it. She's got a whole boxful. All kinds of flowers."

"Those are great," Kate said. "Are you going to make more of them?"

"I need help," Emma chirped. "Can you help me, Mommy?"

Kate gave a firm smile. "Mama's hands don't work like they used to, honey. And Mama and Daddy are pretty tired from their big meeting this morning."

Emma flicked the flower back and forth with her thumb and turned away from Kate. "Did you have a good time at your big meeting?"

"Not really," Kate said. "It wasn't that kind of meeting."

Emma kept her back turned. "Is the lady coming back?"

Adam saw that Emma was pulling the petals off the rose one by one and dropping them on the floor. "Honey, you're ruining it," he said.

"I don't care."

"That's not very nice to your flower."

"I can make another one. Mrs. Nguyen gave me some extra paper."

"Okay, I'd like to work on that with you later," Adam said. "But for right now can you go play in your bedroom for a while, so Mommy and Daddy can talk?"

"SMART PHONE!" Emma yelled. "Birds, birds, birds."

"Okay, just this once," Adam said, hauling it out of his pocket.

Emma grabbed her treasure and tore down the hallway.

* * *

"So what the hell do we do now?" Adam said. "Does Rachel's death make things better or worse for us?"

"Adam, jeez. I know how you feel because I feel exactly the same way, but try not to talk about it like that, okay? If Castro comes back and hears you say something like that, who knows what she might think?"

"So they're sure it was murder?"

"You were there, Adam. You heard Carnap. Not in so many words, but I don't think there's any doubt." Kate craned her neck to see if she could hear anything down the hallway. "Rachel was found in her apartment with multiple stab wounds. Isn't that enough?"

"Maybe she stabbed herself. Maybe she felt guilty about — oh, I don't know — lying through her teeth about us?"

"There it is again," Kate said. "Tone it down, willya?"

"Maybe she found that sharp tool."

"Adam, you've got to get a grip on yourself. This isn't over yet. We can get through this, but we've got to handle it right. Now that Rachel is dead, I don't think her complaint has the same weight."

"Why not?"

"Because there's no witness. There's no affidavit. What she told CPS triggered the investigation, but for them to actually take Emma there'd have to be a court hearing. They'd have to present evidence. And their star witness is dead."

"How do you know all this?"

"I did have a life once, remember? I've worked with a few 'families in transition' in my time. I saw a case once back in Boston where the person who reported the abuse recanted at the last minute. They dropped the charges."

"So we're off the hook?"

"Not by a long shot."

Adam shook his head and scooted toward Kate. "You know what I fucking hate about that wheelchair is that we can't sit together like we used to. Can't I just move you to the couch?"

"I'll need to go to the bathroom first."

"Okay." Adam stood up.

"Hey, not just this second, okay? Stop ordering me around. We've got to talk about this before anything else happens, don't we? Didn't you and Tugg ever have any secrets together when you were kids? Didn't you ever need to get your stories straight?"

Adam swallowed and smiled. "Sure. Of course. But what is it?"

Kate looked at Adam as if he were a puppy dog. "You really don't get it, do you? You're going to be the prime suspect in Rachel's death. The only people who knew about what she'd done to us were Elaine, Tugg and us."

"And the authorities," Adam added.

"Duh, so what? Our lawyer knew too, but he's not a suspect either. Elaine is in Boston and Tugg is off doing wheelies in the desert somewhere. That leaves us."

"You mean that leaves me," Adam said.

"Double duh. Look at me," Kate said. She held out her hands and Adam took them. "But no matter how bad it looks, they can't make a case against you either. It just won't work."

Adam stared at her, uncomprehending.

"Until this morning we didn't leave the house for the last three days, Adam. As alibis go, that's pretty solid."

"I could have slipped out while you were sleeping."

Kate smiled. "But you didn't. I would have noticed."

Adam smiled back. "Oh, really? I slip out with Mrs. Nguyen all the time."

Kate threw her head back and laughed. Adam was overjoyed to see her first real smile in days.

"Yes, that's just who you'd leave me for. A five-foot-tall octogenarian."

"But Mrs. Nguyen has skills." Adam chuckled. "She can cook."

"And she makes a mean tissue rose. Yes, I know. Mrs. Nguyen no doubt has her many attractions. But you're a man of loyalty, Adam. I knew that when I met you."

Adam looked deeply into Kate's eyes. "You're the only woman I'll ever love," he said.

"That's not true." Kate pulled her hands back. "That's a lie and you know it."

"Yes, of course," he said. "Emma."

Kate leaned forward and put her arms around his shoulders.

"You're the only people I really love in this whole damned universe and you're the only ones who love me back," Adam said.

Kate kissed Adam on the forehead then pulled back. "That's another lie. How many is that now, two?"

Adam looked at Kate. She raised her eyebrows and gave a mischievous grin until he finally said it.

"Tugg."

Chapter 6

"It's the lady! It's the lady!"

Adam stumbled down the soft carpet toward Emma's room and heard the knocking on the front door that had probably woken her. It wasn't a nightmare after all. She was afraid of the knocking.

At 7:00 a.m. on a Sunday?

"Daddy's coming," Adam said. He landed in a lump at Emma's bedside, still in his pajamas, and held her. "It's not the lady."

"Then who is it?" Emma yelled.

"Adam?" Kate called from the next room.

"I don't know, sweetie. But it's not the lady."

Whap. Whap. Whap.

"It is too!"

"I don't think so."

"Well, can you go *see*?" Emma wailed.

Adam!

Adam picked Emma up and hustled her back to Kate, where he deposited her on his side of the bed and managed a quick kiss on top of the head.

"I'll go see who it is and tell them to go away." He looked at Kate, who was too busy soothing Emma to ask the question he saw in her eyes.

What if it was the lady?

Adam hurried down the hall. "Coming, coming." He opened the front door.

Different cops this time: Tony Soprano's twin brother and an Asian woman with square shoulders and her hair yanked back.

"Adam Grammaticus?" said Tony's twin.

"Yes. Where's the lady?"

Tony looked at his partner. "Cute, but not funny. Can we come in?"

"I mean, where's Child Services? Where's Lisa Castro?"

"I ain't got a clue, but we'd like to come in anyway."

Adam stood aside.

"Anyone else home?" said the Asian woman.

"My wife and daughter. They're in the next room. Why?"

"We might need to talk to your wife at some point," the woman said.

"What about?"

"Let's sit." Tony indicated a chair for Adam. "So, Mr. Grammaticus," he said, "we'd like to ask you some questions about the death of Rachel Norwood. As I understand it, she was your nanny. Is that correct?"

"I think I need a lawyer present before I can answer any questions," Adam said.

Tony looked over at his partner. "Up to you."

"Adam!"

"Excuse me for a minute." Adam hurried down the hallway and disappeared for a few minutes, then came back to the living room.

"Sorry about that. My wife is handicapped and can't get out of bed by herself. She wants to know if I'm being charged with anything."

"Not at this time," Tony said. "This is just a routine follow-up that we're doing with all of Ms. Norwood's friends and associates. If you'd prefer to have a lawyer present it's your choice, but then let's meet down at the station house."

Adam shook his head. "I guess I don't need one, then. Just go ahead and ask your questions. I'll tell you if I need to stop."

"Right," Tony said. He flipped open a little leather book. "So how did you come to hire Ms. Norwood?"

"My wife hired her. From an agency, I think."

"Adam!"

The cops looked down the hallway toward the sound of Kate's voice.

"Mr. Grammaticus, do you suppose your wife could come out here?" said the Asian officer.

"She can't," he said, getting off the sofa. "She's in bed watching our daughter. Excuse me."

Adam ran back down the hallway. When he returned he said "Yes, that's right. Stadler Childcare Solutions," before he even hit the sofa.

"And I guess we can check with the agency," Tony continued, "but do you know who Ms. Norwood might have listed as an emergency contact? Family maybe?"

"Family, gosh. I don't know if she had any family."

"She said she had a brother!" Kate called from the other room.

The cops just looked at one another.

After some more questions that Adam felt fully competent to handle on his own — whether he was aware of the abuse allegations that she had made against him, whether he had any idea who might have killed her — came the haymaker. "Can you please tell us where you were between ten p.m. and four a.m. from Wednesday night to Thursday morning of this week?"

"He was with me."

Adam yanked his head around and saw a sight that shocked him. Kate had pulled herself out of bed and halfway down the hall, with Emma holding the hem of her nightgown.

"Shit! Kate!" Adam said. He bounded over and picked her up.

"I told her it was naughty, Dad."

"You're right, Emma," Adam said. "Please go back to the big bed and wait for us there. Go now!"

Emma scurried off. Adam hesitated before he brought Kate over to the couch. The cops were standing, awkwardly, with their hands out, as if they could catch her from ten feet away. Adam laid her on the couch and covered her with an afghan, then took a different chair.

"So as I was saying," Adam began.

"He was with me," Kate said again. "We were both here, in this house, with Emma beside us from Monday night till Friday morning. He was with me every minute. He was never out of my sight. The phone records will show that we made calls almost non-stop during that three-day period."

"Even in the middle of the night?" the Asian officer asked.

"Obviously not," Kate replied. "But we were sleeping in the same bed together. I'd know if he left."

Tony Soprano wrote something in his book. "Okay. I got that," he said. "But now that Mrs. Grammaticus is present, can I ask again whether either one of you might have any knowledge of who might have committed this crime?"

Kate jumped in again. "We do not."

"No one who might have had a grudge against Ms. Norwood — that is, except you two?"

"We do not."

"Maybe someone who had the *same* grudge as you?" Tony nudged. He looked at Adam as Adam looked off into space.

Doing wheelies in the desert somewhere.

"No, we don't," Kate said.

"Maybe your husband could answer that question too?" said the Asian officer.

"I — well, no. I already answered that before. I don't really —"

There was another knock at the front door. Lighter this time.

The door pushed open.

Adam thought that Lisa Castro looked surprised to see the cops there. *So this wasn't a set-up?*

"Officer Babcock. Officer Ng. I'm glad I caught up with you. Can we go out to your cruiser for a moment? There's been a development."

"In our case?" Kate called from the couch.

Castro avoided her gaze along with the question and disappeared outside.

"Back in a few." Tony and his partner swung themselves off their chairs and out the front door.

"*Adam*!" Kate hissed. "Go get Emma and take her out the garage door and don't look back."

"What the hell, Kate?" Adam said. "The cops are almost done with us. You saw Castro. She looked surprised to see them here. Maybe she's not here for that. They didn't even seem to know she was —"

"Don't be an idiot! Get Emma and go!" Kate insisted. "Can't you see what's coming?"

Adam stood but hesitated, just as the cops and Lisa Castro reappeared in the doorway. Their faces were stone.

"I'm sorry, Mrs. Grammaticus," Castro said, as she brushed by the cops.

"No!" Kate screamed. "I did not give you permission to enter my house!"

When he heard Emma scream, Adam felt something tear loose inside him. Between Kate sobbing and Emma wailing, he didn't make the decision so much as felt himself a spectator, watching the crazy man in pajamas vault down the hallway.

"Hey, you! Stop! Get back here!"

Adam was dimly aware of the cops closing in behind him, as he met Castro in the hallway, just coming out of the master bedroom.

"Put her down. NOW!" Adam yelled. His pulse pounded behind his eye sockets as he grabbed Castro's arm.

Adam saw a look of horror in the social worker's eyes just before the awful weight came down behind him. Adam fell to his knees, then bucked his head back as he launched again and again at the departing figures.

"Calm down!" Tony Soprano yelled. "Once more and I'm using the pepper spray."

Adam caught one last glimpse of Emma raining a torrent of tiny hands in Castro's face. Then they were gone.

"Cuffs, Julie. Now!" yelled Tony.

An inhuman sound rose up from the living room.

Adam felt the zip of plastic tighten around his wrists.

The cops said something, but he couldn't hear it.

"Julie, for the love of God. Would you just go to her and do something?" he finally heard.

Tony pulled Adam to his feet. "Guess you'll want that lawyer now."

Chapter 7

Adam hurried down the steps of the Multnomah County Courthouse and opened his cell phone. "I'm out."

"Adam! You're out?"

"Yes. Carnap may not be a criminal lawyer, but he sure knows his way around. All charges dropped. I thought I was going to have to spend the night in there."

"Are you all right?"

Adam walked down S.W. 4th Avenue to hail a cab, wondering where Emma was at this very minute. "Yes, I'm fine. Booking, fingerprints, and nine hours in a big holding cell with a bunch of sweaty men, but I'm okay. I definitely wouldn't want to repeat the experience, but it could've been a lot worse. I made it out just before they were getting ready to bunk me for the night. The thought of it gives me chills."

"I'm just glad you're out."

"Me too. Any news about Emma? Are *you* all right?"

"No." Kate broke down sobbing. "I'm not. Just get home as soon as possible."

Adam bolted in the front door and looked wildly around the living room. He saw Kate in her wheelchair on the deck, sitting with Mrs. Nguyen. He rushed over. "Kate!" he said. "What happened?"

Kate nodded toward her visitor. "I'm okay. Thanks to Minh Chau. She's my hero."

"Don't need hero. Need husband," said Mrs. Nguyen. "Hurray." She smiled gently and patted Adam's arm as she got up to leave.

"Thank you — for everything," Adam said. "How in the world did you get the wheelchair out here?"

"This one fold," she said. "Not hard."

Kate smiled. "Thanks."

When they were alone, Adam grabbed Kate and held her. Within seconds the brave front dissolved in a well of tears.

"Any word on Emma?" he said, stroking her hair.

"No. I've been calling nonstop. Between that and you being in jail, I was in pretty bad shape. Minh Chau saved me. Now that you're here, I can finally let it out." Kate cried like a teenager, and Adam held her.

One step at a time they would fix this. He was out of jail. Emma came next.

"Hal called from work," Kate said. "He wants you to call him right away."

"Hal can wait."

"He says he's putting you on paid leave, but that once he's cleared it with the lawyers he's going to terminate you."

There's loyalty for you.

"Based on what? This morning? How did he even hear about that?"

"No, he heard that you were a 'person of interest' in Rachel's death. Don't ask me how. Oh Adam it looks bad."

A call from a reporter seeking comment before they ran a story about a Tektel executive? It wouldn't be long before this hit the papers.

"Have you talked to Carnap?" Adam said, wiping his face.

"Yes — but that's kind of bad now too."

"What do you mean?"

It was another beautiful evening on the lake. The water looked as if it had swallowed another sun. Across the lake someone was roaring back and forth on a Jet Ski. From a distance, the sound was sort of comforting.

"He said that when you attacked Lisa Castro, it confirmed their view that you were an unfit parent. You're too violent."

If they only knew.

Kate continued, "And they think this reinforces their claim that you probably abused Emma. Add to that the fact that they think you had some role in Rachel's death and it looks pretty bad for us. One more mistake, and we may never see her again."

The Jet Ski buzzed past about 50 yards away. So incongruous to be sitting on a beautiful lake, crying, when someone so close was having a good time.

"So how can we get Emma back?" Adam said. "Does Carnap have any ideas?"

"Court," Kate said. "That's the only hope we've got. He's requested a hearing as soon as possible. He said not to do anything stupid until then."

Adam looked down. "And in the meantime, Emma remains in foster care?"

"Yes," Kate said. "Adam, I feel like my insides are bleeding."

Adam heard a buzz again, but it wasn't the Jet Ski. He didn't recognize the number. "Hello?"

"Hey — dude. It's Tugg."

"Tugg, is it you? New number?"

"Yeah, this is a disposable. Lost the other one on the road. You couldn't have reached me anyway."

"Where are you?" Adam said.

"Closer than you think."

Adam snapped the phone shut and squeezed Kate's hand, then walked through the living room toward the front door. When he opened it he saw the big black Harley Ultra Classic Electraglide in the driveway, still ticking in the sunshine.

"Tugg?" he called, looking around. "Tugg?"

The sight of tiny Mrs. Nguyen on her front porch, having a conversation in French with a six foot three, square-jawed beast of a man, wearing a blond goatee and head-to-toe leather almost made him laugh.

Tugg looked over and smiled. "Did somebody call Nannies R Us?"

CHAPTER 8

Lisa Castro sat at her desk with tears streaming down her face. Wanda had left for a home visit two hours ago and the rest of the office was off for the weekend, so at least for a spell Castro had the whole place to herself.

What a glamorous office. What a glamorous life. How many more years could she take it? Burnout wasn't even a question anymore. When you worked in Child Protective Services, you got burned the first day.

Castro leaned back in her squeaky chair and looked at the water stains on the ceiling. Crumbling acoustic tile. A leaky radiator. Mold in the walls that the city never seemed able to fix. Lisa and Wanda often joked that if a stranger walked into their building, he or she would deem it an unsafe environment for children.

Yet this was where the power lay. This was the chance to do some real good in the lives of a bunch of kids who desperately needed it. Even if the public didn't really understand what they were doing and it was easy to paint CPS as the bad guy, it was absolutely necessary to protect those kids, even if their parents — and society — didn't like it.

But Castro doubted she could make it through many more days like today.

Her eyes wandered over to the latest inspirational post-it note that Wanda had stuck on her lamp: *The measure of a man who does his duty is not what others think of him but his own commitment to doing what is right.*

Funny, it didn't say anything about angry parents attacking you. Or screaming at you as if you were a terrorist. The Grammaticus case was far from the worst she'd seen, but in some ways it hit closest to home. Castro herself was living proof that abuse could happen even in a "good" family. And if she could fix things for just one kid — give one girl a chance to escape the nightmares she had experienced — it would all be worth it.

But was it worth her life? Rachel Norwood was dead and Adam Grammaticus was the prime suspect. Was he also a child abuser? It seemed likely. The daughter had "fallen" in his care as an infant. A more recent abuse report had come in from the nanny, who later turned up with knife wounds in her stomach. And the father had assaulted Castro just this morning. Would she be dead next?

Castro picked up a ruler and absently felt its edge.

Abuse cases were the worst, but neglect could be almost as bad.

So many kids and so few good options for any of them.

And all of these Native American kids lately. Where in the world would she put them? Castro was glad that she didn't have to do the home visits and "extractions" on the Indian reservations. Two of the three teams they had sent to do it had asked for a transfer the minute they got back. It was awful to be attacked by an angry father, but almost as bad to have a whole community call you a racist and accuse you of genocide.

"You just don't understand our culture," the tribal leaders had said. "We are a sovereign nation and you are killing our future."

Castro knew neglect when she saw it. The poverty. The easy availability of alcohol. Some of the houses didn't even have any food in them.

"That's because we share food. The kids walk down the street to their cousin's house when they get hungry," came the answer.

That was a new one. Poverty wasn't the same as neglect, of course, but sometimes it came damn close.

And still the cases kept coming. They had a lot of pressure from the governor's office to get the children placed in foster care or group homes right away. An equal amount of pressure came from the tribes to let the kids stay with relatives or Native American foster families, so that they wouldn't be alienated from their culture. Federal law dictated placement of Native American kids with Native American families, if that was possible, but there just weren't enough of them, so they needed to start placing those kids anywhere they could. For once, they had enough money.

The phone rang.

"Lisa, how are you doing? I heard through the grapevine that things got pretty hairy for you this morning. Are you okay?"

Castro straightened up in her chair, even though the governor's chief of staff couldn't see her. She felt guilty for loafing at her desk, even on a Sunday.

"I'm fine, Mr. Beauchamp. Thank you. Are all of the social workers getting special calls today? Or did I just hit the lottery?" Castro bit her tongue. *Stop trying to be clever.*

"If you can call having your arm almost pulled off hitting the lottery, then yes, I guess you did," Beauchamp said.

Castro tried to think of the appropriate thing to say. "Well, at least I had the police officers there. That was a break. After I heard that the father was a suspect in the nanny's murder I went over there to get the kid, police escort or not."

"You're doing God's work," Beauchamp said. "For too long we've felt compelled to ignore abuse allegations from *certain* zip codes. You know how strongly the governor feels about this."

"Yes, I do," Castro said, trying to sound gung ho. "And we're grateful for the support. We have a lot of cases right now. More than I ever remember. But we'll manage somehow. The whole office is working on placements. Especially for the Native American kids."

"You're doing God's work there too. Keep it up. We're counting on you."

"Thank you," Castro managed.

When the line went dead, Castro felt a little better. It was the same dingy office and the same shitty hours, but it was important work just the same.

Out of the corner of her eye, Castro spied an older post-it from Wanda: *be the change that you wish to see in the world.* She blew her nose and turned on the desk lamp against the gathering dusk.

"Time to get back to it," she said out loud, as if someone were listening.

Chapter 9

Adam watched Tugg kneel next to Kate's wheelchair and give her the closest equivalent to a bear hug that was possible under the circumstances. The physical contrast between them was comical. Every time they had greeted in the past, canes or no canes, Tugg had picked Kate up for a full-body hug. Now that she was in a wheelchair, that wasn't possible. This might have to be their new thing.

"He loves you," Adam had once said, in response to Kate's bemusement after one of Tugg's visits.

"He loves that I love *you*," she replied.

Adam watched them, exchanging soft words, greeting like old friends. Kate nodded and Tugg hugged her again as Adam joined them on the deck.

"Tugg, it's so good to see you," Kate said. "It's been awful. Emma hasn't even been gone thirteen hours and Adam just got back from jail. I'm a wreck."

"Understandable," Tugg said. "That's why I'm here."

"You must be a mind reader."

Adam looked around for another chair, but Kate stopped him. "Adam, I'm not feeling well. Physically. I was so hysterical when they took you and Emma away that I took something to calm me down, but all it did was upset my stomach."

"Are you all right?" Adam said.

"I feel like I want to throw up. But I'm just so tired I feel like I could die. I'm wrung out."

"I feel terrible too," Adam said. "Emma is out there somewhere. And it's getting dark. And she's going to have to sleep in a different bed surrounded by strangers."

Tugg put a hand on Adam's back. "Listen, bud, this ain't helping. There's nothing more you can do tonight. Kate, what did you take?"

"Xanax."

"It's worn off by now. Take another. You need to sleep. And Adam and I need to talk. We'll figure this out by morning."

Kate gave a hint of a smile and nodded.

Adam knelt down by her chair. "Okay, but I'll need to figure out where that catch is that Mrs. Nguyen was telling us about. Apparently this thing folds up, but I don't see —"

Tugg leaned down and lifted Kate out of the chair in one movement. "Let's worry about that later. Adam, come put your wife to bed."

Adam followed behind as Tugg carried Kate down the hallway.

"Do you want to go back on the deck?" Adam said.

"Ears," Tugg replied. "It's better in the living room."

Adam closed the sliding glass door and they sat down in opposite chairs, knees close. Grown men, the years dissolved between them.

"Now tell me everything, right from the beginning," Tugg said. "All I know is what Kate just told me: Emma got taken this morning and they arrested you for trying to stop it. Fill me in on everything else."

Adam began, but Tugg stopped him almost immediately. "So the nanny is dead?"

"Yes. You didn't know that? That's what started the whole damn thing this morning."

"Tell me about it. Don't leave anything out."

The whole story took a surprisingly long time to tell. The original charges. The cops. The lawyer. Then Rachel's death. When he got to the social worker coming this morning and his subsequent arrest, Adam started to get emotional.

"First time I got popped, I cried like a baby," Tugg said. "And I hadn't just lost a daughter. Then I toughened up. You've gotta be ice cold in lock-up. Just like you've gotta be ice cold right now, if you want to get Emma back."

"What do you mean?"

Tugg knocked his boots against the floor. "Sounds to me like they think you killed the nanny."

"Maybe they do. But I didn't do it," Adam said.

Tugg just looked at him. "Doesn't matter. As long as they *think* you did, Emma won't be coming home. And if that goes on too long, you won't get her back at all."

Adam swallowed hard. "So what do I do?"

"You've got to think two steps ahead of them. Can you get around the murder thing? They haven't arrested you on that yet, which means they can't prove it. But if they get any evidence, it's over. They'll come after you and Emma will be gone for good."

"But there's no evidence, Tugg."

"You'd better hope not. That gives you a choice. Otherwise there's only one way to go."

"Which is?"

"You find Emma and run."

"That's what I tried to do this morning."

"No, you didn't."

"What do you mean? Of course I did."

"Sorry, bud, you didn't. All you did this morning was trip over your own dick. You didn't have things thought out. You weren't committed."

Adam felt a little pissed. "Tugg, I went crazy when they took her. I didn't know what I was doing."

Tugg held a finger to his temple. "Emotion makes you crazy. This morning you were pissed when they came for Emma and you got emotional. How did that work out for you?"

If the question had come from anyone else, Adam would have been furious.

"You've got to channel your emotion," Tugg continued. "Make it work for you."

"Yeah right."

"You've done it before. I was there."

Adam shrugged. "So you think there was a way to stop this?" He couldn't help the resentment creeping into his voice.

"Yes, and so do you," Tugg said. "You had a decision to make this morning about whether to fight this in court or stop it right then. Instead you did just enough to get yourself arrested. If you want to fight this in court, fine. Do that. But if you wanted to stop them from taking Emma, then you shouldn't have been thinking about anything else. Either let the system work or try to intervene, but don't land halfway between. You're conflicted."

"Conflicted? Over what? They were taking my daughter! Of course I wanted to stop them."

Tugg glared at Adam with the love of a father who had just watched his all-star son miss a dunk shot. "Did you? Were you prepared to give up everything else to stop them? So why did you go for the social worker first, then, instead of the cops?"

"And you would have done better?"

"Yeah. So could you." Tugg stood up and grabbed a heavy metal bowl off the coffee table. "One, two." He swung it in a wide arc against two couch cushions. "A good shot in the skull, and the gun wouldn't even leave the holster. Shock and awe. Then you get the social worker. And then you run."

Adam looked down. "That's what Kate said."

"Good girl. She gets it."

Adam shifted uncomfortably in his seat. "Water under the bridge, I guess," he said.

"Not really. You're still not ready."

"Ready for what?"

Tugg exhaled through his nostrils. "Listen, Adam. Why did you save me that day when we were kids?"

Adam frowned. "I don't know. I had to. There wasn't anything to decide."

"Exactly," Tugg said. "You had nothing more to lose. Well, now you've lost something. Do you want to get it back? Or do you want to keep on losing?"

"Okay, so I wasn't thinking when I killed those skinheads. But I wasn't thinking this morning when I went after the social worker, either. And look where that got me."

"Wrong," Tugg said. "You were thinking too *much*. But you didn't *decide*." Tugg hesitated. "It's been a lot of years, Adam. You've got more to lose now. A wife. A house. A life. Like I said, you're conflicted. But you have to decide. Do you want to get Emma back or not?"

"Yes!"

Tugg nodded. "Good. Then you've got to be prepared to do whatever it takes. Fight it in court first. But if that doesn't work, then you've got to be ready to go with Plan B. Immediately. No hesitation."

"Plan B?"

Tugg shot forward in his seat. "Kill the cops. Kill the social worker. Kiss your wife goodbye, take Emma and run."

Tugg's eyes were wild. Adam extracted himself from the chair and stood up.

"Why is all that necessary? Why do I need to lose everything else to get Emma back? I didn't hurt her. I just want my life back."

Tugg leaned back in his chair. "You haven't lost enough yet. You can't see what I'm talking about. You still think that if you're a good boy it's all going to work out."

"Yeah, okay. I'm a systems guy. And that system has always sort of worked for me."

"Well now it's not—"

"But what you're saying will land me in prison," Adam said. "I got lucky with that once. I won't be so lucky again. I can't risk it."

"Conflicted."

"Fuck you, buddy."

"Fuck you back. I'm just telling you the truth. You don't want to hear it, but I'm here with you anyway. Just like always."

Adam was still mad, but when he looked at Tugg he could see that he had hurt him.

How could Adam be mad at a man who wanted nothing more on Earth than to see him safe and happy? Who understood and accepted him, even when he thought he was wrong?

Adam's anger dissolved. He could not argue with such total devotion. He walked over to Tugg, who stood up to meet him.

"You don't need to say it," Tugg said, embracing his friend. "I know it all."

Adam held it together as best he could, then pulled back and gave Tugg a weak smile. "Is that a Glock in your pocket or are you just glad to see me?"

Tugg laughed. "Both," he said. "But I must be *really* glad." Both hands disappeared into his jacket, where he drew two Glock handguns.

"Regular and bite-sized," said Adam.

"A G23 and a G27. Had to fit under my jacket on the bike."

"Is that all?"

"Well, of course I always carry this." Tugg reached down to his boot and withdrew a giant knife. "Ka-Bar. Don't leave home without it."

"Done yet?"

"A very, *very* tasteful cut-down Remington 870 in the ditty bag on the back of the bike, along with some surveillance equipment and a couple of others things, just for fun."

Adam stared at his friend. "Tugg, let's sit down for a minute."

"What?"

"I need to ask you something."

"So ask."

"When did you get here?"

"What do you mean? You heard me pull up a while ago."

"No, I mean when did you get back to Oregon? Were you here Wednesday night?"

Tugg stepped back. "Hey. What the fuck? You know I'm a peaceful man. After what happened to us all those years ago? And in the Air Force? I still live with that, man. I live with it every day. And I know you do too, Adam. Every goddamned choice you make in life you live with. And you pay for it too. Sooner or later."

"That isn't a no."

"Fucking hell, Adam. What do you want me to say? Would I kill someone if you asked me to? Yes. Did you ask me to? No."

Adam nodded. "This has to be done my way, Tugg. I'm so glad to see you I could cry, but you can't make me do things I'm not ready for. I've got a life now where I can't just —"

"Too much to lose."

"Yes, you're right." Adam let go. "Too much to lose. I don't just want Emma back, I want her back and *happy*. Not afraid all the time. Not on the run. I want her to be with me *and* her mother. Can't you see that?"

Adam saw that Tugg got it. He didn't have to push anymore. Tugg had no wife or kids. All he had was Adam. Tugg's life was simple. His priorities were different. Take shit from no one and make Adam happy. It must be nice to be Tugg. But it must be awful too. Tugg had already lost so much that he must be used to looking for a plan B. But that wasn't Adam's life. Plan A had to work.

Adam heard the sound first. "Kate?"

Adam and Tugg raced down the hallway.

She was sitting up in bed, half crouched over on her side, with a cascade of vomit down her front. "Adam, it won't stop. I feel horrible. What's happening?"

Tugg grabbed the phone as Adam ran to her.

"Ambulance is coming," Tugg said. "Five minutes."

Chapter 10

Adam's ass was still vibrating from the rocket-launch motorcycle ride all the way up the twists and turns to the top of Pill Hill. Tugg was sitting on one of the plastic seats facing the door of the Emergency Room, not really reading the "Do You Have Mesothelioma?" brochure he was holding in his hands.

Adam was at the intake window for the third time, to see if there was any news. "I'm sorry, but it's been seven hours."

"Yes, Mr. Grammaticus," said the pleasant-faced woman at the window. "Your wife is being treated. She was agitated, but she's doing fine now. The doctor will call for you in a few minutes."

"That's what you said an hour ago."

The woman forced a smile. "She's getting the best care possible. Don't worry. We'll call you just as soon as we can."

"Why can't I see her?"

"She's in x-ray."

Adam returned to his seat and looked over at Tugg.

"It is what it is," Tugg said.

Adam thought about changing seats, so that he could avoid the people who looked most contagious. Woman with a baby. Old man rubbing his leg. Teenager with eyes closed and a coat up around his neck.

Tugg's strategy was different. Back to the wall, eyes on the door. Broader field of vision, wider field of fire.

"Mr. Grammaticus? Adam Grammaticus?"

"Yes?"

Adam was up like a shot. Tugg nodded for him to go. Mesothelioma had given way to Human Papilloma Virus.

Kate was in a little curtained area just off the corridor. Probably a better sign than being in one of the ten beds arranged in a circle behind sliding glass doors around the nurses' station. When the nurse led him in, Adam was relieved. Kate was sitting up, face washed and hair brushed, talking to the doctor in quiet tones.

"Is she all right?"

"Yes, quite all right," the doctor said, in a sing-song voice, his blue surgical cap in his hands. No handshake. *Probably for the best.*

Adam looked at Kate, who actually smiled at him. *What the hell?*

Adam sat down and took Kate's hand. "So what was it?" He looked at her carefully, searching for clues, then turned to the doctor.

"Was it related to the MS? Or the tranquilizer? We've been under a lot of stress lately. I don't know if she told you. But maybe it's something worse. What did you see on the x-ray?"

"We didn't do an x-ray."

"Why not?"

"It didn't seem prudent after the blood work came back," said the doctor, smiling.

"What the hell?" Adam said. "Someone had better tell me."

"I'm two months pregnant," Kate said.

Adam looked at the doctor, who was nodding and raising his eyebrows.

"No real danger," the doctor said. "Of course the pregnancy is high-risk due to the MS, but we can deal with that. I understand you have another child, so you've been down this road before. There's no reason that someone with MS can't have a normal full-term pregnancy."

Kate smiled through some tears and nodded.

"Could this explain her physical problems over the last couple of months?" Adam asked.

"We don't know," the doctor said. "MS is a little unpredictable. Some women have worse symptoms during pregnancy, and then things improve after delivery. That doesn't always happen, but it happens often enough. We'll have to see."

"I could go back to the canes?"

"Yes, maybe. I can't make any promises. But someday soon maybe you'll be out of your wheelchair and back on the floor playing with your kids."

Adam felt a catch in his throat.

"I'll leave you to talk."

Except for the beeps and clicks on the other side of the curtain, Adam and Kate were alone.

Kate leaned forward and Adam held her. "Adam, what are we going to do? This had to happen *now*? Really? You remember how tough it was carrying Emma. And with everything we've got ahead of us to get Emma back —"

Adam nodded. "You leave it to me. We'll get Emma back. I don't know how or when, but I'm going to get all of us back under one roof together if it kills me."

"Do you think that's possible?"

"It has to be. Emma's going to be a big sister."

Kate muffled a sob and smiled.

Adam's phone buzzed. "Bet it's Tugg," he mumbled.

"Adam? It's Steve Carnap. Listen, I've got some good news. We've got a hearing before Judge Gordon on Thursday. I know him well. He's a very law-and-order type, but I think that cuts our way on this one. He's a strong brake on government over-reach, and he doesn't like to interfere with parental rights. We couldn't have done better."

"You're sure?" Adam looked at Kate, who must have overheard. He saw the hope reflected back in her eyes.

"Yes, it's set. As you know, there will be a couple of witnesses on the other side. I suppose the cops will testify. But those charges were already dropped. And of course Lisa Castro will be there, but what does she have at this point? A two-year-old hospital intake form? An unsubstantiated allegation from a witness who can't appear? And suspicion on a murder charge against someone with an airtight alibi? It looks promising."

"You're a miracle worker," Adam said. "You can do anything."

"But I don't make house calls."

"Your only flaw." Adam laughed.

"Other than my fee?"

"Well, there's always that." Carnap was laughing now too. "Let me hang up so I can tell Kate." Adam closed the phone and Kate embraced him.

"I heard every word. Now go and tell Tugg. He's still waiting out there by himself. He doesn't know whether I'm alive or dead. What's he been doing all this time?"

"Trying to figure out if he should get the HPV vaccine when he turns 13."

Kate smiled again. "Go."

Adam breezed through the maze of gurneys and IVs and pressed the automatic door pad with his elbow.

When he stepped through the double doors, Adam saw that the room was crowded. It was morning.

Woman with a baby. Old man. Teenager sleeping under a coat.

Where was Tugg?

Chapter 11

Lisa Castro looked at the spreadsheet on her computer and tried to solve the puzzle one more time. If they transferred four more kids from The Longlane Home and put them in foster care, that would free up the beds for kids with special needs, because they had more —

Wanda stuck her head in. "Visitor for you. Want me to stay or go?"

"Who is it?"

"I think it's Rambo," Wanda said. "He says he wants to volunteer as a foster parent."

"What?"

Castro stood up and peeked out her door at the reception area. "Holy fuck. He just walked in off the street with no appointment?"

"He asked for you by name. Do you recognize him?"

Castro peeked out the door again. "Yes, I think I may have seen him when I had the flu over the winter. '*Sons of Anarchy*,' that's it. All I could do was watch TV."

Wanda smirked. "Maybe he's single."

"Not my type."

"A wall of muscle with a heart of gold? What's not your type?"

Castro smiled. "Wanda, you're the devil. Just get out, okay? Show him back, but leave the door cracked open. This is probably a waste of time, but at least I can walk him through the application. God knows we need more foster parents." Castro turned back to her desk and tried to look busy when she heard the tap.

He was even taller up close. And she'd just upgraded him to *The Fast and the Furious*.

"I'm Tugg Morgan."

"Nice to meet you, Mr. Morgan. I'm Lisa Castro."

"Yeah, I know. I'm here to see if I can sign up to work as a foster parent for Emma Grammaticus."

Castro was stunned. How did he know the name of a child in foster care? Maybe it wasn't such a good idea to meet with him alone after all. "Who are you again? And how do you know that name?"

"Friend of the family."

Castro got a sick feeling in the pit of her stomach. Wanda and the rest of the office were right outside, but this didn't feel right.

But this was about the kids, dammit. She needed to toughen up.

"Then you aren't eligible to work as a foster parent for them," she said.

"Why is that?"

"If you don't understand, I can't explain it to you."

Castro didn't like the look that came across his face, but she couldn't exactly read it either. It wasn't anger. It was more like she had touched a nerve and he recognized her from a previous life. *Another bitch,* his look seemed to say. Castro's feet started to twitch, but she refused to be intimidated.

"She's with a stranger now," he said evenly. "How is that better?"

"They've been screened."

"So screen me."

Castro shook her head. This needed to be over. Now. "You'd have to undergo an extensive personal history and background check. Family. Employment. Even then you couldn't choose which child you got placed with. It doesn't work like that. Oh, and we'd have to check your criminal background too." Castro *really* didn't like the look on his face. "So, you have a criminal record?"

"Nothing civil."

"What does that mean?"

"It was under the Uniform Code of Military Justice. You can run an NCIC on me and it'll come back clean."

"I'm sure I could, but I think we're done here." Castro stood up, but wondered if her legs would support her.

"Now just give me a minute," Tugg said. "I'm here to help my friends. If they can't watch Emma, why can't I?"

Castro put her hand on the door and swung it open. "Mr. Morgan, if you don't leave now, I'm going to have to call security."

Tugg got up from his seat and slowly walked by her. "Well, I tried."

Castro shut the door and finally took a breath.

Chapter 12

The courtroom didn't look anything like those polished wood, high-ceiling movie sets from *To Kill A Mockingbird* or *Twelve Angry Men*. This one had industrial carpet, acoustical tile, and anyone could tell that the judge's desk was made of fake wood. The room was tiny and had no windows.

Originally, Adam was glad that the hearing had been scheduled so fast, but it sure didn't *seem* fast. Every day of delay had been another day without Emma. Was she okay? Was she safe? They'd had no contact, no visitation and no suggestion of any time horizon for when they might be able to get Emma back. *But that's what today was about, wasn't it?*

The last four days had been one long descent into hell. From the peak of happy news of Kate's pregnancy and Carnap's optimistic prediction about today's hearing, they'd had nothing to do but worry about every possible thing that could go wrong. Would they get Emma back? Was she going to be psychologically scarred when they did? And what toll was all of this stress having on Kate? And the baby?

Even Tugg had been a little moody. He left the house every day for a long ride to "clear the cobwebs." Tugg never said where he'd gone that day when he left the hospital. Just a cryptic note at the nurse's station saying, "I heard that everything's cool and I've got something to do." *Best leave that alone.* Stress could have a bad effect on Tugg, the military doctor had said. Maybe that explained why he had spent the last three days acting like a hockey player in the penalty box, anxious to get back in the game.

Adam felt marginally reassured by Carnap's presence. And by Tugg, who was sitting in his accustomed seat in the back row. Kate's wheelchair was parked in the no man's land between what Adam guessed were normally the prosecution and defense tables, so that everyone had to go around her when they came down the aisle to approach the judge. For a modern courtroom, there apparently had been little thought of how to accommodate a handicapped defendant.

Lisa Castro was joined at the other table by a very tall black woman. Probably a state attorney. The attorney had shaken Adam and Kate's hands before sitting down, but Castro refused even to look them in the eye. That couldn't be good. She looked pretty agitated, actually, and kept swiveling her head back past the empty rows to look at Tugg. Maybe she couldn't figure out who he was, or why someone with no interest in the case would be sitting there. Maybe she recognized him from a previous life.

"All rise," the bailiff called.

Judge Malachi Gordon appeared from a rear door and ambled to the bench. He looked old enough to have known Thomas Jefferson personally, and peered down at them from comically thick glasses that he'd probably had since the 1980s. Carnap had said he was a good pick for their purposes. Good to hear. But why was a guy that old still presiding over family court?

Emma should be here. This is about her and she should have a chance to show how much she wants to come home. Is she somewhere in the building?

Adam choked up. Emma wouldn't understand all this, of course, but Adam was aching to see his little girl. Why didn't they have Emma here to ask her about the phony report from Rachel?

"Okay, what have we got today, Ms. Loving? Parental fitness — why do so many of these seem to come across my desk these days?"

"I apologize, your honor. We've been a little stacked up." Her voice was smooth and fluid. Must be a killer for the other side.

"Let's get to it, then." The judge picked up a sheaf of papers as if he were seeing them for the first time.

Ms. Loving spoke first. "Thank you, your honor. I would like to introduce Ms. Lisa Castro, Director of Placement for the Multnomah County Office of Child Protective Services."

Not a trial, Adam thought. It all seemed pretty informal. So why did *they* get to go first?

Castro stood and looked straight at the judge. "Your honor, today's hearing was requested by the parents of Emma Grammaticus, a three-year-old girl who came into our custody as a result of a complaint of parental abuse by Ms. Rachel Norwood, the Grammaticus' nanny. There is also a history of other alleged abuse as an infant and, unfortunately, there are other complicating circumstances as well."

Castro still refused to look over, even as she reached out in a vague gesture toward Adam's table.

"Complications? Of course there are. It's family court. We'll get to that, but first let's hear from the nanny."

"Your honor, that is the complication," Ms. Loving said. "Ms. Norwood is deceased."

Steve Carnap shifted uncomfortably in his seat. Finally he stood. "Your honor. My name is Steve Carnap and I represent Adam and Kate Grammaticus, Emma's parents. In the brief you have before you, I've explained the problem with pursuing an allegation of abuse when the party who made the claim cannot appear and there is no affidavit. It is unfortunate that Ms. Norwood died, but it can hardly be held against my clients' interests that her allegation cannot be presented today. If it were, it could be challenged."

"Mr. Carnap, I've seen you in this courtroom before, correct?"

"Yes, your honor."

"Then you know the rules. Can we please hear just a little more about what the claim is before you go trying to refute it?"

Carnap sat.

"So who's going to tell me?" the judge said. "How did she die?"

Castro was still playing staredown with the judge. "She was stabbed, your honor. Eight days ago. Two days after our initial visit to the Grammaticus home."

"Stabbed?" The judge looked around the room. "That doesn't happen every day. Do they know who did it?"

Carnap began to speak, but the judge cut him off.

"And it is too relevant, Mr. Carnap. Do you think I can rule on this without knowing more about the nanny?"

Castro looked about to continue, but Loving touched her arm and took over.

"The police don't know yet, your honor. The investigation is ongoing. But Mr. Grammaticus has been a person of interest. In fact, that is what leads us to today's request, which is that Emma Grammaticus' status be elevated from foster care to protective custody. We wish to terminate all parental visitation and notification of her whereabouts."

Adam heard a sob escape from Kate, as Carnap erupted from his seat.

"Your honor, this is highly prejudicial! Mr. Grammaticus has no criminal record and there is no history of abuse. He has not been arrested for this crime, nor has he been charged with anything. He also has an absolutely unimpeachable alibi. This is all just unsubstantiated paranoia from CPS."

"Mr. Grammaticus *was* arrested recently," said Loving.

"What?" said the judge.

"Yes, for assaulting Ms. Castro, at the time of Emma's removal."

"All charges were dropped," Carnap said.

"You opened the door to his criminal record, counselor," Loving replied.

The judge looked at the ceiling. "Family court, ye gods. Look, we've got a problem here, but let's not get ahead of ourselves." The judge looked at the defense table and addressed Adam. "You can't kill your parents, then ask for mercy because you're an orphan, Mr. Grammaticus. If you're a person of interest in the investigation of the nanny's murder, it doesn't seem quite right that you should benefit from her inability to be here today to testify. I know. I know, Mr. Carnap. He hasn't been arrested, or charged, or even really alleged to have done anything yet, but let's leave that out for a minute. Let's go back to the original charge, can we? Ms. Castro, you never told me what the alleged abuse was."

"Do you mean the recent one or the one before that?"

"There are two of them?"

Carnap erupted again. "There is no prior abuse charge! Can we just settle that once and for all? It's all in the brief, your honor. It's explained."

The judge gave Carnap a skeptical look. "I'll look into that," he said, and turned back to Castro.

"Yes, the most recent allegation —" Castro began.

"The one from the nanny?" said the judge.

"Yes, the one from Ms. Norwood. She alleged that Emma told her one day that her father had hurt her with a sharp tool."

A stormy look crossed the judge's face. "A sharp tool? Something with a blade?"

Adam felt sick.

"We don't know," said Castro. "We did not have time to do a full deposition with Ms. Norwood before she died. And Emma has never admitted to this under questioning."

"Mr. Carnap, what do you have?"

Carnap dropped his papers and just started talking. "Your honor, this is all a series of unsubstantiated allegations and misunderstandings. Mr. Grammaticus is a loving father and a prominent executive at Tektel here in town. Mrs. Grammaticus is confined to a wheelchair and has worked in the past for Families in Transition. Until recently she had been caring for Emma while working out of her home. They hired Ms. Norwood a month ago. We don't know why she made this dubious allegation, but what seems clear is that it was not examined very closely by CPS before they intervened and removed Emma Grammaticus from her home. There has been no proof of anything. It is mere supposition."

"You understand that suspicion is strong enough for family court, don't you, Mr. Carnap? When we're dealing with child welfare, we don't have to leave the child in a risky situation while we gather proof of abuse. It's not about proving past abuse, it's about the danger of future abuse. And the mere suspicion of that is sufficient to remove a child."

Carnap nodded.

"Your honor, that brings up another point," Loving interrupted. "We have recently learned that Mrs. Grammaticus is pregnant. CPS is concerned about parental fitness for that child as well."

Adam exploded. How the hell did they even know about this? "You must be crazy! You want to take our unborn baby, too?"

Kate yelled something incomprehensible and looked like she was trying to stand.

"Bailiff, go over there. Both of you, just settle down."

Blood throbbed in Adam's neck. He wondered if it was possible to have a stroke from anger.

The judge waited for calm, then turned to Castro. "So you want the three-year-old upgraded to protective custody and you want me to consider removing the second child, once it's born. But you haven't offered much for me to go on, have you? I don't need proof, but I need something, Ms. Castro."

Adam felt like he was on a plane in free fall and the pilot had suddenly found the stick.

Loving whispered something and Castro stood up. "Your honor, we know that this is not a criminal court. And we understand that Mr. Grammaticus is entitled to the presumption of innocence on any allegation of his role in Ms. Norwood's death. But I would ask you to defer to my strong suspicions based on the preponderance of evidence: the intake evaluation detailing injury to the infant two years ago, the report from the nanny, Mr. Grammaticus's violent attack on me personally a few days ago, and his role as a person of interest in the nanny's death. All of this makes me very concerned for Emma's welfare in that house. There should be no presumption of innocence where a child is concerned."

"Oh so?"

"With respect, your honor, I am not prepared to prove anything here today. But you said yourself that in family court the standard is different. And I am afraid that when the police have concluded their investigation, they will find that Mr. Grammaticus may have had a role in Ms. Norwood's killing."

"Your honor, this is outrageous," said Carnap. "Now she's claiming to be able to outsmart the police? There is no evidence here, your honor. It is all just speculation."

The judge turned back to Castro. "What about Mr. Grammaticus's airtight alibi, Ms. Castro? Isn't that somewhere in Mr. Carnap's brief?" The judge dropped his eyes and began leafing through the pages.

"Yes, your honor," Castro said. "Mr. Grammaticus' alibi suggests that he could not have physically killed Ms. Norwood himself. But has it occurred to any of the investigators that he might have hired someone to do it for him?"

Castro kept her eyes fastened on the judge, but Loving turned around to look at Tugg. One by one, so did the bailiff, the judge, and even Steve Carnap.

"Oh for God's sake," the judge said. "Who is that? This is family court, not a murder trial. Are you saying that Mr. Grammaticus was smart enough to hire a hit man, then stupid enough to bring him to court? Let's get to the bottom of that, shall we? That's what the criminal courts are for. But I don't see the rush in all this. The child is safe now, right?"

Castro and Loving both nodded.

"Then let's leave her right where she is while the police do whatever investigation they need to do. Motion for protective custody is denied."

"But, your honor," Carnap interjected.

"Sit down, Mr. Carnap. Your motion is denied as well. The child will stay where she is until the police investigation is over. And we'll settle the issue of custody for the baby when that event befalls us." The judge looked down at Kate. "Ma'am, how many months along are, you please?"

"Two," Kate managed.

"That gives us plenty of time," said the judge. "For God's sake, the child isn't even born yet."

Chapter 13

Adam looked out the floor-to-ceiling windows of Steve Carnap's office at the stunning view of downtown Portland with Mount Hood in the distance. Was Emma in one of those buildings? Or was she off somewhere else, beyond the city? Now that the protective custody motion had been denied, maybe they could find out. Or even see her. That wasn't as good as getting her back, of course, but it was better than the wall of silence they'd gotten so far. If they had to wait for the police investigation into Rachel's murder to be completed before they could get Emma back, they'd have to make *some* arrangements to get more information.

Adam and Kate were getting more agile with the wheelchair, which made them fifteen minutes early for their appointment. When they got there, the receptionist brought them straight to Carnap's office and told them to wait, while he finished something in the conference room.

As they sat in silence, Adam reached over and took Kate's hand. They were both so devastated from court that morning that there wasn't much to say. Tugg was off on one of his motorcycle rides so, instead of bothering to go home, Adam and Kate had drifted around Pioneer Square and the park blocks, killing time. If they didn't get Emma back soon, there'd be a lot more of that in their future.

Carnap breezed past them and sat down at his desk. "Sorry about that," he said. "I was meeting with the partners to see if we could get a consensus."

Adam felt as if he were sitting in a doctor's office awaiting the results of a biopsy.

Carnap leaned toward them. "We all think that the best way forward is for you two to split up."

The words hung in the air for a second before Adam realized that they actually had a meaning for his own life.

"I was afraid of this," Kate said in a whisper.

"Afraid of what?" Adam said. "Why would we do that? Wouldn't they see through it? It's just a ploy."

"You'd have to do it for real," Carnap said. "Adam, you would have to move out, and Kate, you would have to file for a legal separation. It's the only way. Adam is the one under suspicion here. If you don't split up, there's a chance that in seven months they could try to take the baby."

Kate winced.

"If I'm charged with a crime," Adam said. "Which I shouldn't be, because I had nothing to do with Rachel's death."

"Yes," the lawyer said, "but think about the short term for a minute. Do you really want Emma to stay in foster care all those months while the murder investigation is going on? Once you're out of the house, Kate can petition to get Emma back. You'd need to find some help around the house, but then you'd be all set."

"All set?" Adam said.

"Adam, I'm sorry but you know that you're the threat here, not Kate. There's no worry of future abuse if you're out of the house. But they'd have to be convinced that you would *stay* out of the house. Then Emma could come home."

Kate had a shattered look on her face, but her voice was clear. "But wouldn't all this look bad for Adam? If the police are investigating and they find out we're separated, wouldn't that suggest I've lost faith in him? That I believe he's guilty of *something*?"

"That's a good point, but we can't help it," Carnap said. "And remember that in a criminal case they'd have to *prove* his guilt, not just be suspicious. It might look bad for him to move out, but that doesn't give them any evidence of his culpability in killing Rachel Norwood. Not unless you testified against him. But I would suggest, Adam, that you get a criminal lawyer to represent you. For Emma's sake, I'm going to have to be Kate's lawyer from now on. I can't help you anymore."

"We appreciate it," Kate said.

Adam watched a tugboat slowly making its way up the Willamette River. The bridges were all raised.

Tugg blew in the front door just before dark, with a serious case of windburn and no trace of a smile. Kate was out of her wheelchair, sitting as close to Adam as physically possible on the living room couch.

"Any word?" Tugg said.

"We're filing for legal separation," Kate answered.

"What?" Tugg's face went from shock, to confusion, to understanding within the space of five seconds.

Adam stroked Kate's hair and turned to Tugg. "Not really a choice," he said.

"For how long?"

"The real deal. File for separation and then divorce, if it drags on that long. Once they clear me in Rachel's murder, we can see where we stand. But until then, if they catch us faking it, we're dead."

"When?" Tugg said.

Adam nodded toward his packed bag sitting in front of the hall closet.

"Take the car," Kate said. "Worse comes to worst, you can sleep in it tonight. Till you get where you're going."

"Where am I going?"

"I don't know." Kate buried her head in Adam's shoulder.

Adam put his arms around Kate and gave her a long tender kiss.

"I cashed in the 401(k) plan. They said the check will be here next week."

"I don't care about money now."

"You'd better," Adam said. "Hal is itching to fire me and Carnap is billing overtime. Even if they clear me and we get Emma back, we'll be broke."

"We've been broke before."

"Yeah, I remember."

From the trailer park to Lake Oswego. Gone in an instant.

"Let's take the bike," Tugg said. "It'll give us more options."

"Okay," Adam said. He stood and walked toward the door, then turned back. "Minh Chau said she'd be over after dinner. Kate, what are you going to do after that?"

"Just go, Adam. I'll figure something out. Families in Transition, remember? We don't need to keep things a secret anymore. I've got some loyal colleagues at work. They're ready to move mountains. I've got the house and the phone. Soon I'll have Emma. We'll be fine here. But leave your cell on, okay? I'll call you when she's home."

"No," said Adam. "No phone calls. They might check. This has to look real. You can't even tell Minh Chau. If we're going to do this, let's do it right. Let's do it for Emma."

Kate raised her arms and motioned him back. "Just one more."

Adam rushed back and they dissolved in a long embrace. "This will work," Adam finally said. "It has to. There's no other way." He rose and walked straight to his bag, bumping past Tugg on his way out.

Everything Adam Grammaticus had built since the age of fifteen, he left behind that door.

Chapter 14

Adam woke to the sweet smell of sagebrush and fescue grass on the high desert. They were still in Oregon, if only barely, having slept last night in a farmer's field just outside Ontario. After spending that first night down near the Columbia River in the worst truck stop Adam had ever seen, they'd taken off at sunrise, riding down the gorge at a blistering pace, straight through till sunset. When they rolled into town, they found a bar and ate, then rode back toward the dark and set up camp in a field by the motorcycle's high beams.

Adam rubbed his two-day beard and sat up. Tugg and the motorcycle were gone. He'd said he would be up with the sun for a trip to town to get some needed supplies. For what, Adam didn't know.

The sun was bright and hot, and looked as close as the Idaho border.

Adam's cell phone rang.

"Adam, it's Kate."

"Kate? I thought we weren't going to use the phone. We should hang up."

"No, Adam, wait. Something's happened."

Adam could hear the desperation in Kate's voice. "Tell me."

"Well, there's a lot. First about Emma. Castro said that even though you're gone, she can't return Emma."

"What? Why not?"

"A lot of reasons. First, she said it was unclear whether I could take care of Emma by myself. I told her I was getting help, but she said it wasn't a stable situation to have a single parent with zero mobility. I'd need three nannies."

"So you just have to line up the child care?"

"No. There's more. Adam, just listen. She got Judge Gordon to reverse the order and they put Emma in protective custody."

"For *what*?" Adam yelled into the cell phone. The nearest building was a barn over a mile away. "That doesn't make any sense. I'll come home."

"No! It's not safe. Listen to me."

Adam stood and paced back and forth in the dense grass.

Kate continued. "Steve Carnap called to say that the police are looking for you in connection with a double homicide twenty-three years ago. Do you remember when they took your fingerprints at the jail?"

Adam felt nauseated. "Yes."

"Well, they claim they got a match. Steve wants to know if you got that criminal lawyer yet. When you do, he said, you should consider turning yourself in while you fight it. It's bullshit, but that's what he said."

"Not going to happen."

"Good, I agree. He said you'd look less guilty, but I told him you're already innocent and look where that's gotten you."

Loyalty, it's a beautiful thing.

"So does CPS know about the fingerprint? Is that why they put Emma in protective custody?"

"Probably. It would make sense."

Adam looked down at the pattern he was wearing in the grass. He considered coming clean, just telling Kate the truth about his past. He'd wanted to tell her a hundred times over the years, but it had never seemed right. That part of his life had been dead and buried, and he wanted to leave it there. Plus, how could he implicate himself without involving Tugg? But Emma was Kate's daughter, too. Didn't she deserve to know what they were up against?

Not over a cell phone.

"Adam, there's another reason you've got to be free, out there with Tugg. I haven't gotten to the worst part yet."

"There's a worse part?"

"Yes. When I heard they were putting Emma in protective custody, I called one of the counselors at work. He said there was nothing protective about protective custody. In fact, he said that they mostly used it as a kind of juvenile detention to protect *society* from the *kids*! He said they'd probably take Emma out of foster care and put her in a group home somewhere off the grid. It's horrible. The kids don't know where they are or how long they have to be there. And they're mixed in with all those other kids."

"So Emma's in danger?"

"Yes!"

"Are you saying you know this, or you're worried? There's a big difference, babe. Did they tell you they were putting Emma in one of these places?"

There was hesitation on the line. "They won't tell me anything. I've been calling them nonstop. I can't know for sure, but does it matter? Are you prepared to leave Emma out there and take the risk?"

"No."

"Neither am I. Adam, I'm pregnant and in a wheelchair. I'm here with the phone and you're out there with Tugg. You have to do something!"

"You mean what we talked about the other day?"

Adam's pulse was pounding in his ears. He could barely hear Kate's words until she screamed them.

"Go get her!"

Adam saw the blue Ford pickup coming down the road in a hurry, so he lay on his belly to let it pass. The sound kept getting nearer, until finally he heard the engine die somewhere at the edge of the field. A door opened and slammed.

Where the hell was Tugg? Now that the sun was up, they had to get moving. How many dominoes would fall if he got busted on a simple charge of trespassing in sleepy little Ontario, Oregon?

"Adam?" It was Tugg.

Adam stood.

"Adam, we've got to go. Get the blankets and gear. We're out of here."

"Where's the Harley?"

Tugg had a resolute look on his face. "We can't go where we're going on a bike. Too conspicuous and not enough room. We'll need to drive all night and take shifts sleeping. We've got room for cargo and there's a cab if it gets cold."

He traded his bike? More loyalty.

But where were they going? And how did Tugg seem to know how much things had shifted overnight?

Adam grabbed his stuff and followed Tugg across the field.

When they reached the truck Adam saw that the bed was filled with something, and covered with a tarp. Adam got in the passenger side.

"Hold the jokes about riding shotgun," Adam said. "Give me the Remington and I'll put it under my seat."

Tugg handed it over and started the engine. They blew down the road with a rooster tail of red dirt behind them.

For a few minutes they rode in silence, until Adam saw the sign: *Idaho four miles.*

"Okay, Tugg. I've got some things I need to tell you. I talked to Kate —"

"Yeah, I know. Give me your phone."

Adam handed Tugg his phone and watched him peel out the battery and SIM card with one hand, while he drove with the other.

"Put all three pieces in the glove box," Tugg said.

More silence.

"I never said a word to anyone, Tugg. Not even Kate. Ever."

"Yeah, I know."

Welcome to Idaho.

Tugg looked in the rearview mirror and seemed relieved by the empty road behind them.

Adam seized the moment. "So what now?"

"I've got it covered."

"What do you mean?"

Tugg kept his eyes straight ahead. "Look, you tried to do everything by the book, right? You were right. You're a systems guy. You built a nice life. You played by the rules. When you got in trouble, you hired a lawyer."

"Yeah."

"And how did all that work out for you? Have you lost enough yet?"

Adam quietly worked the muscles in his jaw.

"Yeah, I have."

Tugg nodded.

After a few miles of silence, Adam asked the question that they both knew came next. "So where are we headed, Tugg? Plan B?"

"That's a negative. We're going for plan Z."

Tugg looked over.

"You're in my world now."

Chapter 15

Come play with us, Emma. You're the new kid. New kids always go first.

I don't want to play. I want to go home.

Come sit in a circle. It's circle time. If you don't follow the rules, you'll make it bad for all of us.

I want to stay at the window. I want to watch for my Daddy.

Your Daddy's not coming. They never do. We're your family now.

No, you're not!

You're going to be with us for a long time, Emma. Maybe till you're grown up. You'll see. You need us. The grownups think they run it here, but they don't. We're your brothers and sisters now.

I don't have any brothers and sisters. Only my mommy and daddy. And they're coming for me.

No, they're not. Someone did something bad. That's why they're not coming.

I didn't do anything bad! Rachel did! My daddy loves me. Rachel lied and that's why the lady took me away.

Your daddy hurt you. He can't find you here. You'll get used to us. Sometimes it's fun here.

I don't want to have fun. I want to go home!

You are home, Emma. We're your family now.

Chapter 16

Adam rolled down the window and felt the hot wind in his face. The highway snaked ahead in a black ribbon that looked like it went all the way to Montana. Tugg took the first exit and headed south.

"Highway 95 — so we're not going to Boise?"

"Not really," Tugg replied. "We'll go south about fifty miles, then cut back into Oregon. Off the main drag."

"Why?"

"It's the next thing."

"Where are we going?"

"Ashland."

"Why?"

"I already told you."

It was no use pushing. When Tugg got into "mission mode" he could be such a pain in the ass; act now, explain later. For now Tugg seemed to know where he was going and that suited Adam just fine. Getting out of Ontario in a hurry probably made sense. If they could triangulate a cell phone call off a local tower he was cooked. Plus he needed some time to deal with the shock waves he'd been pushing back all morning. Emma was lost to the system and he was a fugitive from justice. Somehow he had to work through all that and get her back. But why drive all the way to Ashland? Was that the best place to start? Was that where Emma was? But how would Tugg know that?

"Look Tugg, we've got to make a plan."

"I've got one."

"To get Emma back?"

"Yeah."

Adam could feel the bow string shift in his shoulders. He put his foot up on the dash. *Let's get to it then. Let's hear it.* Adam decided to start the questioning from an oblique angle.

"Where did you get the truck?"

"Friends."

"I thought you always rode alone?"

"I do. I did. I used to." Tugg lit a cigarette and held it out the window.

The road was a bit bumpier than the highway, but Adam guessed that Tugg was keeping the speed down for other reasons.

"What do you mean, Tugg? Are these friends I would know?"

"I doubt it."

"Why?"

"Because they're outlaw bikers. I just met 'em."

Adam just looked at Tugg. *People you'd just met would lend you a truck?* More likely he'd traded his motorcycle for it.

Tugg finished his cigarette and lit another. He kept looking straight down the road.

Adam willed his mouth shut long enough that the silence became a question.

"Look, Adam, the motorcycle isn't gone, okay? I had to sign the title over to an outlaw motorcycle club so I could start the plan to get Emma back. Getting the truck was only the first step. There's a lot more. If this all works out, it can lead us to Emma. But it won't be easy." Tugg finally looked over at Adam. "How much do you want to know?"

"All of it."

Tugg flicked his cigarette out the window and put both hands on the wheel.

"But why would you join an outlaw motorcycle club to get Emma back? That doesn't make sense."

This was the plan? This was what he'd been waiting to hear?

"I haven't joined yet. Joining is a process. I'm a 'prospect.' It's like being on probation. That's where I've been going every day on those rides in Portland. Their main clubhouse is in Forest Grove. The one in Ontario is just an affiliate. There's another one in Ashland. Before you become a member you've got to hang around the club for a while. Meet all the members. Then, if it all works out, they invite you to become a prospect. That's what happened to me before we left Portland. But then you've got to do shit for them. Chores and the like.

You've got to earn your way up. And you've got to sign the title of your bike over to them. If you make it, you get your patch and you're a full member. If you don't, they keep your bike."

Adam's head was spinning. None of this made sense. Could Tugg even pull it off? He wasn't a joiner. Other than himself, Adam couldn't name one of Tugg's friends.

"I still don't get the biker club. What does that have to do with finding Emma?"

The terrain had flattened as they skimmed along the high mesa. Hot sun and tumbleweeds.

"Look, Adam, you can't expect to just go in there like Butch and Sundance and find your daughter. Where would we even start? You need a network. You need resources. And you need information."

"OK but still. If we're going to find Emma, maybe we should start with where she is. Do you even know that yet? No, so I say —"

"I went to see Lisa Castro," said Tugg.

"You *what?*"

"It didn't work. I tried to get her to let me be Emma's foster parent. This was all before the court hearing. She wouldn't let me do it. She kicked me out. But I learned something really important on the way out."

"What?"

Tugg looked over at him. "That becoming a member of the club could help us find Emma."

Adam shook his head. *Not this game again.*

"Tugg, spit it out, willya?"

Tugg looked straight ahead.

"Listen, Adam, a motorcycle club is a lot more than what you see on the outside. There are a lot of people associated with it. Some are women. They aren't patch members. They're usually the 'old lady' of one of the patch members. But they're every bit as committed to the club as the men are. They ride along with them, on the back. They take care of the club. In some sense, they're the *property* of the club. But they've usually got a life outside too. They have jobs. They're the earners. They're out in society, and you probably wouldn't even recognize them."

"And you can?"

"Sometimes. You have to know what to look for."

"Like what?"

"A tattoo. A 'tramp stamp.' Something that flags them as 'Property of the Club.'"

Adam stared at Tugg.

"I know, Adam. It isn't your world. But there are women like that. I've been with some."

"And you saw one of those on Lisa Castro? You've got to be kidding me."

"Not her," Tugg said. "Someone else in her office."

"Who?" Adam said.

"Her name is Wanda."

Chapter 17

Entering Snake River Basin.

"I saw the tattoo when she leaned over," said Tugg. "Above the back of her jeans."

"So she can help us? Did she tell you where Emma was? Is she in Ashland?"

Tugg put his hand up. "Not so fast, bro. She didn't say anything about Emma. I haven't even talked to her yet."

"What? Why not?"

"Because I'm not patched yet. I'm just a prospect. There's a big difference. When you're a prospect they give you your 'cut' — your 'colors.' They give you a leather vest with the logo of the club on the back. Take a look in my bag."

Adam reached over the seat and took the alien thing out of Tugg's bag. He held it on his lap like it was too hot to touch.

The Immortals.

"The top 'rocker' is the name of the club," Tugg said. "Below that's the logo. That's all I get for now. When you become a full member, they give you the bottom rocker with the name of the place where your charter is located. That's when you become a full patch member. When you've got three patches, you're in. But you don't just move up automatically from prospect to full patch. They have to vote you in. And until they do, you sure as hell don't start nosing around asking questions of somebody's old lady at the clubhouse. That can get you killed. I've got to jump through a lot of hoops before I become a full patch. Then I can talk to Wanda. Once I'm a member, then she's a sister, and she's got to help me with —"

"So if you're a prospect, why aren't you wearing your vest?" Adam said.

"Never in a car. That's major disrespect. The colors have to fly freely."

Adam looked absently out the window. "OK so how long does it take then?" Adam asked. "To get your full patch?"

"Minimum six months. I've seen it quicker, but I've seen it take longer, too."

Adam's head shot back around.

"Six months! Christ, Tugg, Emma is out there now!"

Tugg nodded and held his hand up again. "Yeah, I understand. You got a better plan?"

Adam fumed. "Maybe I do. Maybe we should go back to CPS. I could talk to Wanda myself. If you're a member of her club then —"

"Adam, were you listening? You'll get us *both* killed. We've got to follow the rules."

"For an outlaw club?"

"That's right. And one of the main rules right now is that I've got to show commitment to the club."

Adam shook his head. This was all so fucking unbelievable.

"And how do you do that?"

"You mean other than signing my motorcycle over to them?"

Adam drew a breath. "Look, Tugg, I get it. It's not lost on me what you're doing for me here. But clue me in. *This* is the plan?"

"Yeah, *this* is the plan. I've got to do whatever the fuck they ask me to. I don't have any control over it. I hate it, but that's how it is."

Adam could feel his options closing off. He turned his head and looked out the window again. "And these things you've got to do. I suppose they're illegal?"

"I'd do anything for you and your family. You know that. But not everything the club does is illegal. You hear 'outlaw' and you think criminal. But 'outlaw' just means they're a one-percenter club. They don't live by the rules."

Adam's eyes narrowed.

"Look. A bunch of years back some guy at the American Motorcycle Association said that ninety-nine percent of motorcyclists were law-abiding citizens and that most of the trouble was caused by the others who gave motorcyclists a bad name. Some folks took this up as a badge of honor. They're the outlaws. The one-percenters. They don't live by anybody's rules but their own. It's about freedom. They're outlaws, but not necessarily criminals. Get it?"

Adam nodded. Tugg was so free that he wasn't even a one-percenter. He was a millionth percenter. He didn't want to live by *anybody's* rules. Not even a motorcycle club. And he was giving that up for Adam. But would it work?

"So when do you have to start these chores, then?" Adam said.

"We're doing one now."

"What?"

"We're making a delivery."

Adam turned to look out the back window at the truck bed. "Is that what's under the tarp?"

"Yeah."

"What is it? Drugs? Guns?"

"No, Adam. Were you listening just now? Not everything the clubs do is illegal."

"So what's in the back, then?"

"Toys."

Chapter 18

"Toys?" Adam said. "We're driving to Ashland to deliver toys? Please tell me it's to a foster home where Emma might be."

"Sorry, can't say that's the plan," Tugg said. "When I got to the Ontario charter this morning and introduced myself, they asked me to make a toy run. I couldn't say no. They asked me who I was running with and when I said your name, they called a contact from the probation department in Portland. He said you were wanted on a twenty-three year old warrant. I immediately called Kate and she told me the rest. I guess you'd just talked to her."

"So is there a problem?" Adam said.

"There is for them. Like I said, Adam, outlaw ain't illegal. You're the illegal one. They told me not to wear my cut today, even outside the truck. They don't want any flak coming back at the club if you get arrested. They lent me the truck and said you could ride with me, but that's it. We're due back in 24 hours."

"So an outlaw motorcycle club is worried that I might give them a bad name?" Adam said.

"Enjoy your notoriety. The clubs are doing everything they can to clean up their image. That's why the toy run. The big clubs have been doing charity work for years. They want to make it clear to the community that they're not the mafia or anything. They're free souls and want to be left alone, but they aren't a threat to society. That's why I wasn't surprised when I saw one of their old ladies working at CPS. The one-percenters are the ones who beat the shit out of the child molesters in prison. They'd do anything for kids."

Adam had an image of Santa Claus in a leather jacket riding on a chopper. This was insanity. Emma needed to be rescued *now*. But what was a better plan? Breaking into CPS? Threatening somebody? Adam was a fugitive. If he got caught, Emma might be gone for good. If Tugg thought this was the way to go, maybe it was. For now. As long as they kept their heads down, maybe it would work.

"Okay, so what should *I* be doing?"

"You're doing it."

"Bullshit, I'm not just gonna sit around while my baby girl's out there. Maybe we should split up. You're the one who's trying to join the club. You can drop me in Bend and I'll hitch back to Portland. There's gotta be some information I can pick up—"

"You'll get caught," Tugg said. "You need to find Emma but you also need to hide. And what better place for a guy like you to hide than a motorcycle club?"

"You mean gang."

"I mean club."

Adam blew out his breath.

"How do you know so much about all this?" Adam said.

Tugg looked at him. "C'mon Adam, look at me. Give me a helmet and I'm a fucking Viking. They came to me when I was working as a mechanic down in Flagstaff. They started asking me questions. A good mechanic is a valuable asset. I went on a couple of bike runs and a couple of parties. But it wasn't for me. I didn't want the responsibility. It's not like you can join and then get out again. It's not like the Air Force. There's no such thing as a discharge. Once you're in an outlaw club, you're in for life."

"You make it sound like they own you or something," Adam said.

"That's about right."

"Well, if it's not illegal, what's so bad about that? We're out on the road anyway. Now you've got some brothers."

Tugg pulled the truck over in a cloud of dirt and turned to Adam. "Adam, what the fuck? You don't know what you're talking about. This is dangerous stuff. Violent. I'm expected to do anything they ask. *Anything*. And yes, they'd do it for me too, but so what? I'm loyal to you, okay? We're brothers. I get that. But you think I want to get in a bar fight and back somebody up just because he was too drunk to know he was acting like an asshole to someone's wife? And there's a lot of other shit too, that I can't tell you about. I'll be looking over the horizon at jail for the rest of my life."

"Tugg, calm down. I get it. But we're not in any danger now, are we? We're just delivering toys. As long as the cops don't pull us over, I think we're fine."

"You don't know shit," Tugg said, pulling back onto the highway.

"What?" Adam said. "How could delivering toys be dangerous?"

"It isn't always, but it is today."

"What?"

Tugg hesitated, then spit it out. "Because we're driving through The Reapers' territory to do it. The club said they didn't just want the toys delivered, they wanted to make a statement by cutting through rival territory. It would've been easier to go across the Indian reservation and stay on Route 20 all the way to Bend, but they said no. That's why we're in Idaho. We've got to turn back into Oregon a few miles south of here and then we'll be in Reapers' land. Believe me, they'll see us."

"Can't we wait till nighttime?"

"Twenty-four hours, remember?"

Adam felt his pulse bump up. "How will they know us?" he asked. "I thought they told you not to wear your vest."

"That's for law enforcement," Tugg said. "The cops don't know what they're looking at unless they've seen it on MSNBC."

"So how will The Reapers know?"

"We're flying a flag of our own. On the tailgate. Big as a picture."

"I didn't see it."

"And you probably can't read graffiti either, can you? Believe me, if you knew what you were looking at, you'd shit your pants. They'll notice. Any biker would."

Adam looked out the back window again. "So what are we supposed to do, then?"

Sheaville eight miles ahead. Welcome to Oregon.

Tugg lit a cigarette. "You tell me. You're the one with the shotgun."

Chapter 19

Adam never thought that road noise could be so loud, but after a full hour of scanning every dot on the horizon for motorcycles, he decided to close his eyes for a minute and just listen for them instead.

Buzz...zzzz.

His eyes flew open.

"What's up, Adam? If you want to sleep, just do it," Tugg said.

"How can I sleep? I'm listening for Reapers."

Tugg snorted. "Don't look for trouble. It'll come or it won't."

"It usually does these days."

"Now your head's right. But don't drive yourself crazy. Alert, but calm. That's what you're looking for."

"Alert, but calm?"

"Yeah, I'll be alert and you be calm."

Adam smiled and settled back in his seat.

Tugg was right. Adam was already exhausted from bouncing back and forth between the events of the last few weeks: the abuse allegation, Rachel's death, Kate's pregnancy, the court hearing, the fingerprint that led investigators to his role in a decades-old double homicide, and of course the granddaddy of them all: losing Emma.

Adam closed his eyes again and focused on the even sound of buzzing tires on hot pavement. He imagined the rest. A flat plateau leading to a distant mountain range. Shades of blue light pulsing through scrub trees on either side of a two-lane highway. Emma out there somewhere, confused and alone. Kate waiting for him to make it right. An empty road ahead.

Pavement buzzing. Hot sun.

The wind sang a low note through the cracked window.

Adam heard Tugg's lighter flare and clink.
Smell of the cigarette.
Tugg was keeping an even speed. Good man.
Shotgun under the seat.
Drone of the tires.
Bees in a mason jar.
The sound of Tugg taking a long sweet drag.
Kids on a swing pumping their feet as they arced toward sunshine.
Slam of the back door screen.
Adam, you want to ditch school Monday?
It's only a half day.
Yeah, but your stepdad doesn't know that. We can go to my house and have peanut butter sandwiches and grape wine. My mom'll be at work.
I've never had wine.
You'll hate it, but it's got to be done.
Why, if I'll hate it?
To become a man, dickhead. You're fourteen, what are you waiting for?
Laurie Buchansky.
Ain't we all.
Whine of the motor.
Smell of sweet onions from a farmer's field.
Manure and a pulse of water in the distance.
Squirt guns in the back yard.
I want my daddy to come get me.
I'm coming, Emma.
Where are you?
I'll be there as soon as I can.
I want to go home!
We're looking for you, sweet girl.
They said you're not coming.
That's not true.
Daddy, this place scares me!

"Adam, wake up."
The mountains were a little closer, but the road looked the same.
"What is it, Tugg?"

Adam turned 360 degrees, scanning the horizon. Alert but calm had gone to shit.

"I see it. Way out the back. Reapers?"

Tugg checked the side mirror and shook his head. "Cop."

Chapter 20

Tugg had the driver's side window down and his hands on the steering wheel.

"Don't say a word unless he asks you a question, got it?"

"Not sure about that," Adam said. "I say we drop him."

"Adam! He's a county sheriff. We're probably in the clear if we can keep POPO from showing up."

"POPO?"

"Pissed off peace officer."

Adam watched the cop walk past the driver's window until he was about fifteen feet in front of the truck, then he turned and looked them dead in the eye through the windshield.

"Hands in your lap," Tugg said through his teeth. "Don't reach down." Tugg's eye flicked to the keys, and his foot crawled nearer the gas pedal.

The cop walked back to Tugg's window. "Afternoon, boys. What're you haulin'?"

"Toys," Tugg said smiling. "Got a bunch of kids in Grant's Pass waitin' on us."

The cop looked over at Adam. "This your truck?" he asked Tugg.

"No, borrowed it from a friend," Tugg said.

"I'll need to see some ID."

Tugg handed it to him.

"Arizona license with Oregon plates. I'll need to run the reg too."

Adam snapped the glove box open and gave it to Tugg, who handed it to the officer.

"Guess it wouldn't be a bad idea to get your ID too, fella," he said to Adam.

This was it. One query on the computer and it was over.

"I'll have to get it from my bag," Adam said.

"Okay, let me run this first. Don't go anywhere!" The cop gave his best redneck grin and walked back to the cruiser.

Tugg watched him in the rearview mirror. When he was safely in the front seat, Tugg finally spoke.

"Don't touch the shotgun."

"Why the fuck not. We should take him now."

"Whoa. Slow down."

"I thought you said this was Plan Z?" Adam said. "If he checks my ID or frisks you, we're done for." Adam felt a splinter in his brain. "What about Emma?"

"Yeah, but he's checking my ID and plate right now," Tugg said. "And if a cop turns up dead and they trace his last inquiry, who do you think they'll find?"

The motorcycles shot past at something less than the speed of light.

"Fucking hell," Tugg said. "Now we're in shit."

"Do you think they saw us?"

"Fifty-fifty," Tugg said. "But we need to roll."

Adam looked back in the side mirror. Why did it always take cops so long to run a plate?

The bikes grew smaller as the cop finally emerged from his cruiser and sauntered back to Tugg's window.

"Not stolen. Clean record. You boys are free to go."

"Thanks," Tugg said, reaching for his keys.

"Just one more thing," the cop said. "Mind if I take a peek under your tarp? We got a lot of illegal guns comin' through here."

Adam saw Tugg's jaw clench.

"Be my guest," Tugg said.

The cop walked behind the truck and lifted one end of the tarp, then signaled for Tugg and Adam to join him.

"Here we go," Tugg said. "Leave the shotgun and keep your hands by your side the whole time. I'll drop him if we have to."

What the hell? So it wasn't just toys?

Adam hesitated so that Tugg got there first, then joined them behind the truck.

The cop didn't say a word. Neither did Tugg.

Adam's arms felt dead. No weapon. Nowhere to run.

"Not sure what to make of this thing on your tailgate," the cop said. "Latin? My grandson studies it in school. No light Mess or um Tim ear."

"Nolite Messorem Timere," said Tugg.

"What's it mean?"

"Don't fear the reaper," Adam said.

Tugg's eyes widened and Adam could see the smallest trace of a smile on his lips.

"Best song ever," Adam said.

"That may be," the cop broke in. "But you guys are stone cold idiots riding around here with that on your truck. There's an outlaw motorcycle gang called The Reapers up in Malheur. Their motto is some damn thing in Latin. They see this and you just might fear the reaper."

"We'll take our chances," said Tugg.

"Mortui Vivos Docent," said the cop.

"Huh?" Adam said. "I thought you didn't know Latin."

"It's my grandson's school motto. Only thing I know."

"What's it mean?" Tugg said.

"The dead teach the living."

Chapter 21

"You should've let me drive," Adam yelled from under the tarp. "How the hell am I going to handle the shotgun from back here?"

The two dots ahead had grown larger.

"Just let me handle the truck," Tugg said, turning his head to the small window behind him. "I don't think they saw our tailgate when we were with the cop. If we stay back, maybe we're good."

"Why are they going so slow? I thought motorcycles always hauled ass."

"They usually do," Tugg barked. "Stay ready."

Adam couldn't see a bloody thing. Big Wheels. Board games. Stuffed animals of every kind known to man. The tarp was loose now, but he dared not poke his head up till Tugg gave the signal. Then all hell would break loose.

"Maybe the cop called them," Adam yelled.

"What?"

"Maybe the COP *CALLED* them!"

"Shit," Tugg said. "They're down to forty-five. I'm going to back off some more."

Adam felt the truck slow as he fingered the shotgun. "How many shots?"

"FIVE!"

"What the hell?"

"One in the chamber and four in the mag. Adam, just shut up, okay?"

The truck slowed again.

"Adam, they're signaling us to pass. This ain't good."

"When you get alongside just ram 'em!" Adam shouted.

"Can't."

"Why the hell not?"

"It's a biker thing. You don't ram a bike with a vehicle even if he's your sworn enemy. If the club back in Portland found out, they'd kill me themselves."

"Shit, Tugg, you're worried about some biker code? Now? Let's take our chances. We're gonna die if we don't do something here."

"Shotgun!" Tugg yelled. "You wait for my signal." The truck picked up speed at an alarming clip and Adam heard the *braaaaaap* of engines kicking down an octave as the bikes fell behind.

"They see us?" Adam called.

The motorcycle engines picked up.

"How many?"

"Still just two," Tugg said.

"What's happening?"

"They're signaling me to stop."

"You gonna?"

"Adam, *pay attention*! You've got one at each tail light. Ten and two. Go left, then right. Got it?"

"Maybe I can blind them with the tarp."

"Adam, don't be a fucking idiot. You've got one chance. Put your back against the cab."

Heart slamming.

Engines whining.

Pin pricks of light.

A thousand needles at the back of his neck.

When Tugg's voice finally came, the release was sweet as morphine.

Chapter 22

The Big Wheel exploded on the pavement in a shower of red and yellow plastic. The motorcycles swerved to the side and back, leaving a look of shock on the bikers' faces that was visible from 15 feet away, even at 70 m.p.h.

But now Adam was in trouble.

With the element of surprise gone, it was only a matter of time before the bikers got the advantage. Adam had done enough to piss them off, but not enough to stop them.

"What the hell are you doing?" Tugg screamed. "Did you just throw something at them?"

Adam steadied himself against the cab and opened one of the board games. The wind suddenly took it and scattered fake money, board pieces, and bits of paper all over the road. This had a slightly better effect than the Big Wheel, as one of the bikers backed off forty feet, then came roaring back, drawing his finger across his neck in the universal sign for execution.

"Adam, for God's sake, just do it!"

"I've got a plan!"

"No, you don't. Do it now!"

One of the bikers reached into his vest. Adam flinched when he saw bright metal, but it was only a cell phone.

A cell phone?

Adam grabbed a basketball and threw it straight at the biker. He missed by three feet, but the commotion was enough to cause a momentary wobble and the biker dropped his phone.

The wind muffled an indecipherable bark of cursing, as the other biker pulled to within ten feet of the tailgate.

The angle was perfect.

If they fell back again Adam might not get another shot.

He fell on his belly and rolled under the tarp. Adam grabbed the shotgun and slithered through the stuffed animals toward the tailgate.

The roar of the engines was tremendous.

Do it for Kate.

Tugg was holding the truck steady.

Do it for Emma.

Adam popped up and steadied the barrel on the bright blue tailgate.

BOOOOM!!!

A shower of rubber and screaming metal arced into the sunshine. Adam watched as the biker struggled to control the skid and spun off the side of the road in a cloud of red dust.

The second biker braked hard and angled off, but Adam still had a shot at the side of his bike.

BOOOM!

Missed. The biker jumped off and ran for the ditch.

BOOOM!! BOOOM!!! BOOOM!!!

In a shower of debris, Adam saw leather, chrome, and a front tire rise up and fall back to the asphalt.

Adam almost lost his balance as Tugg hit the brakes.

"FIVE SHOTS," Tugg said.

"DONE!"

"You need more?"

"*Done!* Look out the back."

Tugg stopped in the center of the road and whipped his head around. Two dead motorcycles, one smoking and one in flames, burning in the distance.

Adam's lungs were on fire.

"You get 'em?" Tugg said.

"Don't know. We need to go back?"

"What the hell for?"

Adam peered down the road. No sign of the bikers.

"You okay?"

"Yeah," Adam replied. "My ears are ringing."

They were both silent as they watched the smoke rise. Adam climbed out of the truck bed and came around to the cab. The wind had picked up.

"Why did you do that?" Tugg said.

"I needed to take out two bikes. Not two bikers."

"You almost got us killed."

"No I didn't. My plan worked."

"Define 'worked.'"

Fingers of black curled into the aqua sky.

"Someone's going to see the smoke," Tugg said.

"We're almost to the mountains."

Tugg turned his head and looked back one more time. "Good."

Chapter 23

The smell of marijuana, sweat, and engine grease hung in the air like a blanket. The only light in the clubhouse came from a window draped with an American flag.

Adam kept peeling his beer label like it was an orange, trying to get it off all in one piece. The whole room was focused on Tugg, who was finally wearing his colors.

Adam wondered what Emma was doing this very minute.

"That's not what we heard!" a voice boomed. "We heard you threw dog shit at 'em."

The crowd roared.

"Not me, him," Tugg said, pointing.

Suddenly all eyes were on Adam. A dozen bikers and two braless women in black leather vests and Daisy Mae shorts waited for him to say something clever, as Adam kept his attention fixed on his bottle.

"Hey prospect, get your pal another beer," a voice said to Tugg.

Adam looked up and saw green eyes grinning between a thatch of oily black hair and a close-cropped beard. "Filthy Few" his patch said. In another world, he was George Clooney.

Adam shook his head. "Still working on this one, thanks."

"You damn sure? Today you can have anything you want."

Adam had heard one of the bikers call him Spider, and he was pretty obviously the leader. Long and lean, he had a full set of shirtsleeve tattoos running down both arms and a big black spider web etched on his neck.

Spider reached out his hand and slapped one of the women on the ass. "I mean anything."

Adam looked at the floor and smiled. What in the world was he doing here?

"Big Wheels," a huge guy near the door said. "How the fuck did you think of that? Righteous insult. That's what they should be riding."

"He didn't really need the shotgun," Tugg said. "But Adam took the bikes out so they couldn't follow us."

"*He* took them out?" Spider said. "Maybe we got the wrong prospect here."

Everybody laughed except Adam and Tugg.

"But they'd be scared shitless to follow you all the way here," Spider continued. "I love it anyway. Take out their horses and make 'em walk."

"So how you gonna pay us for the Big Wheels?" someone said.

Everyone laughed again.

"Spot those," Spider exhaled. "He can earn 'em off over the next few days."

"I'm sorry," Tugg said. "Wish we could, but Ontario said we had to be back by noon tomorrow. We'll have to drive all night."

"Fuck that." Spider reached for another beer. "Let me talk to 'em. We need you here and you need our votes, prospect. Your friend can just chill."

What was this? They'd have to stay here? While his little girl was out there somewhere waiting for him?

One of the girls walked over and sat next to Adam.

"Okay well then, g'night." Adam jumped off his chair, then flushed red when he realized how that looked.

"Crystal, it's not even dark yet, but this man wants his jammies. Show him where he's staying," said Spider.

Crystal smiled and took Adam's arm.

"I — I —"

"C'mon," Crystal said. "I'll show you."

Adam stole a glance at Tugg, but he looked just like the rest of them. Grinning like idiots.

Chapter 24

"What happens in Ashland stays in Ashland."

Adam looked over at Tugg in the front seat of the truck and wanted to slap the grin off his face.

"I told you, nothing happened," Adam said. "I went to bed."

"Yeah, I know," Tugg said, looking ahead at the strip mall.

"Good. I'm glad you believe me." Adam looked at Tugg. "Why do you believe me?"

Tugg looked over and grinned again. "Because Crystal came to my room last night after you shut her out."

Adam nodded. He was smiling too.

Adam hadn't bothered to ask Tugg where they were going so early. Adam had been up since dawn, afraid to open his bedroom door, and jumped at the chance to get out when Tugg had knocked.

I-5 North, Medford, one mile.

"Where are we going?" Adam asked. "Back to Ontario?"

"First, a Wendy's." Tugg pulled into the parking lot and shut off the truck.

"We going to eat it here?" Adam said.

"No, but I hate the drive-through. Listen, can you go in and get me —"

"Yeah, yeah. I remember." Adam slid off his seat and headed for the door.

The truck engine fired up.

"Hey!" Adam turned his head as the truck pulled out.

Tugg leaned out the window, but didn't stop.

"I've gotta do something for the club today. You can't come."

"What?!" Adam walked toward the truck, but Tugg just kept rolling.

"Don't go back to the club. I'll pick you up here after dark."

"Tugg, what the hell?" Adam just stood there as he watched the bright blue truck disappear into traffic.

Chapter 25

Wendy's. Wal-Mart. An old Phillips 66 station that hadn't changed its sign in thirty years. It went on like this for miles in either direction.

Adam's cell phone was still dismantled in the glove box of the truck. Thirty-eight bucks in cash. *Probably should get off the street.*

Damn Tugg for stranding him here.

He'd headed north, likely for I-5. But where? And why couldn't Adam come with him?

For your own good, Tugg would say. And he was probably right.

A whole day to kill, when he was dying every fifteen minutes.

Where was Emma right now?

Maybe Tugg's plan would work, maybe it wouldn't. But what might happen in the meantime, if it really took six months for Tugg to join the motorcycle club just so he could ask Wanda one goddamn question?

There had to be a better way.

"Collect call from Adam Neighbor. Will you accept the charges?"

"Who? No!" Mrs. Nguyen hung up the phone.

"Sorry," said the operator. "She doesn't seem to know you."

Adam slammed down the receiver.

The sun was higher now and traffic was picking up at the gas station. Whenever a customer pulled up to the pump, the little guy at the counter jumped off his stool and eyeballed Adam as he walked by the bench outside. One of only two states left in the nation where you couldn't fill up your own tank. Probably one of the last to have a pay phone out front, too.

Adam watched as the attendant popped the hood and checked all the fluids as the gas pumped.

He picked up the phone and dialed again.

"Collect call from that nice young man with the motorcycle who came to visit your neighbors. Will you accept the charges?"

"Who? Yes!"

"Go ahead, please."

"Mrs. Nguyen, it's me. Adam Grammaticus. I'm sorry about the trick, but I'm desperate. If I call back in fifteen minutes, can you have Kate come to your phone?"

"No. You shitty. You leave her. Why don't you call your own phone?"

Adam swallowed hard. He cleared his throat and tried to channel some of Tugg's charm.

"Mrs. Nguyen, you've always been such a great friend to our family. What you're doing now for Kate is wonderful and I'm sure she appreciates it. But I didn't leave her. If you go get Kate, I'm sure she'll be happy to talk to me."

"While I pay."

"We'll reimburse you for the call. Please don't hang up! Just get Kate and ask her to answer your phone when I call back in fifteen minutes. Would you do that for me?"

"For her, not you. She pregnant. Why don't you come home?"

The attendant closed the hood and stood by the driver's window with his clipboard.

"I can't right now. But I might if I can talk to her. Will you do it?"

"Still shitty."

"Fifteen minutes."

"You already said."

"Kate? It's me."

"Adam, are you all right? Where are you?"

Naturally there was a break between customers and the little guy was sitting at the counter just a few feet inside the open front door, pretending to read a magazine.

"We can't talk about that, but yes, I'm fine. Are you okay? Have you heard anything?"

Ding. Ding.

A car pulled up and the attendant hopped off his stool. Adam turned his head so he didn't have to look at him.

"No. Nothing. Adam, what's going on?"

"Kate! Quiet for a minute. Someone was listening, but he's gone now. Tugg and I have got a plan."

"Minh Chau is standing right here."

"Okay, just listen then. We think we might be able to find out where Emma is, but it's going to take some time. Have you heard anything that I don't know already?"

"No, nothing."

"Any contact with Castro?"

"She won't talk to me. Adam, they're looking for you."

"Yes, you might tell that to Mrs. Nguyen, so she understands why I can't just pop back home."

There was a pause on the line.

"She's been terrific. Some people from work have been helping me during the day, but Minh Chau has been staying over every night. I couldn't do it without her. Not with you gone."

"Still shitty," he heard in the background.

"I'm doing the best I can," Adam said. "I miss you." His stomach felt hollow.

"We'll get through this. I'm doing okay," Kate said.

Mr. Goodwrench was headed for the door.

"I'll call again when I can. Send Minh Chau my love."

Adam heard some sharp tones in Vietnamese as the phone hung up in his ear.

"Steve? It's me, Adam Grammaticus."

Outside a Wal-mart now, on a pre-paid cell phone. No sense having some ambitious cop trace too many collect calls back to Ashland.

"Adam, is that you?"

"We still privileged, Steve? Can I talk to you?"

"I told you before, I'm not a criminal lawyer. And I'm not your lawyer anymore either. You need to get one and come in. Didn't Kate tell you?"

"She told me, but I'm looking for Emma. Do you know where she is?"

"I can't tell you that."

"Can't or won't?"

"Both."

"What the hell does that mean?" Adam caught his voice.

Couples were milling through the parking lot, drunk on the hot sun, as Adam sat near a coin-operated rocking horse, under an awning at the front of the store.

"It means it would be better for everyone if you came in," Carnap said.

"Is Emma in danger?"

"She's not with her parents. Any time a child is in that situation, there's a risk of danger."

"Stop being a lawyer for five minutes and just talk to me, okay?"

Adam saw a woman staring at him as she came out of the store.

The line was silent.

"Steve, are you still there?" Adam lowered his voice. "What can you tell me about Emma?"

"That it would be better for her if you came in."

"You're the one who told me to leave Kate."

"I didn't tell you to become a fugitive. There's a warrant out for you now."

"In Portland?"

"Statewide. Wherever you are, you'd better come in."

Adam dropped his voice to a whisper, but said the words firmly. "I'm not coming in. I'm going to find my daughter."

More silence.

"Steve? Steve? Did you hang up?"

A boy ran out of the store and jumped up on the plastic horse. "DAD! Can I go around just a couple of times? *Please*?"

The father fished a couple of quarters out of his pocket, as the kid started bucking back and forth. "Yesssss!"

"Sorry, I'm not your lawyer anymore."

Chapter 26

The new cell phone had been dismantled and discarded ten hours ago. $17.07 left in cash. Adam sat on the curb next to the Wendy's and looked out at the dimly lit parking lot.

10:00 p.m.

Had he misunderstood Tugg saying he'd meet him back here after dark? Or maybe something had happened?

Adam had no one to call. Nothing to do but wait.

One restaurant crew had already left and another had started a few hours ago, which was why Adam had decided to eat all of his meals at Wendy's. At least they'd be less likely to kick him out of the parking lot.

Once they closed at eleven that worry would disappear, but new ones might arise.

Every passing set of lights gave Adam hope, until they either went through the drive-thru or parked. And since when did the shitload of blue trucks arrive in the world?

"Sir? Sir?"

Adam looked up and saw a teenage girl in a Wendy's hat and uniform standing over him under the streetlamp, holding a small paper sack.

"Yes?"

"We took a pool and bought you a potato skin and a Frosty. We decided not to call the cops, but you've got to leave soon. You're creeping everybody out. That's all I've got to say."

Adam couldn't quite make out her face, given the backlit halo of light.

"So you drew the short straw?"

"Huh?"

Adam stood and took the bag. "Thanks." There was no use explaining. In fact, the less he said at this point, the better. Adam was walking toward the street when he saw the headlights wink twice on the opposite side of the road.

"Tugg, you're hurt!"

"Yeah, you could say that."

Even in the dark cab, Adam could see that Tugg had cuts and bruises all over his face.

"Move over. I'll drive," Adam said.

Adam got in and eased the truck into traffic. After a couple blocks he looked over and saw that Tugg's hands were swollen.

"Tugg, what happened?"

"Pull over."

"Huh?"

"Just pull over."

Adam bounced the tires off the curb.

Tugg opened the door and went around to the tailgate, where he gingerly stepped up and into the bed of the pickup.

"Got to lay down," he said through the rear window.

"Tugg, are you okay?"

"I will be. Can you make it?"

"I don't know the way back."

Tugg arranged the tarp, grabbed a couple of stuffed animals that had been too dirty to donate and lay down on them. "Doesn't matter," he groaned.

"Should I take you to the hospital?"

"No!"

Adam pulled back into traffic. "Okay, but how will I get back to the clubhouse?"

Tugg shook his head as he cuddled up to the spare tire.

"Not going to the clubhouse. Head back to Ontario."

Chapter 27

The morning sun was bright as Adam rattled down the bumpy pavement. The map showed this as a state highway, but on an Indian reservation maybe they got to choose how they used government funds.

A string of hills stood shoulder to shoulder like monks on either side of the road. A small house or trailer appeared every five miles or so. If there hadn't been any telephone poles, you'd swear it was uninhabited. Half an hour ago, Adam had seen a pack of wild horses bolting across the highway. One mustang reared up in front of him, as if he were on a Hollywood set. *God, Emma would love to have seen that.*

More bumps.

Tugg was still asleep, against all odds. After seven hours, Adam was getting pretty tired himself.

Tugg hadn't said much more last night than "Take the short way back, through the reservation. We're cool now." Then he promptly fell asleep.

The air was getting hot. They'd have to stop soon for gas and water. But where?

Adam had come to a couple of conclusions about Indian reservations over the last few hours.

First, they were huge. Adam had no idea when he'd looked at state maps all his life that those big blocks of sacred territory were actually hundreds of miles across and barely developed. This must have been what Oregon looked like two hundred years ago.

Second, there was almost nobody here. He didn't know what the population was, but it was pretty clear that there was plenty of land to go around. If you did the math, there were probably a thousand acres for each inhabitant. Still, nobody seemed very rich.

Third, you didn't know poor until you'd seen rural poor. A couple of times Adam had seen a cluster of houses with seven or eight kids running around, chasing a dog or maybe just raising a cloud of dust. Didn't they have parks or playgrounds? How far away were the schools? Was there even a town of some kind in the middle of all this?

Adam remembered reading once that Indian reservations had their own laws, even their own police force and courts. This was a separate, sovereign nation, and it wasn't subject to the same rules as the rest of the state or even the country. But how could that be true? If you had a money laundering operation or tried to build a bomb on Indian land, he'd bet that the FBI would be right on you and drag you back to Portland for trial. A serious crime was surely subject to prosecution anywhere in the state.

But what about state gambling laws? Didn't some tribes have their own casinos? They probably had a couple of loopholes like that, but Adam doubted anyone could get away with a serious crime here. Even sovereignty went only so far.

Tugg hadn't moved in the flat bed for hours. Another pickup truck passed going the opposite direction and the driver waved, so Adam waved back. Maybe a town was coming up.

Adam saw the small hand-lettered sign for food and gas peeking out from a curve in the road up ahead.

After they ate and gassed up, maybe Tugg would take a shift.

"Is this a restaurant? Are you open for business?"

"We don't have any restaurants on the reservation, but I can feed you."

Adam looked at the tall, lanky man in the blue-checked shirt standing next to the stove. His smooth dark face and lean build suggested he could have been thirty, but the long grey braid snaking down his back betrayed him as closer to sixty.

"You want to eat first or gas up?"

"Let's eat," Tugg said, taking a seat at the single rickety table next to the window. An oscillating fan hummed in the silence.

"I'm Edward White Robe. I can serve you breakfast. Eggs, toast, and coffee. That's it. Okay with you?"

"Great," said Adam.

Edward disappeared in the back as Adam turned to Tugg. Tugg's face was swollen and looked awful.

"Tugg, you want to tell me what —?"

"Look, Adam, I still feel like shit, okay? I don't feel like talking. We've got a long way to go yet. Wait till we're back in the truck."

Edward reappeared with a carton of eggs and a skillet. A fly circled the room aimlessly, never landing.

"So, gas and food," Adam said, turning back to Edward. "You must corner the market around here, with it being so desolate." Adam winced before the words were even out of his mouth. This was going to be an awkward breakfast.

"Not much of a market," Edward said. "But if you need it, I've got it. Beer, magazines, belts, boots. Everything but meth. That's out *there*." He pointed out the window with his spatula as a pat of butter sizzled in the pan.

Adam looked out the window while Edward continued.

"When I was a kid, it was liquor. Still is, for most. But ever since I came back, the drugs are getting worse and worse. Especially for the kids. If you want something to drink, just go ahead and grab a can of Coke over there by the door."

Adam shook his head.

Tugg's eyes were half closed slits, which, with the swelling, gave his face the appearance of a pumpkin. Was he listening or sleeping?

"So you left and came back?" Adam said.

"Yes. Been back almost forty years. Left when I was a kid. One summer night I lay down in the grass with my mom and sisters, and the next morning I was in a room with four walls off the reservation. I didn't know where I was. That was 1965. I thought it was a dream or a joke or something. But they kept me for twelve years. Put me in boarding school. I never saw my mom again."

Adam watched Edward stir the eggs in a big lazy circle. "Never?" Adam didn't know what else to say.

"She killed herself before I got back," Edward said softly. "My sisters were still here and they told me what happened. I never could figure out why they took me and not them, but that's what they did. They said my mother was an alcoholic. And they cut my hair. We don't cut our hair unless there's a death in the family, but when I got back I found out that's exactly what had happened. Far as I'm concerned, they killed her. Killed a piece of me too. Since then, I've never left."

"That's terrible." Adam wanted to get up and shake the man's hand. Do something for him. Say the perfect thing. "Did that happen to other India — err, I mean Native American — I mean, was that common for the time?"

"It's okay," Edward said. "We call ourselves Indians mostly. Some don't like it. But I feel like 'Native American' is a word that the government made up for us. Or you can say tribes. Just don't say 'redman' or shit like that. We don't like it."

Tugg was definitely asleep. The fly was crawling on his shirt and he hadn't bothered to brush it away. If Adam did, it would wake him.

Edward put the eggs on a plate, then disappeared in the back again, re-emerging a minute later with four slices of white bread, which he put in the pan.

Edward kept his eyes on the pan and started talking again. "So to answer your question, yes. It was pretty common back then. Until the Indian Child Welfare Act got passed in 1978. Too late for me. That was when they stopped kidnapping Indian kids and started putting them with other Indian families. I'm not saying we never have any problems. Some kids need to be protected. But most weren't taken away for abuse. It was 'neglect,' which is a pretty easy target if you take a look at what we've got around here. But the sad part is that today we're almost back to where we were."

"What do you mean?"

Edward turned to look at Adam, in the same way you'd be careful before putting your fingers in a cage to pet a ferret. Then he turned back to the pan and flipped the toast.

The fly finally flew outside.

"My friend Hinney has a daughter who left the reservation to study nursing in Bend. Then she came back and had twin boys. Two years ago the social workers came and did the same shit to them that they did to me. Said Hinney's daughter had stolen some prescription drugs where she worked. That was a lie. So they took his beautiful grandsons and put them in a group home in Salem. He can't get them back."

Adam wondered if he should confess his own difficulties with the foster care system. Show some solidarity. But he decided to remain silent.

Edward flipped the toast onto the plate. "Now I'll make the coffee." He disappeared in back again and came out with an aluminum pot and coffee can.

"It's okay," Adam said. "Skip the coffee. Let's eat before it gets cold."

Tugg stirred.

"Okay. You're right." Edward slid some eggs and toast onto a second plate and brought it to the table.

Tugg found a fork and said, "Please, join us. Have a seat."

Edward shrugged and pulled a stool over to the center of the floor, watching them as they ate.

"Edward was just telling me a story about what happened to his friend's grandsons," Adam said to Tugg.

"Yeah, I heard." Tugg was halfway through his eggs already. "So the Tribal Court can't help him?"

"I wish they could, but I haven't told you the worst part yet," Edward said. "This is going on all over the reservation. It's happening to other tribes too. We've got 700 people here on the reservation and they've already taken thirty of our kids. They're kidnapping them. Between that and the meth, we're losing a generation. It's genocide."

Adam looked over at the Coke, but Edward was already off his stool. He cracked two cans and set them on the table in front of Adam and Tugg.

"But why?" Adam said, taking a long swallow. "Why is this happening now?"

The muscles on Edward's jaw tensed. "We have our suspicions. We've talked about it at council. They're bypassing our social workers and bringing state social workers in from Portland and Salem. That way they have no ties to the reservation, and they can put the kids in a group home. That's how they make the real money."

"What?"

Edward seemed surprised that they were surprised. "You guys are probably from the city. I guess it hasn't made the papers. The government is making a living off our children. Indian kids make up half the children in foster care in Oregon, even though we're only something like five percent of the population. It's about money. The state gets thousands of dollars from the federal government for every child it takes into foster care. So far it's something like fifty million dollars."

"Where does all that money go?" Tugg said.

"To the state. Then the state's supposed to pay it out to the foster families who take the kids. But most of the Indian kids don't go to foster families. They go to a private group home in Salem. That's where Hinney's grandsons went. The Longlane Home. It's the biggest foster care provider in Oregon, and they got a ten million dollar no-bid contract to take our kids. They're getting rich off it. The twins alone made them something like $30,000."

"I wonder who else might be there?" Adam said, looking at Tugg.

Adam set down his Coke and reached for his wallet.

"When you've got a government that's making money to put kids in foster care, what's the incentive for keeping them out?" Edward said. He looked at Adam and shook his head. "No, no money. You can pay for gas, but the breakfast is free."

"Are you sure?" Adam said. He looked around the broken-down room and the proud man on the stool in the middle of it.

"Sure. When you white guys aren't around, we just give shit to each other. It's the Indian way. Didn't they ever teach you that in school?" For the first time, Adam saw Edward break into a grin.

Chapter 28

It was a long way over to Salem. Double back through the middle of Oregon, with no more direct route than Highway 20 all the way to Bend, then over the mountains for the rest of the way.

Adam should have tried to sleep, but even with Tugg at the wheel he couldn't drop off. The state capitol was in Salem. The Childrens' Home was in Salem. If Emma was in protective custody, maybe that's where she was too.

He could sleep tonight. It was 7:00 p.m. and the kids would almost surely be inside for the rest of the day. Doors locked: dinner, then lights out.

Coming into the valley, the temperature had warmed and long shadows raced along the green landscape. They were in the homestretch. They'd had nine hours to hatch a plan.

"Look I know they've got a snatch-and-grab protocol," Adam said. "I'm not the first dad to think of this. We've got to play it smart and make sure she's there first."

"Now you're talking," Tugg said. "Once we've seen her, we can figure out the rest."

"But we may only get one chance," Adam said. "When we see her might be the best opportunity to –"

"You want to get her, or do you want to get her and get away? There's a difference." Tugg rolled his window down and let the breeze roll through.

"You know what I want."

"Yeah, I do. So let's stake out a place where they can't see us and wait till they take the kids outside."

"How do you know they'll be outside?"

"State law. Emma's under five, right?"

"She's three."

"Then she's got to have at least one hour of outdoor recess every day, unless the weather is for shit."

There was no use asking how Tugg knew this. From experience, Adam understood that when Tugg said something like this it was true. Adam rolled his window down too and let the cross currents whip his hair, giving him renewed energy despite his lack of sleep.

"Sounds like tomorrow," Adam said. "We'll need daylight. But I've got to be close enough to see her."

Tugg looked over at him. "You remember all that surveillance equipment I had on my bike? You think I *left* that on the bike back in Ontario? It's behind the seat here. Binoculars, taps, every kind of tracking device you've ever heard of. Most of it's legal."

"And that won't look funny. Two guys watching a bunch of kids with binoculars."

"It is what it is. We'll make it or we won't. But when the time comes and we get near Emma, you've got to control yourself. If she sees you and starts yelling 'Daddy,' we're through."

Adam's stomach was doing back flips Maybe this would work.

Salem, next three exits.

"I want to go over it again. One plan for if we have a chance to grab her right away and another for –"

"Adam, geez!" Tugg barked. "Calm down. You're the same as you were as a kid. Always overthinking. You can't plan everything. Opportunities will present themselves and you have to be flexible enough to take advantage of them. If you're too locked in to a plan, you'll miss something."

"Yeah, but it's what I do."

"And I let the river come to me. It's what *I* do," Tugg said. "If I hang on too tight, it just makes me crazy."

And it makes me crazy to take chances with my daughter's freedom.

Tugg wasn't a father. He just didn't understand.

"So where did you learn that?" Adam finally asked.

"The Air Force. Life, I guess."

Adam put his hand out the window and felt the wind flowing like water over his palm. "I guess I missed that. Life taught me a different lesson."

Tugg hesitated, but took the bait. "Which is?"

"Always have a 230-pound biker in your corner."

Chapter 29

The binoculars were back in the truck.

After a quick recon of the area last night, Adam and Tugg had found a motel and slept like the dead for twelve hours, before returning at 8:00 a.m., good to go.

Whatever genius city planner had put the State Prison and the Longlane Home within two blocks of one another probably wasn't thinking about stalking. But that was criminal, considering that a good number of the residents in this particular neighborhood were ex-cons, some of whom had been locked up for sex offenses.

That wasn't why ex-cons settled here. At first it made no sense. Then it made complete sense. Why would someone who had just gotten out of lock-up want to live within a few blocks of the prison walls? Maybe because his old lady rented an apartment nearby while he was inside, so it would be more convenient for her to visit. Then, when he got out, guess where he would be living?

The neighborhood was not-so-lovingly called "Death Row," and it was populated by a score of thrift stores, greasy spoons, check cashing outlets, and pawn shops. White trash Fifth Avenue. You could get lost for hours. Best of all for Adam and Tugg, a medical building with offices on the third floor had a communal waiting area with a big fat window that looked out over a green space behind a high fence, which just happened to be the playground for The Longlane Home.

Adam and Tugg sat facing the window, indistinguishable from the handful of other patients who were waiting for their appointments. Tugg might have been an ex-con in for a chest x-ray. Adam could be a neurotic parole officer who had migraines. Who knew?

The playground was empty and some clouds had rolled in. It was raining lightly.

"Janice Thompson?" The stocky nurse in green scrubs seemed to feel the need to shout, despite the fact that only four people were in the room, and the elderly black man sitting on the other side of the room with both hands on his cane probably wasn't Janice Thompson either. Janice vaulted out of her seat and disappeared with the nurse.

Adam leaned in close to Tugg.

"Don't even say it," Tugg said. "All day if necessary. How the hell do I know what time recess is?"

Adam turned back to the window.

At 10:00 a.m. Adam saw the door on the back of the Longlane Home open. A ton of little kids ran out, each in identical yellow hooded slickers, headed straight for the monkey bars.

"Shit," Tugg said. "I hadn't thought of that. Will you be able to spot her?"

Adam leaned forward against the cool glass.

A boy?

No.

Too tall?

No.

Wrong shape?

No.

Adam scanned the rest and decided that two different kids might be her, but he really couldn't be sure. "There's got to be a better way."

"No, there's not," said Tugg. "We'll wait for second recess in about four hours. But let's get out of here for now."

Second recess, it was raining hard. A teenage girl opened the back door of the school and ran out into the rain straight for the fence, but two guards came and pulled her back, as she melted in a tantrum that Adam could almost hear through the plate glass window.

"Tomorrow?" Adam said.

"Tonight, we may have something."

"What? How come, all of a sudden?"

If Tugg's gaze had been sunlight, the rain would have dried by now. "See that guard down there? On the left? We were stationed together at Holloman. His name's Paul something. And he's got a record."

"What?"

"Yeah," Tugg said, finally turning away. "He got kicked out. I never saw him after that. I'm sure CPS wouldn't have hired him if they knew about his record. Even if it was military. That's our in."

Adam could feel hope welling up again. They were close.

"So we come back tonight then?"

"No. We watch the parking lot until Paul leaves. Then we follow him home. It'll be easier that way. Less chance of getting caught."

"Let's go to the truck."

"Good idea."

By the time they hit the street, the rain was falling harder. One block to go and they decided to make a run for it.

"I'm driving," Adam said. "I want you to watch out the window."

Adam put the truck in gear and headed down the block for a parking place just across the street from The Longlane Home.

He swung in and shut off the ignition.

The rain made a metallic pop as it bounced off the roof and hood. For a minute or two it came down so hard it was almost comical.

"Shift change probably won't happen till closer to five," Tugg said. "But we've got to wait here just in case."

"The cars are all out front. There's only one door. This should be easy," Adam said.

"Should be. When it gets closer to time, let's change seats so I can drive."

"Okay." Adam fiddled with the keys and gave the wipers a quick spin. "Hey, Tugg—"

"Yeah?"

"Paul What's-his-name. What was he busted for? What'd he do?"

Tugg put his boots up on the dashboard and settled back in his seat. "Got drunk and assaulted another airman. The guy gave him a chance, but Paul was too drunk to notice. When he pulled a knife, the other guy hit Paul so hard it blinded him in one eye. But they let the guy off. Self defense. Paul got tossed because he started it."

"How do you know so much about it?"

"The other guy was me."

Chapter 30

The little brick house wasn't technically in the "Death Row" neighborhood, but it was close. Couple of blocks off the strip mall. Close to work. Probably best not to drive too far if you only had one eye.

Tugg had been in there a long time.

If Tugg could get him to talk *and* Emma was there *and* they could come up with a plan for getting her out, then this could be the best lead they'd had since what Adam had come to think of as Emma's kidnapping.

To hell with the state. Something was at the bottom of this and, once he had Emma back, Adam could start digging and find out what it was. Edward's story back on the reservation was a wake-up call. CPS was out of control. They took kids whenever they wanted and didn't much care who objected. Damn Lisa Castro. Was she part of some ring that put kids in foster care for money? Is that why they took Emma? Had Rachel maybe gotten a kickback for what she'd done?

It was all too wild to contemplate. Adam wanted his little girl back, but he also wanted to figure this whole thing out. Maybe he could go back to Edward. The tribe would protect him. Maybe they couldn't arrest him if he stayed on the reservation.

This was getting ridiculous. Once they got Emma, it would be all he could do to run without getting caught.

The front porch light went on and a few seconds later the door opened.

Tugg walked slowly to the truck.

"Well? What did he say?"

"Drive. I'll tell you on the road."

"She's not there?!" Adam said the words out loud again, as if his skepticism could somehow erase their truth. "Are you sure? Could he have been lying?"

"No, he wasn't lying. Paul got religion. He said he told his employer all about his service record and his stint in rehab. They hired him anyway. The new Executive Director is a born-again Christian and she said Paul deserved a second chance."

"So why did he tell you anything? And how do you know he wasn't lying?"

"Adam, he just wasn't. You could see it. He told me that protective custody kids never stayed there anyway. They go to private homes in secret locations. They tend to be out in the boondocks. They're usually poor families who take in six or eight kids and live on the stipend. The only way they leave is if they're adopted out."

"And he didn't know where any of them were?"

"I didn't ask. Secret, remember? Wanda or someone who works in that office might know, but they sure aren't going to tell a guard at a group home. That would defeat the whole purpose of protective custody."

Adam felt like his chest was going to collapse. He wondered if he was having a heart attack right here, but the pain was prickly more than piercing. He fought to stay on the road.

"I still think Paul might be lying," Adam said. "Maybe he doesn't know any of the kids. Maybe they put them in there under false names. That would be the best kind of protective custody. Where no one knew anyone's real name."

"C'mon, Adam, the kids know who they are."

"But maybe they don't tell the guards. Maybe they try to keep it a secret. Did you ever think of that?"

"Couldn't be."

"Why not?" Adam could tell by the look on Tugg's face that he was losing it. Adam choked up. Tugg put his hand on the steering wheel and glided them over to the curb.

"Because I asked him if he knew any Native American twin boys and he knew who they were," Tugg said.

"He knew them? Are they there?" Adam gasped at the shred of good news, even though it wasn't for him. "Maybe we can get them instead and bring them back to Edward."

"No, we can't do that. We go back to Plan Z and head to Ontario."

Adam put it in park and shut off the engine. "I can't drive anymore."

They shifted seats over and under without opening the doors. Tugg sat for a minute, then fired up the engine.

Adam was silent for the first few miles, then said in a whisper, "I would like to have seen the look on Edward's face when he told his friend we'd found his grandsons."

"Yeah, I know. That'd be great, but it just can't happen."

"Because we might get caught, and then who would rescue Emma?" Adam said.

"That and another reason."

"What?" Adam said, his eyes finally dry.

"Because someone adopted them a year ago."

Chapter 31

The rain stopped somewhere over the Cascades, but the sky was still black. They were back in the high desert, the "other" side of Oregon that no one talked about.

"I can take a shift now," Adam said.

"Okay." Tugg pulled off to the side of the road and took a long piss, then climbed in to ride shotgun.

Adam suddenly felt the call and jumped out for his own relief, while the open door dinged insistently. It was too dark to see the painted hills, but he could feel them. Smell them. They were close.

Adam climbed back in and pulled onto the road. "Exit coming up ahead. You want to head back the way we came?"

"No, just follow 26 all the way to Ontario. It's quiet. If we'd wanted to make time, we could have gone up to Portland and taken the Interstate."

Adam flipped off the high beams as another car passed. "Too much risk near Portland — and I guess too much risk from the Reapers if we head south again."

"That's not a worry anymore," Tugg said. He had his boots off and his feet up on the dashboard again. The swelling on Tugg's face and hands was better, but the bruises looked worse.

"I appreciate what you did for me back there," Adam said. "It couldn't have been easy to see a guy who probably hates you so much."

Tugg stirred for a second and repositioned himself on the seat, but his eyes stayed shut. "Paul doesn't hate me. It was embarrassing. He said that what I did to him was the great wake-up call that put him on the road to Jesus."

"Seriously?" Adam hesitated, then said it anyway. "Shit, Tugg. Maybe you should punch people more often."

Tugg shook his head, but still had his eyes closed. "That was a period in my life when I had plenty of fights and believe me, I didn't heal anyone. My philosophy was always 'if we're going to fight, we're going to fight.' I don't go for all of that pushing and shoving, and I never took the time to curse someone out. One punch to the face as hard as I could before he even got his arm cocked. That always ended it. But I stopped after what happened to Paul. Mostly."

The road was quiet, so Adam flipped the brights back on. Prineville was behind them and they were headed up the mountains again. The darkness at the edge of the high beams swallowed everything but the road.

"But not completely?" said Adam.

"Not until way later. Just before they put me in prison."

Here it was. The pain was right there, as obvious as the cuts and bruises on Tugg's face. When they'd first gotten married, Kate had said that love meant sharing everything. That there should never be any secrets between them. So there weren't any — except, of course, that one. But men were different. If you loved someone, sometimes you let things go.

Tugg never opened his eyes, but the words started coming. Adam kept his hands on the wheel and stared straight ahead into the moonless night.

"I was assigned to temporary duty at Incirlik Air Base in Turkey. Our F-15s were flying down the Syrian border into Iraq so they could patrol the 33rd parallel, also known as the no-fly zone. Most of the guys were living in a tent city and had to take a bus in every day, but I got special permission to live off base and take my bike in. It was just like a regular job, you know? I rode in, worked on the planes, rode home. I always felt pretty lucky not to be in the shit. Everybody back home said the Gulf War ended in 1991, but that was just bullshit for TV. When I got there in '97 we were still enforcing the no-fly zone and we kept on doing it all the way until the war started up again in 2003. I could see what was coming, so I thought about getting out after my enlistment was up. I'd saved some money. Then it happened."

Adam was silent.

"One day out of the blue they assign me to transient aircraft. Just my luck, I got a radio call that a TA was coming in with an in-flight emergency. Apparently he'd just faced off with an Iraqi pilot who had a death wish. He was code three — all fucked up — and on top of that, he'd over-g'd the goddamned thing."

"What's over g'd?" Adam asked.

"You know 'over g.' Too fast. He'd pulled too many g's. Anyway, I thought, 'I'm going to be here all night fixing this shit.' This kind of thing happened all the time, but it never made the news. An Iraqi pilot would take off and head straight for the no-fly zone, then stop just short of the 33rd parallel. Our guy would engage and then the fun would start.

"Anyway, after the emergency crews were cleared, I parked the jet and debriefed the pilot. He wasn't one of mine, but I reminded him he owed me a case of beer for the over-g. In addition to all the regular maintenance, over-g's require an additional two hours pulling panels on the aircraft to check for cracks.

"Sometimes it's fun to get somebody else's jet. Are they as good as you and all that. I was lucky that night. Just a couple of write-ups from the pre-flight inspection and I could start pulling panels. When you're a Crew Chief you learn to look at everything because your pilot's life is in your hands."

Adam thought he saw two glowing embers at the periphery of the road. He'd have to watch for deer. No one else was on the highway.

"So about this time a flight line expediter from another squadron pulls up and calls me over. He says, 'How much longer are you gonna milk this one, Morgan? I need you for jets for tomorrow and this thing isn't even ours.' I noticed that the Maintenance Commander was riding with him, so I extended some military decorum instead of saying what I wanted to say. I said, 'I just have the over-g inspection to do and it's finished, sir.' He says, 'How long's that going to take?' I said, 'No more than a couple hours.' He rolls his eyes and says, 'Bring me the aircraft forms.' He looks 'em over and says, 'This jet's in fine shape. Just sign off and let's get going.' I tell him, 'Sir, this guy over g'd with a lot of weight on board. I've got to pull those panels.' He says, 'That wasn't a request, Airman Morgan.' I correct him, 'It's Sergeant Morgan, sir.' And he says, 'I said *Airman*. You get my fucking point? I am ORDERING you to sign off on this plane.' He's standing right on top of me, screaming in my face. I could feel my fist tighten and I could see the punch shattering his cheek. Then I looked over at the Maintenance Commander. I'd never pencil-whipped anything before and I'd be damned if I'd start now. So then I just did it."

"You hit him?" Adam said.

"No, I signed off on the plane."

Adam had a sickening feeling that he knew the rest of the story. Tugg's jaw was clamped and his face glistened in the ambient light.

"It went down on the return. I didn't even know the Captain's name. They paint it right on the side under the cockpit and the last thing I usually do before I sign off on a plane is write the name in my notes. Makes it more personal, you know? But I didn't that time. All I had was the tail number, so I knew I was the last guy to sign off, which meant I was going before the board."

Tugg straightened himself in his seat and peered out into the blackness.

"Of course neither the Expediter nor the Commander backed my story. They didn't want to go down for this. By that time I was facing a dishonorable and a year in jail. There was nothing more they could do to me at that point. My life was as bad as it could get. That's what I thought, anyway."

"So why did you end up going to prison for five years?" Adam said.

"The expediter made one more mistake. He walked into the NCO Club that night while I was drowning my sorrows about losing the pilot. I beat him unrecognizable. Took out eight of his teeth and broke his left eye socket. Then I got my hands around his throat. They had five guys trying to pull me off. When I heard an M9 jack a round behind me, I finally let him go.

"For a while they were talking about trying to put me away for life, but I had a good JAG. The story about the pencil-whipping came out. The Maintenance Commander rolled over on the expediter and they both ended up doing time. In other circumstances, I would've been cleared. But I got five years for what I'd done to the expediter. And by the time I got out, everything was gone."

"They kicked you out?"

"They betrayed me. I was loyal to the Air Force. Aim higher and all that crap. I did the job they trained me to do and then some. But when the time came, no one had my back. All they cared about was what I'd done to a senior NCO, justified or not. So it was off to Leavenworth, and that's where things got worse."

"Ummm — you, uh —"

"Way worse."

Oh shit, Adam thought. This is it. He never should have let Tugg tell him the story. "In a military prison?" Adam said. "Tugg, I can't believe it. You always hear about that kind of thing in a state prison, but —"

"Adam, just stop. No one punked me while I was inside. If you mind your own business and you look like a gorilla, you're golden. But the problem is your life stands still and everybody disappears. You can't protect anything. They limit your contacts. Hell, I couldn't even contact you until I got out, remember? That's what I'm talking about."

Adam was confused, but he dared not ask. What a relief that he'd been wrong about what had happened to Tugg in prison. Time to change the subject.

"You're a man of great loyalties, Tugg. I'm sure your buddies back on base heard the real story. I'll bet they were on your side."

"Fuck 'em."

"What?"

"Fuck 'em. They never contacted me once. Not when I was inside, not when I got out. After that, I never joined anything again. My loyalty goes to damn few."

Adam thought of the outlaw motorcycle club they were heading back for. The humilities of being a 'prospect' and the things Tugg was expected to do that he wouldn't even talk about.

"And now you're giving that up for me."

Tugg turned toward him. "For you, buddy. You're all I've got left."

Adam was sick of secrets. He owed his pal more than that. If Tugg had something he had been carrying around with him, Adam should've helped him with it. Relieved his burden. Loyalty ran both ways.

"So what did you have to do back there in Ashland that you can't talk about?"

Adam was surprised to see Tugg smile. "Same reason I couldn't bring you, I can't tell you."

"You're protecting me again."

"Damn straight."

They drove in silence for a while. Adam still didn't know everything, but maybe things would be better now. Tugg had finally confessed his big secret. And Adam had learned a big piece of the puzzle behind Tugg's PTSD. Maybe that would help.

The fir trees had thinned in the higher elevation and the sky was a little brighter. Were those stars overhead? They must be near the summit.

"I guess after your mother died it's like I was your only family."

Tugg was quiet for a moment and the smile disappeared. "Who said I never had a family?"

CHAPTER 32

Lisa Castro pulled the rose-colored curtains back in the second bedroom of her tiny condo in the West Hills of Portland. Breaking dawn was always her favorite time of day. If she looked in the mirrors on the closet doors, she could just make out the outline of Mt. Hood in the distance, all lit up from behind, like a crown on her majesty. In a few minutes the room would be flooded with sunlight. When she'd chosen this room to be her home office, morning light had been the essential factor.

Of course, in some ways it hardly mattered. If she wanted to work in bed all day, she could. If she wanted to eat over the sink, she could. Lisa lived alone and could do as she pleased which meant, of course, that she had to pay for everything, too. The condo was too expensive. She could have gotten twice as much for her money across the river in East Portland. But the views were worth it. She was worth it. If you sacrificed having a husband and kids — and let's face it, even a social life — for your job, it was important to take care of yourself. Somebody had to.

Lisa flipped on the desk lamp and booted up her computer. Wanda had chosen a hell of a week for a vacation. The office would be a zoo, and it was best to get a head start. The requests for foster placements just kept coming. She'd better get cracking on finding some new ones. She'd have to get creative on where to put those new kids coming in from Alameda and Goose Hollow. These weren't the customary places that foster cases in Multnomah County came from, but no one said that you had to place them in their own community. That was just for Native American kids. And they weren't even doing that these days.

The screen lit up. No matter how busy, Lisa always started her day with a quick scan of news stories that had been tagged by the electronic clipping service for CPS, then a quick read of the *Oregonian*. The first was usually uneventful, but she wanted to make sure she didn't miss anything. There'd been a car accident overnight in Gresham that killed both parents, but the kids survived and were in CPS custody; a foster Mom up in Camas, Washington, had been convicted of running a prostitution ring out of her home; the warrant for Adam Grammaticus was still outstanding.

Lisa knew that she should start working on the new placements, but she couldn't help but be drawn back to the ones she'd already made this month. Those were done — a success — so she should have crossed them off her list and barreled forward. But she couldn't help it. The Grammaticus' grief had been so real, and familiar to her in a way that an extraction from poor families sometimes wasn't, that Lisa couldn't help but feel their pain. But that was silly. She admonished herself for such unexpected snobbery. Was she turning into a conservative all of a sudden? Abuse could happen anywhere. Rich parents were probably just better at hiding it. They had lawyers and resources and often managed to stay out of the system. But that was changing.

Still, Kate Grammaticus didn't seem like an abuser. Likely she wasn't. Just duped by her husband, as Lisa's mom had been. That didn't make it right. You had to stand up for your kids. Even if you couldn't stand. But damn it, Kate Grammaticus couldn't even take care of herself. If one case haunted Lisa, this was it. She'd stopped taking Kate's calls last week, but surreptitiously Lisa was still checking up on her. Kate seemed to be getting some social support from her friends at work and she had help around the house. Maybe if that continued, and the husband stayed away once the baby came, Emma Grammaticus could go back to her mother. Lisa could help her find enough nannies. She probably owed her that.

In the meantime, at least Emma was safe. Lisa had hand-chosen one of the best placements she knew: a two-parent family with two of their own kids and six foster kids out in Troutdale. Not much money, but a good placement all the same. A group home wouldn't work for Emma's situation. Too vulnerable. Emma's father and that scary-as-shit Hells Angels type he was palling around with were out there somewhere, probably roaming the state looking for her. Maybe the police would pick him up soon. Good. If they did, Lisa made a mental note to call Steve Carnap and tell him that Emma could go home to her mother.

Selfish dad. He was the reason his daughter was in foster care. A double murder two decades ago, and he'd probably killed the nanny too. No sense even considering sending Emma back while he was still out there.

The sun rose clear of the mountain, bathing the room in brilliant light. Particle or wave, beam or supernova, the instant blast of sunlight always caused Lisa to marvel at the path it had traveled. All the way from the sun through 93 million miles of empty space, somehow the light had found its way to her tiny little office. If sunlight had a smell, Lisa had decided as a child that it would be hyacinths or lilacs. Something purple. Rich and fragrant.

Lisa enjoyed the warmth crawling like a cat along her shoulders. She leaned in toward her computer screen. It was time for the newspaper: a proposal to treat river water for use in the state drinking system had been defeated in the Legislature; the state budget was still in a mess; the Governor had pardoned someone named Richard Norwood.

Why did that name sound familiar?

Chapter 33

The compound for The Immortals looked more like a cross between a military base and a wrecking yard than a motorcycle hangout, but maybe that was the point. Once they got past the swinging chain link gate, Adam saw the distinctive half dome of two Quonset huts, one of which said "Iron Horse Garage" on its large metal door. The other building looked like some sort of barracks, which probably made it the clubhouse.

Tugg pulled the truck over to a graveled area, got into his bag and put on his colors.

"Hey, prospect!"

Adam turned to see a small, dark man in black boots walking toward them. The patch over the left side of his chest said "sergeant-at-arms" and another triangular patch on the other side said '1%' just above a third that said '13.'

"You're fucking three days late. You're already out," he said to Tugg.

"What?"

Adam could see the horrified look on Tugg's face.

"Doc's pissed. He said to bring your cut directly to him when you got back. Now!"

Tugg looked at Adam but didn't say a word.

Adam stood by the truck and watched Tugg crunch his way across the gravel behind the little man, who suddenly turned and said, "Hey, citizen! You're part of this too. Get going."

Adam fell in behind. Tugg shook his head and held his finger to his lips. Whatever this was, it was Tugg's show.

The garage was dark and choked with exhaust fumes. There was a deafening roar from what looked like a vintage World War II motorcycle and sidecar that two men were fussing over. When Tugg and Adam came into view, the taller man ran his finger across his throat and the other one cut the engine.

The guy looked like every father's nightmare. Doc's hair was kinky and combed straight back, but his skin was alabaster white, ghostly even, except for a swirl of red and green snake tattoos coiling around each arm, disappearing inside the armpits of his leather vest. His eyes were huge black circles and, as he ambled around from behind the bike, Adam saw that he had a prosthetic leg.

"First fucking job we give you and you fuck it up."

"I — I —"

Adam remembered Tugg's advice. *Explain without making excuses. And show respect at all times.*

"You what?" Doc said, pulling out a cigarette.

Tugg pulled himself up straight. "I have no excuse. Spider said he was going to call, but I should have done it myself. I meant no disrespect."

Tugg found no purchase in the two lifeless disks staring back at him and started to pull off his vest.

The laughter broke somewhere over Doc's shoulder from the back of the garage. Now that his eyes were adjusted, Adam could make out the dim outline of twenty or thirty people. Doc grinned and his mouth worked the cigarette over from one side of his face to the other.

Spider stepped out from the shadows.

"Prospect, I feel thirsty after my long ride. Why don't you get us all some beers?"

Tugg handed Adam a beer, then opened his own and took a long swallow.

"Tomorrow's our bike run," Doc said. "You made it back just in time. All the charters in the whole state are gonna be here. Maybe we'll give you your bike back instead of making you drive the chase truck."

Tugg nodded and took another pull at his beer.

"What about his friend?" the little sergeant-at-arms bellowed. "Put him in the back of the chaser. I hear he shoots a mean Remington."

Laughter rose from the forty or fifty bikers and the handful of ridiculously underdressed women who were standing around in the garage.

"We'll make a biker out of him yet," someone called out, which provoked another round of laughter.

What the hell was this? High school run by pirates?

"Yeah," Doc said, turning to Adam. "You showed some class for the club, so we ain't gonna put you in the chase truck either. But you sure as shit *ain't* going to ride a bike with us, and you *ain't* going to ride on the back of this prospect's bike like a couple of pussies." Doc glared at Tugg, then his face lit up.

Doc motioned Adam over to the vintage motorcycle he'd been working on, but when Adam got there he could see that what was attached to it wasn't a sidecar but some sort of oblong wooden box with a metal wheel on the bottom. It was a mini-coffin, complete with R.I.P. painted in black across the top.

"Ain't she beautiful?" Doc said.

"Yes," Adam said. "What is it?"

The group hushed, as if Adam had made a major faux pas. Or maybe a sermon was about to befall them. Or both. Whatever it was, they'd obviously heard it a million times before.

"That's fate," Doc said in a low voice. "That's my leg."

Adam didn't get it at first and then — all of a sudden — he got it all too clearly.

"You cremate someone and they give you the ashes. You lose your appendix and they put it in a jar. But what the hell do you do with a leg? You don't bury it. You don't throw it away. After the accident, I made the doc give it back to me. Now I carry it with me as a reminder. It balances my ride. And nobody *ever* fucking asks for a ride in my sidecar, do they?" Doc glared at the crowd.

Adam slowly realized what was going on. He couldn't be serious. They expected him to ride with *that*? Adam could see by the look on everyone's face that he was being exalted in a way that bordered on deification.

"I'm honored," Adam said softly.

"Plenty of room. You'll have to leave your shoes with your pal for him to carry while you're in there. We can cut it open halfway so you can sit up straight. You'll be fine. Just don't kick it. You do that and I'll make you walk."

"No sir," Adam said.

If this was what it took to get Emma back, so be it. If riding around like a lap dog for the President of the club would help them get next to Wanda, he was all in.

Doc looked out at the crowd again. "Any of you goofs take out two Reapers with five shots from the back of a pick-up?" Silence. "I didn't think so."

All eyes turned toward the gate, where the sound of twenty unmuffled choppers was working its way up the road. When the bikers arrived, someone opened the gate and motioned the crew toward the gravel courtyard.

"Forest Grove," Adam heard one of the bikers say.

"Yeah, they cut it close," Doc said. He limped toward the front of the pack and greeted the squat man out front with a kiss on the lips, after which there was much whooping and hollering as everyone from the garage ran out to meet their comrades.

Tugg walked over to Adam and stood with him for a minute, watching the scene unfold in the distance. Helmets came off, everyone embraced, and there were a few more kisses on the lips.

"Weird shit," Adam whispered to Tugg. "He wouldn't let me ride on the back of your bike but he kisses a man on the lips."

"It's to shock the civilians," Tugg said. "They're a tight crew. Closer than brothers."

"But they like their women, right?"

"Yeah, no gay men allowed in an outlaw club. They *love* their women. Like that one over there."

Adam gazed at a voluptuous figure clad completely in black leather, who was just getting off the back of some guy's bike. Even if she hadn't just taken off her helmet, there'd be no mistaking her for a dude.

"I see what you mean," Adam said.

"Not yet you don't."

"What do you mean? What's so special about her? Besides the obvious."

Tugg smiled. "Because, my friend, we just caught our first break all week."

Adam stared at the curvy stranger.

"That's Wanda."

Chapter 34

Thank God for goggles.

Adam knew that he must look like some sort of lunatic Nazi general riding out front, in a homemade sidecar, with a hundred motorcycles roaring behind him. The wind was fierce and somehow it didn't help that he was down so low, with every bug and bit of gravel nicking him in the face. Tugg had said that a bike run usually traveled at about 80 m.p.h, but at this height it felt like it could have been two hundred.

The bike formation behind him was an impressive sight. Adam had looked back a couple of times and saw the choppers all lined up, riding 18 inches off one another's tires, with Tugg in the far rear with a couple of other prospects. Since Adam was with Doc, he was out front, the place of honor, but he felt more like a mascot than a celebrity.

And then there was the subject of the leg.

Adam had his socks on, but his shoes were back in Tugg's saddlebag, so he kept his toes scrunched up and refused to extend his feet all the way into the sidecar. Was the leg wrapped up like a mummy? Just sitting there? He was afraid to ask. Adam hung onto the sides of the mini-coffin and gritted his teeth, trying to smile every time Doc looked down at him.

When he could forget about the leg, the country was beautiful. And the smells were tremendous. Years back, Adam had ridden dirt bikes with Tugg all over Tillamook County the summer before he went to college and Tugg went into the Air Force. After that Kate had happened and – once her multiple sclerosis set in – she'd made Adam promise to give it up. No sense both of them ending up in a wheelchair. Of course he'd agreed, but every now and then he remembered that summer. Riding in a car with the window down, you didn't get the full effect. On a motorcycle you weren't looking at a picture you were *in* the picture. A slight change in temperature. A whiff of whatever crop was growing in the field. He was hurtling down the highway in a wooden box, swimming through the scenery. It was stolen time.

How long was this ride supposed to be? They'd been on the road for hours. Whether they were going somewhere or just making a big loop, Adam couldn't tell. Surely they'd stop sooner or later, just to take a pee. Adam had to be stoic. This was all necessary, he told himself, to get Emma back. Being accepted by the club had to be good for Tugg, and that had to be good for getting next to Wanda. Maybe they wouldn't have to wait the full six months now that she was here.

Adam tried not to get his hopes up, but it was impossible. If Wanda was the key to this whole strategy, wasn't this their best chance to get the information they needed? Damn protocol, wasn't he sitting in the leader's sidecar? Maybe like a pet Chihuahua, he reminded himself, but still it was better than nothing.

Adam wished he could have talked to Tugg some more before the bike run had started. Had Tugg really had a family? But the last thing Tugg needed was for Adam to push him about some ancient history. Wanda was what mattered now.

There were a couple of signs now and then along the road and Adam spied a house and barn way off to the left. Maybe they were getting near a town. He hoped so. Adam couldn't even feel his *own* legs at this point.

Adam looked up and saw that Doc had put his left hand in the air, gloved in black leather, clenched in a fist. Then he pointed to the right at an upcoming building and put his hand back on the handlebars. When Doc pulled off into the parking lot Adam could see that it was a motorcycle repair shop. The formation broke and everyone roared past like a hive of bees, then lined up their motorcycles along the road, one after another, like a row of dominoes.

Doc took off his helmet. "You good?" he said to Adam.

"You know it." Adam gave a thumbs-up and another smile. He hoped Tugg would remember to bring his shoes. He had to pee.

"Stay put," Doc said. "We ain't here but for a minute. Bar up ahead two miles where we can stop and eat. This is just for fun."

Adam nodded and sat back down.

Three of the bikers got off their motorcycles and walked toward the garage door, like cowboys in a Wild West movie. They stood outside the open door, obviously talking to someone inside, then one of them suddenly broke ranks and stepped into the building. When he came out, he was holding a guy by the hair. A couple of the bikers laughed as the guy hollered, obviously scared to death. Adam saw why. One of the three bikers threw him in the dirt, then the other two started taking turns kicking him.

Adam's stomach tensed. What the hell was this?

First one would hit him in the face and knock him to his knees, then the other would kick him in the stomach, flattening him out. When the guy was lying flat on his face in the dirt, Adam heard Doc yell, "Prospects!"

Tugg and two other guys walked up the line of motorcycles toward the scrum.

"That's what happens when you're chickenshit," Doc said in a low voice, speaking like an incantation, as if Adam weren't there.

Adam had a horrific sensation that he knew what came next.

One of the other prospects took the first swing. Tugg took over, tackling the guy, then climbed into a full mount so he could whale on his chest.

"Good man. He gets it," Doc said.

Adam was so angry he knew he shouldn't speak, but then he asked the question anyway. "What'd he do?"

Doc looked over, as if surprised to remember that a mascot could talk. "Huh?" Doc said. "He's a former member. Problem is there ain't no such thing. We tried to explain that to him. Now we come down about once a month and explain it to him all over again."

One of the other prospects tried to move in, but Tugg waved him away and just kept whaling.

"We wouldn't take him back now anyway," Doc said. "He's fish food. Damned good example, though."

Adam watched Tugg rise up and deliver a savage kick to the man's genitals.

"Ohhhh!" The crowd gasped and there was a smattering of shouting and applause.

"He's done," Doc yelled. "Let's eat!"

When Tugg walked back, he passed within a few feet of Adam, but he didn't turn to look at him. Tugg's face was stone and his eyes were focused on his place: at the back of the pack.

After Tugg went by, Adam leaned over the sidecar and vomited in two big lurches. A rivulet of liquid made its way toward the metal wheel but mercifully stopped just short.

When he sat up, Adam could feel Doc's eyes upon him.

"Dude, the only reason you ain't walkin' back is you missed the leg."

Chapter 35

Adam had spent the last two weeks walking across emerald lawns, attending classes, secretly feeling like someone must have made a mistake.

No one he'd grown up with had ever gone to college.

Why did it seem like everybody already knew everybody else? Or that he was the only kid on financial aid?

Still this was his chance. He'd never go back to the trailer park. Now that his Mom was dead – and Tugg was in the Air Force – maybe he'd never even go back to Oregon.

But you couldn't just study, right? Adam found himself walking down a dark street, in a bacchanal tide of insecure freshmen, where all streams seemed to empty into the houses on fraternity row.

It was Friday night.

The music poured out of the open windows and all the lights were turned up bright.

Alpha Beta Nu, Chi Psi, DKE, Psi Upsilon – he had his pick.

Technically the drinking age in New Hampshire was 21, but that would be like busting someone for loitering in Times Square.

He followed a rivulet of people up the brick walk to one of the frat houses.

"Men to the left, women to the right," called out a big drunk frat brother at the door.

The line was clotted on Adam's side, but the women seemed to be getting in just fine.

"Freshmen men, sorry," said another guy. "You're too pathetic. Just go away."

Adam spied a couple of girls he had classes with whom he knew were freshmen, who had just gone inside.

Adam turned to leave.

"Hey, dude. Blue shirt. Dude!"

Adam turned and saw a short kid waving at him.

"Ec 10 right? You're the guy who's going to get me through. Go right in."

Adam didn't know the kid's name, but recognized him as a sophomore in one of his classes. "Thanks."

The air felt like a swimming pool. The noise and smell of beer was overwhelming. A couple of guys were playing electric guitar – badly – over in the corner, not even the same song that was blasting over the speakers. The crowd was massive and everyone seemed centered on a row of silver kegs on the opposite wall, huddled around them like a fireplace in winter.

People drank from funnels. Girls laughed way too loud. A couple of guys had their shirts off and their baseball caps turned backward.

Are we having fun yet? Who needed this shit?

Adam jostled his way back toward the door when he saw the crowd part quickly as a girl fell down on the warped wood floor.

"Whoa. First time away from the convent?" The guy was wearing a red sweat shirt with the sleeves torn off, and some sort of logo stenciled on the back. He reached down a meaty hand and pulled her to her feet.

The girl was small and Asian, and her eyes had the glassy look of animal fear.

"I think she'd better lay down somewhere," said a guy in a cowboy hat standing a few feet away. "Sleep it off."

"Good idea," said red shirt, grinning.

He gripped one hand on her bicep and the other around her opposite shoulder and began guiding her unsteadily toward the stairs.

"Nyuuuuh." She tried to pull away.

Adam turned away from the door and walked over.

"Hey, what the fuck?" Adam said to red shirt, moving between him and the bannister. "Too drunk to walk or talk means too drunk, period."

"Huh?"

"I said she's too drunk." Adam had to raise his voice to be heard over the pulsing music.

"Who the fuck are you? Who let you in?"

The guy with the cowboy hat was suddenly in Adam's face. "What are you her Dad?"

Adam ignored cowboy hat and stepped to the side so that he was facing red shirt again.

"Get your fucking hands off her."

"Are you shitting me? No."

Adam's fist exploded so fast he couldn't even remember throwing the punch. He felt the nose crumple as a shower of blood leapt into the air.

When the guy let go, the girl staggered over to Adam, as red shirt held his hands up to his ruined face.

"Fuck!!!" yelled cowboy hat.

The next few seconds were a blur of punches and yelling, then Adam had the bright idea to duck under the crowd. A few seconds later he found himself with the girl's hand in his own, running for the door.

"Motherfucker broke my nose."

"Where is he?"

Adam blazed out the door, hearing the wild drunken commotion fall away behind him.

The September air was humid, but felt cool compared to the frat house. Adam jagged left across the lawn, pulling on the girl's wrist.

When they hit the next street he finally slowed down.

"Where do you live?"

"Shh, shhoom, krr–"

"What?"

"Dorrrrm kevvvv–"

"OK, I'll just take you to the infirmary."

Adam sat in a black painted chair, staring out the window opposite the Dean's desk.

"Not a very auspicious start to your college career, Mr. Grammaticus."

Dean Sisson was standing behind his desk, while the man in the black pin-striped suit – whom Adam took to be the college attorney – sat in a high-backed wing chair off to one side.

"Yes, I know," Adam replied. "I'm pretty disappointed. What kind of a college are you running here?"

"What did you say?"

Adam knew he should just shut up. Pretend he was sorry so maybe they wouldn't kick him out. Maybe if he were a rich kid, and had someone to back him up, that'd work. As it was, he was pretty sure he was screwed anyway.

"She was too drunk to give her consent. That guy was five minutes away from raping her." Adam worked hard to keep his voice under control, but it was pretty tough under the circumstances. "Didn't we just go through a two hour sexual assault training during orientation? I was actually listening."

"Were you?"

"Yes, I was.

The lawyer hadn't said a word, but he was writing furiously on his yellow pad.

"Well since you were paying such close attention during orientation," the Dean said, "maybe you also noted that physical violence is grounds for expulsion."

Here it came.

"What about the kid who was going to attack her? Is he getting expelled too?"

The Dean's eyes narrowed and he leaned across the desk. "Mr. Barnaby was the VICTIM of a crime, not the perpetrator. I think you're confused on that point, Mr. Grammaticus."

Barnaby. Barnaby. Like Barnaby Hall over on North Campus?

"So here's where reality sets in," the Dean continued. "The Barnaby family have said they won't press charges if we handle all discipline within the college. So I'm inclined to –"

"You mean they don't want the story to get out," Adam said.

"I believe you'd do well with a semester at home, Mr. Grammaticus," the Dean said, straightening his posture.

"I don't have any place to go."

"Then perhaps you'd like to leave school completely. Find another college and start over again next fall?"

Adam noted that it was phrased as a question. There was still time. But time for what? Time to learn to kiss ass when he'd done nothing wrong? Fuck it. If he was going to stay it would have to be on his terms.

"Okay, Dean, I guess I can do that," Adam leaned forward. "But since I don't have any place to go I think I'll stay right here in Hanover next year. I've always been interested in journalism. Maybe I can get a job over at the Valley News. Write a few stories from a student's point of view."

All of a sudden the college attorney stopped writing. He looked over at the Dean and clenched his jaw.

"Well now that's very interesting," the Dean said. "Perhaps we can both dial this thing back a little. There's no need for threats. We always like to keep this sort of thing within the college."

Maybe that's the problem, Adam thought.

"And now that you mention it, we are going to investigate the incident at the fraternity. It seems that some minors were served alcohol, in violation of college policy. That deserves at least a look see."

Adam shook his head in disgust.

"Is the girl ok?"

The Dean hesitated at first, as if he couldn't remember who they were talking about. "Yes, of course she's fine. Why wouldn't she be? Nothing happened."

"That's good, I thought maybe she'd died of alcohol poisoning or something."

"Dear God, no. Everything is fine."

Adam nodded and put his hands on the chair to stand up.

"Hold on a moment, Mr. Grammaticus. We're not done yet. If you stay at the college, as we're now prepared to allow you to do, you'd still have to be punished for what you did. I think a semester's probation is in order."

Adam snorted and continued to rise.

"Yeah, fine."

"And you'd have to promise not to do something like what happened at the fraternity house EVER again."

"Fuck you!"

"What?"

"You heard me, I said fuck you. If I ever see that again I WILL step in and stop it. And you should too. You've got a problem here and you don't even see it. Someday you will."

The lawyer looked over at the Dean and violently shook his head. Adam was standing now but the Dean dropped into his chair.

"But I can promise you this," Adam said. "I won't be going to any frat parties ever again, if that's what you're worried about. Who needs that shit? I came to Dartmouth to make a better life. I worked my way out of a bad situation at home and I'm here to study and make something out of myself."

The Dean's mouth didn't move as the next words came out. If someone had told Adam that the lawyer was a ventriloquist Adam wouldn't have been surprised.

"Then I suggest that you do that."

Chapter 36

"Bikers sure know how to party after a bike run, huh?"

The long-haired freak was obviously drunk out of his gourd. Adam couldn't figure out why he'd come over to talk to him. Adam had been sitting alone in a corner of the Quonset hut/clubhouse just watching the scene: a river of beer, topless women everywhere, music that seemed like a continuous loop of the Allman Brothers, while most everyone talked at once, except for the small contingent, including Tugg, who were playing pool by the back door.

The guy's patch said "Prospect," same as Tugg's. That explained it.

"So are you a friend of Doc's or something?"

"No," Adam replied. "I'm just visiting. I'm here with Tugg Morgan."

"Yeah." The guy belched and sat down across from Adam. "I know. You guys are hot shit or somethin'. They said you shot two Reapers."

Adam wondered when Tugg might make his way over to try to talk to Wanda, but maybe that was wishful thinking. She was always around the red-bearded guy she came in with, obviously his girlfriend or something, unlike most of the other girls in the room who seemed to be some sort of community property and were treated in a way that the term "sexual harassment" didn't cover.

"So you're not a prospect, then?" the guy said to Adam.

"That's a HELLUVA good question," said a voice behind them.

Adam looked up and saw the small guy with the sergeant-at-arms patch who'd been in on the joke when they first arrived. He was hammered and had a silly grin on his face. Adam was sure he must be one of the toughest guys in the room. Short guy usually was. A neighbor from childhood had told him a story about his strategy in the Navy of walking up to the biggest guy in the bar, clocking him, and then sitting down for a peaceful drink, once it was clear that nobody else should screw with him.

"What's the '13' stand for?" Adam said.

"Depends who you ask," the short guy said. "Thirteenth letter of the alphabet. Could be Motorcycle. Could be Murder. Which do you think?"

"I think I should keep my mouth shut," Adam said.

"Now see," the guy said, stepping over and pawing at Adam's collar, "that's the kind of answer that makes me think you're a Prospect. You don't ride and you look like a schoolteacher, but anybody who can handle a shotgun and take out two bikes and not even hit the men on them makes me curious. Size of the fight in the dog, you know."

Adam grimaced at the evil breath fogging in his face, but nodded.

"I know that myself," the sergeant continued. "I fought my way up. Now I'm third in line after Doc. No shit."

Tugg appeared and sat down next to Adam.

"Prospect, meet Prospect. And Prospect." The sergeant pointed at Tugg, then the long-haired freak, and then at Adam. "You!" He pointed at long-hair. "Get your fellow Prospects some beers." "And you!" He pointed at one of the topless women. "Get over here and keep his seat warm." A couple of other bikers came over and sat down on either side of the topless woman. Adam tried to look away. Unbelievable. They must be fake.

"So what's the story with you guys?" the sergeant said to Tugg. "You guys fags or somethin'?"

"Not hardly," Tugg said, smiling at the woman. "My friend's married and he's got a daughter. That's why he's here. We're looking for her."

"I'm somebody's daughter," the woman said.

"You're everybody's daughter," the sergeant said and the little group erupted in laughter.

Adam felt sick.

"So how old is she?" the sergeant continued.

"She's three."

"Shit. What happened to her?"

Long-hair came back with the beers and handed them around, then took the clue and left when he saw that his seat had been taken.

"CPS took her," Tugg answered. "Out of the blue. That's when he called me."

The sergeant appeared to have regained his bearings somewhat. "You hurt her?" His stare made Adam uncomfortable.

"No, our nanny lied. We think she might have hurt Emma. We don't know. Anyway, they came and took her away."

"Yeah, we know." The sergeant blinked a couple of times. "Just wanted to hear you say it. Your friend told us you had a warrant out when he took the truck a few days back. That's cool. You're sort of hiding out. Good place to do it."

"I like to hide things," the woman said.

"You like a lot of things, darlin'," the sergeant said.

The bikers laughed and Adam looked down.

"See, I told you he was a bad boy," the sergeant said, pointing at Adam. "Wanted by the law. Handles a shotgun. All you need's a tattoo and a cut and the cops'd never find you."

Adam tried to laugh a little, then turned serious. "But then I'd never find my daughter."

"Yeah, that sucks. But hey, wait a minute." The sergeant looked over at the other bikers. "Jed's ol' lady works for CPS, don't she? Maybe she can help." The sergeant rose unsteadily on his feet, then sat back down. "Darlin', go get Jed's girl, willya."

The girl rose in such a hurry that her breasts seemed caught by surprise. They bounced up and down as the bikers on either side stood up as well.

The trio walked over to Jed, who nodded and made a gesture to Wanda. She understood instantly and walked toward Tugg, Adam, and the sergeant.

Though she was fully clothed, Adam's mouth went dry.

Chapter 37

Wanda nodded at the sergeant-at-arms, then looked quickly at Tugg. She glanced at Adam, then back at Tugg, and gave a tight smile.

"Nice to meet you guys," she said. "I've been hearing the stories."

Adam could see that she recognized Tugg, but wondered if the sergeant would notice. In his current state of stupor, probably not. But they'd better be careful. Wanda must have already decided that it wasn't in her interest to reveal that she knew who they were, or she would have told someone long before the bike run. Of course, it wasn't in Tugg or Adam's interest either, but they were the ones at risk. If Wanda got mad and ratted them out, things could get ugly in a hurry.

"Sit down here and help us out for a minute," the sergeant said.

Wanda took a seat where Miss Plastic Surgery had been a few minutes ago, but Adam could see that this was different. Wanda clearly had standing because she belonged to Jed. If the sergeant really was number three in the club, then he outranked Jed, and that presented a golden opportunity. It was a calculated risk, but maybe they could get the information they needed.

The sergeant fancied himself the chairman of this little meeting. "So Wanda, these boys are looking for a girl. *His* girl. A little girl. CPS took her. You know anything that can help them?"

Tugg looked calm, but Adam knew that under the surface his brain must be racing. Tugg's way wasn't analytical, but more situational. He was like a tiger lying in the sun across the river, watching the gazelles.

"No, I'm sorry I don't know anything about her," Wanda said.

"Hon, we haven't even told you her *name* yet," the sergeant said.

Wanda flushed, but Tugg never took his eyes off her. If she broke, they'd have to make an exit like Al Capone.

"What'd you say her name was?" The sergeant was talking to Adam, but Tugg answered.

"Emma Grammaticus. CPS in Portland pulled her about two weeks ago. Put her in protective custody."

Wanda smiled at the sergeant and knitted her hands. "See, that's why I can't help you. I don't have anything to do with safe house placements. Those are confidential. Even from me."

Adam felt the ropes pull in his stomach. Had this all been a waste?

"Shit," the sergeant said. "I thought you *worked* for CPS. You're tellin' me there's nothing you can do to help them? This ain't just a Prospect and a civilian askin', darlin'. This is *me*."

If Wanda wasn't scared before, she looked a bit more intimidated. Her eyes were locked on the sergeant's as if he were Darth Vader. Apparently Tugg wasn't the only apex predator in the room.

"Kurt, I'm being straight with you. With them. There's no way I can get any information about a safe house placement. The only way I could get it is to break into someone's computer."

"Which you'll do if I ask you."

"Yes." Wanda nodded. "But maybe there's another way."

"Okay." The sergeant slapped his knees and stood up. "I'm done playing matchmaker. You work it out. Prospect! Your friend needs to come with me. I got an idea of my own. Help him with the legal part of his problem, anyhow."

Adam looked at Tugg, but had to go. All this time the plan had been for Tugg to talk to Wanda. Here it was on a silver platter.

The sergeant put his hands on Adam's shoulders and lifted him out of his seat. "Gonna make a biker out of you yet. I saw you lookin' at Candi. That girl's got hidden talents. Makes a man think about doin' bad things. Get over here."

Adam heard the crowd laugh as the sergeant-at-arms began to shout: "Bad Ass comin' through. Got us some prime beef."

Under his breath Adam said Emma's name like a prayer and knew that she was worth it.

Chapter 38

The tits were coming at him full in the face again, but all Adam could do was grin and bear it. Strong arms held him down on both sides. It would've been impossible to move even if he'd tried.

"See, it don't hurt a bit, does it?" the sergeant said.

Candi swung over the top again as her nipples grazed Adam's cheek.

"Okay, so what'd you say your girl's name was again?"

Adam turned his head. "Emma."

"And that's with one M or two?"

"Two."

The needle felt like a hornet dancing on his bicep, as Candi contorted herself into a better position.

"This'd be easier if I had a chair," she said to the bikers. "Let him go now. He'll hold still."

The bikers loosened their grip and Adam repositioned himself on the table, then tried to sit as still as possible.

"Give him some other girl's name and scare the shit out of his wife," one guy said.

"This is a family man," Candi said, finally sitting down. "This tattoo's for his little girl."

Candi's enormous breasts kept brushing Adam's arm, but the pain of the tattoo was sufficient to fight off any stimulation. The crowd seemed to be enjoying the spectacle, but after a few minutes, once Adam wasn't struggling anymore, they all drifted away as Candi continued her work.

"Got my first tattoo when I was thirteen," Candi said. "But you can't see it unless you want to."

"That's okay."

"Your friend's had some work done. He with someone?"

Adam tried to see if Tugg was still talking to Wanda, but Candi's endowment was blocking his view.

"Huh? No. He's single," Adam finally said.

"That's very interesting. How old's your little girl?"

The buzzing of the tattoo needle sounded like a vibrator. In and out. In and out. Adam couldn't look, but he hoped it wouldn't be awful.

"She's three."

"My girl's six. She's with her father. Her name's Eden."

The line of sight past Candi's boobs finally opened up. Adam saw Tugg and Wanda talking intently. Alone. Over by the chairs.

"That's a pretty name," Adam said absently, trying to keep up.

"Yeah. Well. She's a good kid. She deserves better than her dad and I had when we were together. Her father's like you. He's a good man."

Adam caught Kurt's eye across the room. Kurt tipped his beer bottle in a salute, then held his hands out in the universal male sign for "juggs" and raised his eyebrows.

Adam forced a smile and looked at Candi's face. "How long since you've seen her?" he said.

"Three years."

"They took my daughter two weeks ago. It already feels like a decade."

"Something bad happen?" Candi's voice was husky as she kept her face close to her work.

"No. Just a bunch of liars. Common story, I guess."

Candi shook her head. "I didn't fight the custody. Sometimes I think I should have. But she's better off now."

Change the subject. Quick.

"Hey, I heard you did the tattoos on a couple of the guys here."

"Yeah. It's kind of my thing. I do 'em then I do 'em. You know? I don't belong to anybody here yet. Just come for the parties. Your friend seems nice."

Adam looked over at Tugg again. The freaky guy with the long hair was standing over them, talking to Wanda.

"He's great. My best friend in the world. Other than my wife."

Candi looked up. "If you want I can give you a blow job when we're finished. It'll help with the pain. Better than a Tylenol."

The bikers' voices over by the window were loud, like someone had just gotten to the punch line. Kurt, Jed, Doc and Spider were all standing with a crowd of other guys. Adam saw Kurt raise his foot, then cry "Ohhhh," as he was obviously reliving Tugg's moment of glory earlier that day at the motorcycle garage.

"Thank you, no," Adam said quietly. "You're beautiful, but my wife is home waiting for me. It just wouldn't be right."

"That's okay. We're almost done." Candi's voice didn't sound like she was hurt. Maybe she was numb.

Adam swiveled his head to Tugg's side of the room and saw that the voices were raised over there too. But this wasn't a joke. The skinny freak had his hand on Wanda's shoulder and Adam could read Tugg's lips: *back off.*

"You ain't the fucking *king* yet!" The guy had yelled just loud enough that everyone in the room could hear him, but still there was a moment's hesitation as things grew quiet and Adam watched freaky-boy slip his hand underneath Wanda's vest.

In an instant, Adam was off the table, holding the tattoo gun.

Jed yelled, "What the hell?"

Adam took three steps and leapt into the air just as Tugg was going for his Ka-Bar.

When Tugg saw Adam, he fell back and yanked Wanda out of the way.

Adam landed on the freak with the point of the needle right at his neck.

Half a dozen bikers ran past Candi to the other side of the room.

"No! No! I didn't mean it!" the guy wailed.

Doc leaned down and grabbed a handful of hair and brought the guy to his feet. "Well, Jed, I guess you'll do the honors."

"You're goddamned right I will," spittle flying.

Jed looked down and gave a nod to Adam. Tugg held his hand out as Jed took the knife, then perp-walked the dude outside as most of the crowd followed.

Wanda looked over and gave Adam a blank stare.

After a few seconds of shouting and whistling Adam heard a piercing animal-like scream, immediately followed by an echo of "OHHHHHH!!!" from the crowd.

Candi shrugged her shoulders. "Ain't a blow job in the world's gonna help with that."

Chapter 39

Adam thrilled at the satisfying crunch of gravel as his motorcycle sped across the compound. This time he turned with plenty of room as the fence rushed toward him.

"Different feel than a dirt bike, huh?" Kurt said.

"Yeah and that was twenty years ago."

"It'll come back. Like riding a *bike*!"

Kurt was laughing so hard, Adam thought he was going to soil himself. This *was* different, but still at times it felt like no time had passed since his Honda XR-200. That was 220 pounds versus 870 for this Harley behemoth. Adam goosed the throttle and sped back the other way.

"I think you're ready for the road," Kurt said.

"You sure?"

"No, but let's do it anyway."

Adam couldn't wait to show Tugg his progress. He'd been at it for three solid hours. It was 11:30 a.m. now, but Tugg still hadn't shown his face. Few people had. After all the beer and debauchery last night, Kurt must be an iron man to have gotten up so early, let alone offered to teach Adam how to ride a street bike.

"We can get you on the road in four hours," he'd said.

"Really?"

"It won't be pretty, but it's possible. And we just happen to have an extra bike today.

Adam probably should've felt guilty about taking the guy's Harley after his spectacular ejection from the club last night. By the rules, the bike didn't belong to him anymore, but Adam supposed it could've been worse.

"He'll live," was all Kurt had said.

"But he's gone?"

"Well, he ain't going to be sitting on a bike for a while."

Adam sped back and forth across the compound a few more times.

"Let's do it," said Kurt. "Let me go down to the garage and get you a heavy jacket and some boots, and I'll get my bike. I'll ride with you for a piece down the road so you can see what the highway feels like. Next bike run, you'll be ready."

Adam smiled. He put his kickstand down and killed the engine but left his helmet on, while he watched Kurt disappear down the path. He wondered how he looked in the helmet, but the mirror on the handlebars was too small to give the full effect.

Adam had spent a long time at the mirror that morning looking at his arm. The swelling was still pretty bad but, except for the "E," at least the thing was readable backward. Candi had done a pretty fair job, but Kate would still have a fit.

Yesterday a tattoo and today a Harley. Everybody joked about him hiding out with the club, but all Adam could think about was waking Tugg so he could hear what he'd learned yesterday. Then maybe they could get out of here and find Emma.

Finally.

Tugg stood in the doorway, with his hand up like a zombie in the sunlight. He walked over to Adam on the bike.

"What, too badass?" Adam said, removing the helmet.

"Something's missing. Maybe it's a leather jacket and some actual experience."

"Kurt's getting the jacket now."

Tugg just shook his head.

"Listen, Tugg, we don't have much time. What'd she say?"

"Hold on, easy rider. There ain't much."

"What?"

Tugg's face was pinched against the blazing sun as he looked directly at Adam. "She wasn't lying when she told Kurt she didn't know. She doesn't. Her idea for 'another way' was that we figure out this Indian thing. She thinks it might be connected."

"You mean what Edward told us on the reservation?"

"Yeah," Tugg said, opening a fresh pack of cigarettes. "She confirmed what he said. The placements in Salem. The cash. How much of a push there's been to get this done in a hurry. But then she told me something we hadn't heard before."

Adam knew that Tugg was probably feeling pretty rocky. Hungover. No coffee or food. And he'd probably been up all night with Candi to boot. But Kurt was coming back any minute. "Yeah, what?"

Tugg took a drag on his cigarette. "She said that almost overnight there were five or six white kids from the suburbs coming through the system. Emma wasn't the only one. And Wanda said it seemed like there was pressure to get those kids run through real fast, just the same as there was pressure a few months back to get the Indian kids. Might be coming from the same place. So maybe they're related."

Adam spied Kurt walking up the trail carrying a leather jacket and some boots. He was about 50 yards off.

"So it looks like back to the reservation," Adam said.

"I guess." Tugg stepped on his cigarette. "Whatever happened to Emma has been happening to other kids. There must be a pattern."

Adam didn't want to solve a conspiracy. He just wanted his kid back. This all sounded pretty thin, but it was all they had. The holy grail of a conversation with Wanda was now behind them. Time to move forward.

"When do we go?"

Tugg made a grimace. "Let's do it now. I'll drive the first shift. To tell you the truth I can't take much more of this shit. I'm starting to lose it again."

Adam stared at his friend's face and noticed his hand tremble as he knocked the pack for another cigarette.

Lose it. With Tugg that phrase could cover a lot of ground.

Adam saw that Kurt had veered off and gone straight for his bike and was signaling him to come over.

"Okay," Adam said, "let's get you out of here. But forget the truck. We'll go like we came."

Tugg looked puzzled.

"Gimme another hour and I'm gonna be a biker."

Chapter 40

Fifty miles an hour was a long way from bad ass, but after four hours on a motorcycle, Adam was ready to redefine the term. At least they hadn't gone through Idaho this time and had just headed west, straight for the reservation. Still, this being his first day back on a bike — with no spills yet — Adam didn't want to press his luck.

Tugg was right beside him, probably going out of his mind. Another drawback to taking the bikes was that they really couldn't talk. Not to mention the amazing vibrating ass problem. And what they'd do if they happened to spot any Reapers.

Tugg was flying his colors, but Adam wore a plain leather jacket. Apparently one could ascend only so many levels of cool in 24 hours.

Adam scanned the low, flat mesas and reminded himself that they weren't in Reaper territory. But the sun was getting low and it'd be hard to see what was coming at them once it got dark. The bike carried a real sense of vulnerability that he hadn't thought of before he'd tried it. The freedom was great, but it came at a cost.

Tugg fell back a bit, then shot forward at what looked like 80 m.p.h., then he fell back and shot forward again. He must be going crazy. Finally, Tugg signaled and pulled off to the side of the road. Adam pulled up behind him and shut off his bike.

"I've had it, we're done for the day," Tugg said.

"What? There's no place around for miles. We're still 90 miles from the reservation."

"That's why we're stopping." Tugg took off his helmet. "For God's sake, Adam, you just got your legs back under you this morning. Don't push it."

"I haven't been."

"Yeah."

Adam took off his helmet. "But I thought I was doing well."

"You are, but have some pity." Tugg got off his bike and turned his back to take a piss.

"Where will we sleep?"

Tugg zipped up and turned around. "Out there." He gestured toward a flat area near some rocks and a couple of scrub trees. "I've got some blankets, food, a lighter. Trust me Adam, I do this 365 days a year."

Adam nodded.

Tugg mounted his bike and fired it up, then pulled off the highway and rode toward the rocks. Adam followed, bouncing over the scrub brush.

Where was the XR-200 when he needed it?

Adam hadn't been camping in twenty years. But this was *real* camping. No tent. No sleeping bags. Just a campfire and some blankets and your best friend leaning up against his motorcycle, picking his teeth.

"Good meal?"

"Sure." Adam tried to sound enthusiastic. Peanut butter sandwiches and a little diced ham weren't bad actually, under the circumstances.

"Why didn't we cook something over the campfire?"

"Too hard."

"So why the campfire?"

"You really want to know?"

Adam wondered if it was time for ghost stories.

"Cougars and coyotes."

"No shit?"

There was a crescent moon overhead but the entire sky was filling up with stars. Millions of them. Stars you never saw in the city.

"Cooked food would just attract them, but a campfire means smoke. They'll smell the ash, even when it's out. They won't come near us all night."

Adam's eyes flashed in the firelight.

"And I've still got the Remington, my Glocks, and the Ka-Bar. I think we've got it covered." Tugg took a swallow of water, then doused the fire in a hiss of smoke.

Adam had just enough light to find his blanket and spread it on the grass next to his motorcycle. "Guess we should sleep," he said.

"Your ass is going to wish you had in the morning. You'll feel it when you get back on."

Adam looked up at the brilliant sky. With no fire, the stars were even brighter now. How could he sleep through this?

"Guess you didn't get too much sleep last night, did you?"

"What do you mean?" Tugg said.

"Candi."

"Adam, please. We're both tired, okay?" It was silent for a minute, then Tugg started again. "I didn't sleep with Candi last night, if you gotta know."

"You didn't?"

"No. That girl is seriously fucked up. She's like an animal looking for shelter and it wasn't gonna be me."

Adam kicked off his boots.

"But you could've had her just for one night, right?"

"Women aren't that scarce. And I've got a simple rule: don't dip your dick in crazy."

Adam saw Tugg's lighter flare, then the red tip of his cigarette.

"It's just not worth it," Tugg continued. "Not fair to her or to me." Adam heard Tugg exhale, then saw the tip glow red again. "Some things just ain't right."

Adam had been with Kate so long he couldn't remember what it felt like to be with another woman. He'd had his chances, but Tugg was right. Some things just weren't right.

"Most men don't learn that until they get married," Adam said. "Some not even then."

"Yeah, well my wife's dead and my daughter's gone." There was a silence as Adam saw the tip of cherry red in the darkness. "But that's all history. I never told you because it happened while I was in prison."

Adam waited a second, then filled in the obvious. "This was after the plane went down."

"Yeahhh." Tugg's voice was flat and hollow. "After the plane went down."

Good Lord. Any piece of Tugg's story by itself would have been enough to explain the PTSD. The plane crash, prison, the war — but Adam knew this was something deeper.

"Look, do you really want to hear this?" Tugg said. "You've got a wife and daughter of your own now and you don't want this rattling around in your brain, trust me. Let's just get Emma back. Then you'll be all right."

"And what about you?"

"I'll be okay."

"You're protecting me again. You don't need to do that."

Adam saw the lighter flare. Third cigarette in ten minutes.

"It's *my job* to protect people. That's the problem. When you're in prison, you can protect yourself just fine. But what do you do about the people you leave on the outside?"

At first Adam thought that Tugg was laughing. What the hell? Then he knew what was happening. He heard Tugg spit and suck in a shuddery breath.

"Tugg?" Adam waited for a reply through the blackness. "Tugg?"

Adam had the eerie feeling that he was alone. He found his way over to Tugg's empty blanket, then stood up and looked out over the landscape.

There he was, about twenty feet in the distance, standing on a little hill. Adam never would have seen him, except there was a Tugg-shaped hole in the middle of the starry sky.

Then there was no mistaking his location.

The scream must have echoed for miles on the open desert. Adam wondered if he should go to him, but then another scream came and then another. Tugg would come back when he was ready. Some losses you wanted company for and some you didn't.

Adam listened for an echo in the distant hills, but he couldn't hear any coyotes.

Chapter 41

Kate was running so fast. She still had two laps to go but her nearest competitor was back on the straights and Kate was already at the half turn.

The crowd was going wild.

DART-MOUTH! DART-MOUTH!

Senior spring and Kate was about to win the all-Ivy championships, which put her in line for Nationals and maybe a spot as an All-American.

It didn't get any better than this.

Adam looked around the stadium. Students holding banners, laughing with their friends, spilling beer, a couple of bright green painted faces. Desperately hanging onto the last few months of adolescent freedom before the real world closed in.

Who was this girl?

They'd been together two and a half years and Adam already knew she was the one.

Smart, beautiful, and a loving heart the likes of which Adam had never thought he'd find.

Just lost her parents last year in a car crash. She went to the funerals, cried, came back to school, and just kept going. How? She'd said that Adam was her life now. There was nothing to stay home for. Adam sure didn't have anything to return to at the Cedar Shade trailer park. He was going to propose on graduation day, then they'd build a life together, just the two of them, come what may.

Kate was smooth as glass as she approached the full turn. Thighs glistening. No sex for two weeks before the matches! They'd have time tonight after she won. Adam was already out of the competition long ago, sitting in the stands watching Kate work.

C'mon Kate.

The girl behind her was closing.

Kate didn't look back. She never did.

The crowd erupted.

FAS-TER! FAS-TER!

Suddenly Kate stumbled, like she'd caught her foot on something.

Adam shot to his feet.

The girl behind rocketed forward as Kate took another bad step.

What the hell?

It was like she'd tripped. Or had a muscle pull or something.

C'mon Kate, keep going!

But then, to Adam's horror, he and the crowd could only watch as the nightmare unfolded: Kate started to swivel her hips hard, from side to side, taking big exaggerated steps like she was having trouble just staying on her feet.

The girl in second place had long since passed her. And now, one by one, the girls from the other schools were shooting by too.

Even from this distance, Adam could see that Kate was crying.

She was still moving, but her steps were getting weirder.

Was it an electrolyte thing? Like that woman at the marathon a few years ago?

Whatever it was, Kate was in trouble.

Adam raced down the steps and looked for his opening to get onto the field.

Adam broke through the scrum just as Kate was waving away the medic and her teammates. She sat crumpled on the in-field grass, sobbing.

"Adam!" She could see him now. "Just come here and hold me."

"Kate, what the hell's the matter? Are you all right? Why aren't they taking you inside and figuring out what's wrong?"

The tears were still glistening on Kate's cheeks, but her mouth was resolute.

"All I need is you," she said. "I already know what's wrong."

Adam looked at her uncomprehending as she continued to wave everyone away so he could come over to the grass and sit down next to her.

He held her for a long minute as she sobbed again. Then she looked him directly in the face and the awful secret came out. She'd known for about three months now. Had suspected, really, for most of her life after she'd gotten the test when she was twelve. Her parents would never tell her; said they'd do it when she was 21. Then they died with the result. How could they do that to her? Every twitch and glitch for the last ten years she'd panicked, hoping it was just her active imagination. That she wouldn't have to live with what her aunt Kathy had been through. But now the dreaded day was here.

"Kate, my God. Why didn't you tell me?"

The stadium erupted in a burst of cheers as the next race began. The forgotten couple sat together on the ground, heads close, lost in their own world.

"I thought you wouldn't love me or something. Shit, maybe I thought I wouldn't love me. I don't know. If I didn't talk about it, maybe it wasn't true."

"So you kept it inside all this time? Worrying?"

Kate nodded.

"You think I'm some shallow guy who can't handle tough times? After what I went through with my Mom? You and I have a lot more than that, Kate. A lot more."

"I know it." Kate looked so defeated that Adam just held her and kissed her forehead. "But I thought you'd want to have kids," she continued.

"Yeah, well, I DO want kids. I want YOUR kids. I want to spend the rest of my life with you. How the hell does that grab you?"

Kate looked up and smiled through her tears.

"Yes, Adam. Yes! You know I want that too. But our kids would be at risk. You know that, right? If we had a daughter she could end up like me. She could –".

"Yeah, well I hope she DOES end up like you. In every way but one. And if she does have MS we can cope. Just like we cope with everything. You can't stop living, right? You've got to keep going. And you know I'll always protect my family. No matter what."

Kate lurched forward awkwardly and threw her arms around Adam's neck, knocking him back until she was laying on top of him on the grass.

For a long minute they just lay there, gently kissing.

Adam could hear a few whistles and cat-calls from high up in the stadium, all but drowned out by the cheering as Dartmouth took the lead in the 440 relay.

"So can you walk at all or do I have to carry you?"

"Oh, I'll be able to walk," Kate said. "It comes and goes, but it will probably deteriorate over time. Eventually I'll need a cane, then maybe – if I'm unlucky – a wheelchair. But that's not for years. As long as I don't push myself, I should have a few good years left."

"They're all good years," Adam said. "You don't know what the future brings."

"Neither do you. It could get bad. Worse."

"For better OR worse. That's what I want."

Kate nodded her head. Just once.

Chapter 42

Adam opened his eyes to the sound of wood snapping and the scent of instant coffee in a metal cup.

The sun wasn't quite up yet, but it was already pretty bright. Tugg had his gear laid out on a blue plastic tarp, packing it neatly.

"How's your ass?"

Adam was grateful for the question. Any dialogue was hopeful after how things had ended last night. "Don't know yet. How should it be?"

"Still attached," Tugg said. "You'll need it today."

Adam sat up and looked at the horizon.

Another two hours on the motorcycle meant two hours in a bubble, unable to speak to Tugg. He'd better get it out now.

"You okay?"

"Yeah fine. Why wouldn't I be?"

Adam accepted reality for what he needed it to be.

"So what's next after the reservation?"

Tugg looked over and spilled the dregs of his cup onto the ground. "Depends what we hear."

"No, I mean after that. Now that we've talked to Wanda, we're done with the club, right? You're out from under?"

Tugg shook his head. "Not hardly."

"What do you owe them? You don't want to go back, do you?"

"No, Adam. Were you listening last night? I don't trust people. The military. A motorcycle club. It's all the same thing. You think I want to be a part of that?"

"So don't go back then," Adam squinted into the sun. "We've got what we need."

Tugg laughed, but his eyes were pebbles. "It's not my motorcycle anymore, remember? Yours either. Not to mention the cut I'm wearing. They'd crawl through hell to get that back, and I mean that literally. They'd find us. Even if I gave everything back at this point they'd want to know a reason. And they'd kill us if they knew the truth."

Adam shook his head. "So how are you going to pull out once we find Emma?"

"As long as I don't get my full patch, there's still time. Once that happens, it's over. I might as well be back in prison. Or dead."

Adam shook his head. "So don't go back then. Let them come find us. We need the bikes and we need the cover. I say we go to the reservation, then find Emma, then deal with the club later on, if we have to."

"You don't know shit."

"Maybe not, but I'm still right."

Tugg cinched a rope around the blue tarp and carried it over to his saddle bag.

"Yeah, I guess you are. Dead now or later, there's not much difference. But we've gotta find Emma first. Then I can make my peace."

Adam stood up and walked over to his friend.

"I'm not going to let anything happen to you, okay? The club isn't gonna get you and I'm not going to let you kill yourself either. We'll find a way."

Tugg looked over and forced a smile that his eyes couldn't match.

"You've come a long way, dude. You finally got your priorities straight. Emma comes first. You aren't conflicted anymore."

Chapter 43

The same lazy fan was still pushing hot air from one side of the room to the other. Adam held out his hand to Edward White Robe and nodded toward the stove.

"You still serving breakfast?"

Edward gave a firm grip and a tiny smile creased his face.

"Got addicted to that free Indian food, huh?"

Tugg and Adam headed over to their table near the window.

"Looks like you've made a few changes since last time," Edward said. "New motorcycle, new man?"

"Something like that," Adam said.

"Might not have recognized you without him here."

They both glanced at Tugg. "I do tend to make an impression."

Adam and Tugg took their seats as Edward disappeared in back. This time he came out with all of the fixings at once and started in.

A portable black and white TV was set up in the corner of the room with the sound on low. "Wheel of Fortune."

How to broach the subject? Ask more questions about the reservation? Casually bring up the foster care issue?

"We went to The Longlane Home, but your friend's grandsons weren't there," Tugg said. "I talked to someone who said they were adopted last year. I'm sorry."

Edward looked over cautiously and then back at his frying pan. He flipped the eggs and remained quiet. "You didn't have to do that," he said.

"Yeah, but we were already there."

Edward brushed the back of his hand across his face. "You're good men."

"You gave us a free breakfast."

"You were good before that." Edward turned off the stove and spooned the eggs onto plates. He walked over to the table, then grabbed his stool and pulled it toward his customary spot.

"So you didn't go to The Longlane Home just to look for Hinney's grandsons, right? There must have been a reason —"

Tugg looked at Adam, whose eyes gave permission.

"We were looking for his daughter. CPS took her a few weeks ago. We thought she might be there, but she wasn't."

"Your wife an Indian?"

"No," said Adam.

Edward nodded and looked lazily out the window. "I'm sorry you didn't find her. Did you come all the way back just to tell me about the twins?"

"No," Adam answered. "But we think that what happened to my daughter might be related to what's been happening to the Indian kids. You said last time that a lot of you had been talking at council. Can we talk to some of the other people?"

"Council is only for members of the tribe," Edward said. "But this is important. Let me see what I can do."

"When?" Adam said.

"Whenever we say. This sounds like a good enough reason to have council tonight."

Adam nodded at Tugg, who had pushed his empty plate away.

"Better let me drive over and talk to some folks," Edward said, standing up. "We arrange these face to face. I'll be back in a couple of hours."

"Okay," Adam said. "You want us to come back?"

"No. Better pull your motorcycles behind the garage. You two can wait in my room in back. Rest for a while. But you need to stay out of sight."

"Why?" Adam asked, already knowing the answer.

Edward nudged his head toward the television. "No state cops on the reservation, but best to be safe anyway. A jacket and a motorcycle can only hide so much."

Chapter 44

Whatever stereotypical images Adam might have harbored about what an Indian council meeting might look like were shattered the instant he entered the room. There was no peace pipe. Just a hundred or so chairs in a rough semi-circle around a table in a dilapidated school auditorium. It could have been a PTA meeting in any town in America.

The faces of the inhabitants, however, told a different story. Adam didn't see a smile among them. Old men in jean jackets and women with young kids sat stiffly in their chairs, staring at him and Tugg. Adam heard none of the friendly small talk one might expect amongst people who knew one another so well, or any welcoming gestures from the community. Instead, these looked like people waiting to hear a jury verdict.

Whatever Edward had said about the purpose of the meeting, clearly this wasn't normal. A couple of kids stared at Tugg with wide-eyed interest, then disappeared behind a man Adam took to be their grandfather.

Edward was sitting in one of the chairs at the table, next to another man. Was that the chief? Handsome and thickly muscled, he had obsidian black hair pulled straight back from his face. Too young to be any sort of "elder," he was nonetheless clearly in charge. He wore a brown jacket and matching pants that didn't look like they were trying to be a suit. His snakeskin boots gleamed against the dull floor.

"I'm Tommy. Council tonight was called by Edward. He brought some visitors who have some information about the foster care situation here on the reservation. Edward, introduce them, please."

Edward stood. Adam could tell that Edward must be a man of great standing within the community. All eyes were upon him.

"These men are named Adam and Tugg. They're from Portland. Adam's daughter was taken by social services a few weeks ago. These are good men."

Edward sat down and the crowd's gaze turned to Adam and Tugg.

Was that it? After an awkward silence, Adam jumped in.

"I'm sorry, but we don't actually have any new information about the reason for the abductions from social services. We have our suspicions, but we're here to learn from you. Maybe we can help one another. Can someone tell us what's been happening here? Edward told us a bit, but I wonder if someone can tell us what *you* think is behind all this?"

After a brief silence, there was a tiny voice.

"It's the governor and his greed."

All eyes turned to the back row, where Adam spied a young woman holding a baby. Next to her was a man about Edward's age, worrying his hands on a wooden cane.

After another silence, Adam said, "Edward told us that you were suspicious about the governor. But can someone fill us in? Why would he specifically be coming after your children here on the reservation? And if he is doing that, I wonder how my daughter fits in?"

When no one spoke, Adam looked at Tugg, who just shook his head.

They looked at Tommy, who just stared blankly back at them.

Edward stood.

"These are *good* men. They drove all the way to Salem to see if Hinney's grandsons were still at The Longlane Home, then they drove all the way back to tell me they were adopted. He's looking for his daughter. We need to help them."

Adam watched the crowd fidget. The man with the cane started to tear up and his daughter put her hand on his shoulder. Everyone looked around. Finally a beautiful woman about 35 years old walked over to the table and spoke.

"My name is Tulie Price and I'm a child welfare worker for the reservation. How much do you already know?"

Adam took over. "Ms. Price, thank you. Just treat us as if we don't know anything. Please start at the beginning. Once we know what you know, we'll be happy to share our story and answer any questions. Is that all right?"

Tulie nodded and put her hand on Edward's shoulder. "Some of this was in the newspaper a few years back, but I'm going to tell it all again, from our perspective. When he was Lieutenant Governor, our current Governor was also the Executive Director of The Longlane Home, which is the largest foster care business in the state of Oregon. Most people thought that was okay, because the Lieutenant Governor's position was part-time and had just been newly created by the state legislature. It paid no income and carried no duties. It existed only as a governor-in-waiting just in case the current governor died or resigned unexpectedly, so there was no perceived conflict of interest. Lots of states have this kind of system.

"Of course then, as we all know, Governor Gibbard died unexpectedly. At that point, Lieutenant Governor Halliday resigned from his position at The Longlane Home and assumed the governorship. That's when all of the changes started for us. Everybody knows that the governor inherited a huge state budget deficit. The Longlane Home started to get all of these no-bid state contracts for foster care. When the kids flooded in, so did a tide of federal money, some of which went to the deficit and some of which got filtered to The Longlane Home."

Adam didn't know whether it was appropriate, but he raised his hand anyway.

"Yes?" Tulie said.

"I'm sorry to interrupt, but I'd like to ask a question, if that's all right."

Edward jumped in. "Adam, you can just go ahead. We don't have any false politeness here because we don't need any. When you actually respect someone, it's okay to be blunt."

Tulie nodded and gave the smallest glimpse of a smile.

"Okay, then let me play devil's advocate for a moment," Adam said. "I can see where this is going, but the governor's ties to The Longlane Home were in all of the newspapers when he assumed office. It was investigated. Everybody knew that there might be a conflict of interest, which was why he resigned from The Longlane Home and stepped down from its board. They said he put all his assets in a blind trust."

Someone snorted.

"Don't you think it's a little weird that all of these kids started going to foster care right after he assumed office?" Tulie asked. Apparently bluntness cut both ways.

"Yes, sure," Adam said. "But lots of people said it was because he was an expert on child welfare issues and this was a long-neglected area of state government. It made sense that he would attend to it."

Tugg came to life. "Yeah, but then why would so many of the kids just *happen* to be Indian? I guess this is a question for both of you. Adam, if he was just fixing a deferred problem, why did so much of it fall on the reservations? But Tulie, if he was just trying to fix the state's financial problems, why would he have it in for the Indians?"

A murmur went through the room.

Tulie cleared her throat and continued. "This is where we got burned before. For the newspapers, it wasn't enough that 50% of the kids who were taken were Indians. They thought they could explain that by looking around here. You rob the bank because that's where the money is. In some ways they blamed us. The foster care problem was largely an *Indian* problem, everyone thought, because look at how we live. Everyone was too polite to say it outright, but that's what they thought. It was the same b.s. they did to us back before the Indian Child Welfare Act was passed. Since then, the foster placements are supposed to be *within the tribe.*

"But right now, we have qualified Indian foster parents who have *never* been contacted for a placement. Did they put that in the papers? No. So they did have it in for us, didn't they? They violated federal law by making most of the Indian kid placements in group homes like The Longlane Home, rather than within our own community."

"So it's racism," said Adam.

"Our whole history has been due to racism," Tulie said. "But that's too easy. This smelled like something more. We got suspicious about the financial angle and started to do our own digging. This time we didn't rely on the newspapers. We wondered not only why so many Indian kids were going into foster care, but why they weren't going to Indian foster homes. Why would the state so brazenly violate the ICWA? And why were so many of the placements made to The Longlane Home?"

Adam was on the edge of his seat, but he could see that everyone else in the room except him and Tugg must already know the answer. Edward was looking at him as if in apology, nodding.

"We found out that under the federal reimbursement formula to the states, any foster child with a special needs designation got a payment that was *four times* the regular amount. And then we found out that someone in the state house had designated ALL Indian children in Oregon as special needs!"

Adam heard a couple of righteous interjections from the crowd.

His head was reeling. *All of them special needs? As if being Native American were somehow a handicap?*

Adam was pissed. He could see why all of those in the crowd around him were so upset, too. But a tiny piece of him died when he heard this, because if all of this were true, how could it explain why Emma was taken?

"That's when it happened," Tulie continued. "The Indian kids started disappearing overnight. They sent in whole teams of social workers from Portland and Salem. They didn't use our social workers and they didn't make placements with our own foster families. The same thing happened at the reservations in Warm Springs, Umatilla, Paiute, and Grande Ronde. Most of the kids went to The Longlane Home. And they haven't come back."

Adam felt sick. This might not be related to Emma, but it was one of the biggest injustices he'd ever heard of. A system *that* corrupt might involve other abuses that could explain what had happened to Emma. Didn't Wanda say that they had taken a spate of white kids from the suburbs? First it was the Indians, then it was the rich kids. Maybe there was a connection.

"So the Governor is dirty," said Tugg.

"Yes," said Tulie. "We think he's making a profit from this. He's at least using the Indian kids to balance the state budget deficit. But then there's the question of why so many of the kids are going to The Longlane Home, rather than to Indian or even white foster families. The state gets its cut either way. But the rest of the payment goes to the group home or to the family that actually does the care. So it's got to be the money. They're going to The Longlane Home because that's where the governor has his financial ties."

"Can you prove this?" Tugg said.

"No, but it's probably still true. Maybe the trust isn't as blind as everyone thinks. Remember the 2012 presidential election? Everyone said that Romney had a blind trust, he wasn't involved in the day-to-day affairs at Bain Capital. Then it came out after the election that if he'd won he still would have been receiving Bain money in his blind trust, even if he wasn't directing the company.

"There's blind and then there's dumb. Halliday's still got a pension coming from The Longlane Home. He's not an idiot. And who's managing the trust?"

Edward stood up again. "This is what I was afraid to tell you two the other day. We haven't told anyone else about this. We don't trust the government and we don't trust the newspapers. If we handle this wrong, who knows what they could do to us? Take the rest of our kids?"

Adam fell back in his seat, while Tugg sat shaking his head. "My God," Tugg said. "How can we help you?"

"How can we help *you*?" said the woman with the baby. "You know who I am right? Thank you for looking for my sons. You said that his daughter was taken too. Is she Indian?"

Adam shook his head.

"Is she special needs?"

Adam shook his head again.

Hinney's daughter frowned in thought.

For the first time, Tommy spoke. "We all trust one another now. That's a big first step. Maybe we can learn something from *your* story."

"I'm sorry, I've got nothing," Adam said. "My daughter was taken when our nanny made a false report about child abuse. As I said, Emma is white and she's not special needs. We think they put her with a foster family, then they put her in protective custody. One thing we know for sure is that she's *not* at The Longlane Home. We checked."

"Could they be making money off her in a different way?" Tulie asked.

Adam shook his head again. "I don't see how. Nothing beyond the regular reimbursement, anyway. We know someone from CPS who said that there have been a lot of removals lately from suburban white families. That'll cause a firestorm of publicity. If there's a river of money flowing in from federal reimbursements, the last thing they'd want would be publicity. Why kill the golden goose?"

"Maybe you could go ask your friend again," Tommy said.

"It's worth a try," Tugg said, turning to Adam. "We could at least bring the motorcycles and the jacket back."

Adam's jaw tightened.

"Be careful," said a woman in the back. "Keep to back roads, so the police don't find you. Well, the state police anyway."

For some reason, everyone turned to Tommy.

"I'm a sheriff with the reservation police," he said. "I don't work for the Oregon State Police or any other municipality. I work for the tribe."

A few people smiled.

"You can come back here if you need to," Hinney said. "We're a better sanctuary than a church even."

Adam turned around to thank him and a few people smiled warmly.

"What happens on the reservation stays on the reservation?" Tugg asked.

"Just about right," Tommy said. "Most white people don't know the half of it."

A chuckle passed through the crowd.

"Just like that free food," Edward said, grinning from ear to ear.

Chapter 45

Adam and Tugg sat in the last booth of the Denny's, near the restrooms. Tugg had his customary spot — back to the wall, eyes on the door — while Adam was still making love to his pancakes.

Edward was a fine man, but damn. Sometimes you just needed to eat food that was hot all at once. Pancakes, eggs, bacon, toast, orange juice, and a side of fruit salad. Adam would have licked the plate if no one were watching.

The place was jumping. First restaurant outside the reservation made it feel like the Capital Grille.

Adam drained the rest of his juice and looked at Tugg. Neither had spoken much since the council meeting last night, probably because both were thinking the same thing. Maybe the two cases *were* connected. It was all beginning to make sense now.

When they got back to the clubhouse, they could ask Wanda for her thoughts and share what they'd learned. Why would the Governor want to create false abuse charges against suburban families when he was trying to avoid publicity for what amounted to false removal of Indian kids into the foster care system?

Tugg finally looked at Adam.

"Only about a hundred miles to go, right?" Adam said, wiping the plate with his toast. "Then this biker thing will be over."

"Yeah, this biker thing. You done?"

"Almost."

"Okay, let me hit the head —"

Tugg got up and disappeared into the bathroom, while Adam put his hand up to wave the waitress over with the check.

Like a shadow over his shoulder, Adam could feel them at the front door. Something about riding a motorcycle seemed to give you a sixth sense for the presence of another biker.

They just stood there for a second, looked around, then turned and left. No colors. No patches. And no motorcycles except Adam's and Tugg's in the parking lot.

Tugg got back to the table just as the check arrived.

"You ready?"

"Yeah, but listen. Something weird just happened."

"What, like you paid the check?"

"No," Adam said. "While you were gone two bikers came in, gave everything the once over, then left."

Tugg's eyes immediately went to the parking lot.

"Were they Immortals?"

"I don't think so. They weren't wearing any patches."

Tugg leaned over the table for a wide view out the window, then grabbed a tooth pick.

"Well, if they were Immortals, they'd be wearing patches. But if it was some other club, they'd have to have a death wish to wear a rival patch in here. Maybe they were just regular AMA types passing through. Or they didn't like our bikes, so they ran."

"So why did they come in, then?"

"Good point."

Adam dropped some money on the table and stood up. "How far does the Immortals territory go?"

"It stops right at the reservation," Tugg said. "Even bikers don't mess with the Indians."

"Do you think they might have been Reapers, then?"

Tugg stepped outside and held the door for Adam. "No, like I said, we're outside the Reapers' territory. And I told you back in Ashland, that issue is dead now."

When he got outside, Adam heard the unmistakable sound of twin mufflers disappearing in the distance.

Chapter 46

Adam was trying to do a better job of keeping up, riding side by side with Tugg on the open road.

At this pace, they'd be back at the clubhouse in a little over two hours. He hoped they could talk to Wanda, delicately try to extricate Tugg from the club, then try to find some alternative means of transportation and resume the hunt for Emma, wherever the trail might lead.

That was a lot to ask. Maybe it couldn't be done. But by now, Adam was getting the hang of Plan Z. Some things just couldn't be planned. First order of business was to find his daughter. The entanglements with the club might have to be dealt with later. At this point, Adam wasn't even sure how solving the conspiracy — if they could do that — would lead to Emma.

The clock was ticking. Adam was still a wanted man. One slip-up before they found Emma, then where would they be?

The air felt cool against Adam's face. He was getting in tune with the bike. The engine pitch seemed to change like a bird in flight. Speed and elevation, nearness to another bike, even the wind could change the road noise from moment to moment. It was all part of the experience. You didn't just drive the miles, you lived them.

Tugg's engine whined and Adam wondered whether he'd changed to another gear. Tugg looked down, then swiveled his head and took a quick look behind him. Was something wrong?

Tugg looked over at Adam and flashed a peace sign at him.

Adam smiled and flashed one back.

Tugg shook his head and made the gesture again, more insistently.

Two more miles to a stop?

Change to second gear?

Threat level two?

Adam heard the engine whine again and realized it wasn't coming from Tugg's bike. It was coming from behind them.

When Adam turned his head, he saw two bikers, closing fast.

Chapter 47

Adam held his speed as steady as he could, while Tugg remained right alongside him. So far nothing had happened, except that two motorcycles had passed them.

The colors on the jackets were clearly visible.

The Reapers.

But the two had become four, then six, with the bikers riding in a pattern around them so that Adam and Tugg were flanked on all sides: an eight of spades traveling down the highway.

Adam's heart was slamming like tennis shoes in a dryer.

The two guys out front were dropping their speed. Adam and Tugg had no way forward and no way around. Adam saw that Tugg was backing off, so he did too. The speed kept dropping, as Adam saw the biker on the far left begin to crowd into Tugg.

The intention was clear. *You are going to stop.*

But they hadn't attacked them, signaled them or even spoken to them.

Yet.

Maybe they just wanted to talk? *Fat chance.*

Would it make a difference that this was Immortals' territory?

Finally, the whole scrum drifted off to the side of the road at about 10 miles an hour and the guy out front held up a fist.

All of the bikes halted. Adam noticed that only the two out front put down their kickstands, so Adam kept his up, same as Tugg.

A beefy guy with chaps and a cigarillo planted somewhere in the vicinity of a mouth behind a dirty yellow beard took off his helmet and began walking toward Tugg. Tugg took off his helmet.

There was zero traffic on the road and the hot sun was beating down.

"Are you the guys?" Yellow Beard yelled at Tugg.

Adam decided to take off his helmet.

Tugg was cool. Tugg was always cool. Tugg had weapons all over his body and he could get to them at a moment's notice, but the other bikers would have weapons too, so maybe the point was to leave them where they were as long as possible.

"Get the fuck off our territory," Tugg said to the leader.

Yellow Beard seemed stunned, then gave a hearty laugh.

"Are you the same guys who shot up two of our motorcycles from the back of a blue pickup a couple weeks back? It sure didn't matter to you that you were on *our* territory *then*, did it?"

Tugg didn't respond.

"Our clubs settled this," Tugg finally said, low and threatening. "And part of the settlement was that you stay the fuck off our land."

Yellow Beard threw down his cigarillo. "Well, I don't seem to remember that, so we still got payback comin'. And that happens now."

Adam saw one of the guys on the flank make a gesture toward his jacket, but Yellow Beard waved him off.

"Bullshit," Tugg said. He put down his kickstand and walked up to Yellow Beard. "We set it up in Ashland last week. And we settled it like men. I fought three of your guys."

"You?" Yellow Beard pretended to laugh, but his eyes said he believed it.

"Yeah, I think I still got a couple of teeth in my boot somewhere. But the deal was if I won, there'd be no war. Your club agreed to stay off our land and I got to walk away."

Yellow Beard laughed some more, then turned around. He just wouldn't stop laughing. Now he was doubled over. Was he insane?

When he stood back up, Adam saw that the guy had a handgun and it was pointed right at Tugg's heart.

"Maybe you walk away, but your friend here ain't a patch, is he? We never agreed to anything about *him*."

The other bikers nodded and looked at Adam.

A guy at the flank spoke up. "That's the shit who took out my bike. I saw him."

"You sure?" said Yellow Beard.

"Unmistakable."

"Game over," said Yellow Beard. "You can go or you can stay here and watch, but your friend is dog meat."

Chapter 48

The heat rose up from the pavement, as Adam lived a lifetime in the next moment. Seeing what was about to happen, like film on a broken reel.

The rest of the kickstands went down and five bikers began to walk toward him.

Tugg was down on the ground with a gun pointed at him.

What would happen to Emma? Would Kate get her back?

Adam saw a girl of about six falling off a bike, her knee shiny with blood.

A fierce middle-schooler, slashing the ball into the net.

A brunette beauty of about 18 at the top of the stairs, flashbulbs popping.

Then wearing a white dress, walking through a garden, holding the arm of a grey-haired man Adam did not know.

"Ok Dad, how you doing there? Getting enough air?"

"I'm fine," Adam replied. "Just take care of her."

Kate was on the table, fully awake, with her head lolled over to one side staring straight at him. The surgeons were hard at work, just on the other side of a little blue drape that looked like a ping pong net between Kate's chest and belly.

"You don't worry about what's going on down there," the anesthesiologist said. "Just talk to your wife."

"How're you doing?" he said to Kate.

She nodded, then grimaced.

Adam could hear the pulling and cutting, and feel the movement of Kate's body jostling.

His whole life was on that table.

"Is he going to pass out?"

"No, he's going to be ok," said the anesthesiologist.

"Watch that finger please," said the surgeon. The resident was pouring a river of sweat off her forehead.

Kate turned her head to the other side, so Adam looked down at the floor and said a silent prayer.

"This is taking too long. We need to get that baby out."

Kate turned back to Adam with tears in her eyes.

"Everything's going to be fine," he said. "I promise."

"Hands now," said the surgeon.

The table rocked a bit from side to side.

And then it happened.

The loud screaming startled him at first, but then he saw the baby, covered in blood, held up like a prize on the other side of the blue drape.

Kate's eyes were wide.

Their new baby girl gave another lusty cry.

"Wow," the surgeon said. "Welcome to the world. That's a perfect ten APGAR."

Kate had broken into a full smile and was trying to peek over the curtain.

"Hold still, Mom. We haven't sewn you up yet."

Adam watched the doctors pass the baby from one person to another, until the last person in the bucket brigade wiped her off with a little towel and laid her down in a transparent bassinet.

"Dad, would you like to come over here and see your daughter for the first time, while we close the sutures?"

Adam looked at Kate. For the last nine months his entire world had been in one place. Suddenly it was two.

"Go," Kate said. "I'm right here. Emma needs her Dad."

Adam eyeballed the surgeon, who gave him a wink as he kept his hands busy.

Adam got up from the little stool and walked over to the bassinet.

Perfect nose. Perfect lips. Tiny little ears with fuzzy black hair on them. What did he expect, a pink ball of play doh?

"Would you like to hold her?" the nurse said.

"Can I?"

They handed him a thick blue drape, then the nurse deposited Emma into his arms.

He looked down and whispered.

"Well hello there, honey bun. I'm your Dad. I just met you, but I'll always take care of you. You and your Mom. You're my world now."

Emma gave another long cry, then her face scrunched up and Adam felt warmth on his arm.

"Uh.....I think something's happening."

The nurse smiled. "Yeah, sometimes that happens. At least she didn't do it ten minutes ago. You'd better get used to it. Here, you can do her first diaper."

They wiped Adam off and handed him a tiny white diaper.

He could just catch Kate's smile over the top of the drape, as he turned his back to do his duty.

You waited your whole life for this moment.

You imagined it. Acted it out when you were a kid to see how tough you were. Then spent the rest of your life hoping it would never happen.

Now it was here.

How dare they take this from him? His past and his future.

Adam felt sparkles of light as his head and neck flushed.

He would not go gentle into that good night.

Chapter 49

Running from the law. Two weeks in a biker club so he could have one ten-minute conversation. A ride in a sidecar with an amputated leg.

What's in the bag boy?

Emma was out there waiting for him. Maybe hurt and alone.

Three skinheads had Tugg down on the sidewalk, whaling on him.

Go get her! Kate screamed.

Yellow beard still had the pistol pointed at Tugg's chest.

Have you lost enough yet?

Adam picked up the branch and launched it at the skinhead's perfect white dome.

"Hey you," Adam called to yellow beard. The blood sang in his ears. "Fuck you and your friends. And fuck your mothers too while you're at it."

When they all started coming at him at once, Adam just laid down with his bike.

He heard the gunshot, but couldn't see if Tugg had been hit.

One. Two. The fists were raining down.

Adam heard a ferocious scream, followed by another gunshot.

At first Adam tried to cover his head, but then the body kicks started coming. Pain exploded in his ribs. What had he been thinking? If only he could get to his feet. Adam cocked his legs and rocketed sideways off the motorcycle's seat. Suddenly free of the crowd, he scrambled up and took off.

Tugg was on the ground, with a pistol in his face.

If he could just get to Tugg's bike.

An old joke came to him. *I don't have to be faster than the bear, I only have to be faster than you.*

Adam changed direction up the road with a bunch of bikers clomping after him. College track versus cigarette lungs. The pain seared through his chest.

Tugg hadn't made a sound. Was he shot?

Adam zigged left, then zagged right when he heard the footsteps begin to fall away behind him. After ten more steps he cut back on a semicircular path toward Tugg's bike. The bikers who moments ago had been behind him were caught flat-footed, no longer between him and Tugg's bike.

Yellow Beard looked up at what was coming and swung the gun toward Adam's face.

Yellow Beard's legs shot out from under him as Tugg was on him in an instant.

Adam heard the siren behind him, but couldn't tell how close it was.

He leapt toward Tugg's bike.

Maybe they'd reach him before he got it. This was his only chance.

Tires skidded along the road as Adam tore the shotgun out of Tugg's ditty bag.

"Hah! Fuck you!" he screamed. "Five shots!"

The closest biker was right in his sites.

The police car looked like it was about to run over the bikers, which put it on a direct path for Adam next. He jumped out of the way and saw that Yellow Beard's gun was now in Tugg's hand.

"You guys! Drops the weapons!" The deputy had the door swung open and was perched behind it with a shaky handgun. Miraculously, he hadn't run over the bikers.

Tugg slid the handgun out on the pavement, but that was all he surrendered. Adam put the shotgun on the ground at his feet and raised his hands.

Before he knew it, Adam was lying face down on the hot pavement with the other bikers, a row of trout on a stick.

Now the shakes started coming.

Would they even have a paddy wagon in a small burg like this? If they did, the sheriff would be awful proud.

Chapter 50

Welcome to Harper, Oregon.

Any dreams of escape were dashed by the time two other squad cars showed up with a pair of bulky farm boys whose glory days of high school football were about ten years behind. They executed a quick pat down on all of the bikers, which turned up both of Tugg's Glocks, his Ka-Bar, wallets, keys, and a pirate's bounty of weapons from the other bikers.

The ride back to town was amazingly short. They'd had the good sense to put the guys in Reapers jackets three and three in the back of two squad cars, and loaded Tugg and Adam in the third one. But when they walked into the police station Adam saw that it was just one big holding cell for all of them. Maybe that weapons search had been a blessing in disguise.

Now came the fun part.

Adam had been smart enough to ditch his wallet a week ago, figuring it was better to be picked up for driving without a license than to face down a murder warrant. His odds were slim, but it might slow them down a bit. He didn't see any wanted posters. Did they still do that?

"Mike, you gonna do 'em one by one or should we just bring 'em over to Vale tonight?"

Farmboy Mike took out a set of keys and stood over by the holding cell. "Inside, gentlemen." He turned to the other cop. "Let 'em wait. Let's figure out who we got first. We can do 'em all at once."

The cell door slammed and Mike took out a bag of wallets. "Let's see. We got eight men and seven wallets. Who am I missing?"

When no hands went up, Mike dug into each wallet and did a little game of concentration with the photo IDs, until he finally got to Adam. "Did we miss your wallet? You were the guy holding the Remington, right?"

Adam just looked down. "I lost my wallet."

"What's your name?"

"Sorry."

"Your name is sorry? That's what it's gonna be."

The cop's face turned red and Adam stole a glance at Tugg. Would things get harder or easier in the next few minutes when the other bikers discovered a triple murderer in their midst?

Mike looked at the other bikers, but their faces were stone. Even if they'd known Adam's name they wouldn't have told him.

The enemy of my enemy is my friend.

Adam didn't fool himself. Tonight the alliances would shift back again.

"Guess who's got the first strip search?"

Adam supposed he should feel a little lucky that they hadn't already recognized him, given all of the media coverage over the last few weeks.

"Step out of the cell."

The door swung open and Adam stepped out.

"Right here?" he said.

"Right here." Mike looked delighted with himself.

The jacket came first. Mike was smart enough to grab it and drape it over a chair. Maybe he had enough experience with bikers to know that he was asking for trouble if he let it hit the ground.

"No patches. Are you an Immortal or a Reaper?"

"I'm an Immortal," Adam said.

A couple of Reapers in the cell snorted.

"Yeah, well, he sure had the drop on you freaks when I drove up."

Adam felt a rush of adrenalin that he recognized as pride.

"So you ain't even a Prospect then, like the other guy?"

"He's just a hang around," Tugg said from the cell. "He gets his Prospect patch next week."

Mike nodded and turned back to Adam. "Well, let's see how the rest of it's hangin' then, Mr. Hang Around. Boots and jeans next."

When Adam was finished, he felt glad that there was a difference between a strip search and a body cavity search. But what happened next?

"Hold on just a second," Mike said. "They got scrubs over in Vale, but here you get your own clothes back."

Mike picked up the pants from the floor and started to go through every pocket. After the boots, he started on the jacket.

Even though Adam could hardly have considered his single arrest as much experience with the criminal justice system, he could already spot a flaw in this procedure. What was to stop a guy in the holding cell from handing his contraband to a friend before they searched him, then getting it back when he returned to the cell?

"Whoa, what's this?"

Mike pulled his pudgy fingers out of a small interior pocket and held up the driver's license like it was a crackerjack prize. He glared at Adam. "Randall Oppenheim. Geez, I hope they give you a nickname once you're patched." Mike narrowed his eyes and peered at the picture. "Doesn't do a thing for you. Here." The cop handed Adam back his clothes, but kept the license.

"Now, I got to run all these, but Randall, I can see already that you're a naughty boy. This license expired four years ago. What else am I gonna find when I run your NCIC?"

If Adam were playing poker, he'd surely win this hand. *How the hell should I know?*

Chapter 51

The bench along the wall had only four seats, and four of the Reapers had taken them. Tugg and Adam sat on the floor opposite two more Reapers.

No one had made a sound, but a couple of hand gestures were sufficient to get the point across. You didn't need a Ph.D. in biker science to understand that two fingers in a V at the throat didn't mean "I love you."

The other cops had gone for the night and Mike was sitting alone at his desk with his back to the cell, speaking in a low voice on the phone.

Earlier he'd said that they might go to Vale overnight, but now it looked like no luck. If Mike left, it would be over. They'd come back in the morning to see who was belly up in the fish tank.

Adam tried to make out the words, but Mike's voice was too low. Tugg hadn't said much, but after twenty years of non-verbal communication, Adam suspected that Tugg must still have a weapon somewhere on his person. Unless it was a six-shooter, they were probably still overmatched.

Would Kate even learn what had become of him? All the news would report was that Randall Oppenheim and Tugg Morgan had been killed in a small town jail. Unless she read the report, or someone told her, how would Kate ever put two and two together to figure out that it was really Adam?

Maybe he should confess. If he told Mike who he really was, surely he'd take him out of the cell and transfer him tonight. He couldn't leave a triple murderer unattended with these guys all night. For their own protection!

But what a waste of luck to blow the fact that somehow Adam hadn't been recognized so far. He'd hold on for now. He could decide at the last minute. Incarceration was better than a death sentence, wasn't it? And somehow he'd convince Mike to take Tugg along.

Mike's voice was a little more animated. Maybe he was talking to a higher authority, who was giving him instructions on how to handle so many prisoners. Maybe they were telling him he had to stay all night and keep an eye on things.

Adam could only hope.

When Mike hung up the phone, Tugg shot to his feet. "I will fucking kill *all* of you tonight," he screamed. "I'll cut your balls off. My club will hunt down your families."

Geez, where did this come from? Had Tugg gone crazy?

The Reapers looked stunned. Yellow Beard was off his seat and over in Tugg's face like a shot.

Adam couldn't remember the moment he decided, but the next thing he knew his fingers were full of Yellow Beard and he had his knee in the man's groin.

The other guys erupted toward Adam and Tugg's side of the cell, when Adam heard the shotgun cock.

"Hands up, gentlemen," Mike said.

Everyone froze in place as Adam suddenly understood Tugg's gambit.

"Officer, you can't leave us in the cell with these guys overnight," Adam said. "It's six to two."

"Okay, everyone in Reapers jackets, face down on the floor."

"Oh hell," Adam heard from the pack. "Goddamn home town sheriff."

"Shut up," Mike said.

When the Reapers were all down, Mike opened the cell door and let Adam and Tugg step out. After he locked it again, he did something that was shocking. He put down the shotgun.

"Okay, you guys. You're free to go."

"WHAT?" Yellow Beard roared.

Mike gave a scowl, then turned back to Adam and Tugg. "You guys can follow me." He led them over to his desk, where he opened a drawer and retrieved Tugg's Glocks, his Ka-Bar, the Remington, and his wallet. Then he handed Adam back "his" driver's license.

"I just got off the phone with Doc at the clubhouse. He says you guys are due back in Ontario tonight."

Tugg checked the magazines on his Glocks and buried them in his pockets.

Adam was too stunned to move.

"Randy, let's go," Tugg said.

"Huh?"

"Let's go. It's time." Tugg turned back to Mike. "Can you get us our bikes?"

"They're out front."

Another cry of protest came up from the cell, but Mike and Tugg ignored it.

Adam looked over. "So what happens to them?" Adam asked the cop.

Mike gave a tiny smile. "Doc said to hold 'em for 48 hours. Then he'll be down. We don't screw around with turf disputes. This is Immortals country. We let you settle it yourselves."

Mike stared off into space for a minute, then looked back at Tugg. "But Doc said he wants you guys back pronto. He wouldn't say why."

"We must be late. Randy, let's go."

"Yeah, that's kind of funny," Mike said. "About being late."

Tugg already had the door open, but Adam hesitated. "What's funny?"

"Randall, you must owe back dues or something. Doc said he thought you'd been dead five years."

Chapter 52

In a thousand years, Adam never would have thought that an outlaw motorcycle club would look like home. Sealed in the bubble of his helmet and unable to talk to Tugg for the last hour, Adam had spent the entire ride alone with his thoughts. *Thank God we escaped.* But how much more did they still have in front of them?

The wheels on his Harley bit into gravel as Adam followed Tugg's taillight up the road to the clubhouse. What came next he wasn't sure.

The Indian situation made sense, but how did Emma fit into it? Maybe if they told Wanda what they'd learned at the council meeting, she would be able to help them put the pieces together.

Adam saw a light by the gate up ahead and one of the members swung it open for Tugg. Adam sped up so they didn't have to wait for him.

Adam parked in the yard, took his helmet off, and took a few ginger steps off the bike.

"Hey, prospect." It was Kurt, the sergeant-at-arms, coming out of the shadows. "Good ride?"

"Decent," said Adam. "I didn't fall. I had a good teacher."

"Yeah, but we heard you had a little side trip. Handled it well, though."

Kurt looked happy, then feigned irritation as he turned to Tugg. Last time Adam and Tugg had arrived in the compound, Kurt had greeted them with an elaborate practical joke.

"Hey, *other* prospect."

"Hey, Kurt," Tugg said, slapping the dust off his jacket. Tugg wasn't even off his bike yet.

"We've been waiting for you. We really appreciated that little call from Mikey telling us you'd be home for supper. It gave us time to set something up."

Adam looked at Tugg, whose eyes never left Kurt. Was this another joke?

"What?"

"Your last little test for the club."

"Okay," said Tugg.

Adam didn't think that Tugg did a very good job pretending to be excited, but maybe it was a macho thing. Until you actually got your patch maybe you weren't supposed to show that you expected it. But who *would* expect it this soon?

"Yeah." Kurt spit on the gravel and broke into a smile. "We've seen that you can ride, that you can fight, and that you'll defend the honor of the club — but now we need to see if you're a man."

Whatever this was, the stakes had just gone up. Pass this test and Tugg was stuck. *Maybe he should try to muff it on purpose?*

"Okay," Tugg said. "Where to?"

"In the clubhouse." Kurt yanked his thumb up the driveway. "Now."

Tugg put down his kickstand and got off his bike, then looked at Adam.

"So you're gonna come too, right?" Kurt said.

"Well, should I? I'm not really a prospect."

"Are you a fag?" Kurt said.

Adam's blood pressure went up. "No." *What the hell is this?*

"Then you'll want to watch. C'mon." Kurt took a step toward the clubhouse, with Tugg following close behind him.

Where is everybody?

The walk across the compound seemed endless.

They must all be inside. Good. That meant they'd probably see Wanda.

Chapter 53

Adam had never seen so many nude women in his life. With the exception of Wanda, who was fully clothed and standing next to Jed, the crowd consisted entirely of men, smiling and laughing, overjoyed to see the look on Tugg's face when he caught a glimpse of the fate that awaited him. On the ground, lying face down on a strip of carpet, lay eight naked women, all lined up side by side with their asses in the air, waiting for him.

The crowd erupted.

"Some test!" somebody yelled.

"I wish I was a prospect again!" said another.

Oh no. How could Tugg intentionally screw this up?

Doc and Spider stepped forward and stood on either side of Tugg, like coaches with some last-minute advice before their fighter steps into the ring.

"Okay so you've got a pretty good idea of what happens next," Spider said, suppressing a grin, "but here's the catch."

"Hey, let me tell him," Doc said. "This is the best part."

Tugg stood staring at the women, some of whom were looking back at him and smiling. A few wiggled their hips.

"You've got to do what you've got to do," Doc said. "But you've got to do it WITHOUT COMING!" He broke into a horse laugh and slapped himself on his good leg.

"One after the other," Spider continued. "While we watch. You got to do all eight in a row and you can't blow it until the LAST ONE!"

"The girl who makes you come gets a hundred dollars," Doc said. "You last all eight and you get your patch. Then we party."

The girls were cat-calling him. Slapping their asses, some reached back to spread themselves even wider.

Adam was horrified.

How the hell could Tugg get out of this one?

Could they just turn around and leave? Could Adam fake a heart attack?

Tugg nodded and walked up the line. Not a glance at Adam.

The crowd broke into a cheer.

Kate was at home sitting in a wheelchair and he had to endure *this*?

"I've got to go," Adam said, turning toward the door.

Was it wrong to abandon Tugg at a time like this? Would he want him to stay? All Adam knew was that he couldn't watch this happen.

"He's probably goin' to call his wife!" somebody yelled.

"No, I think he's goin' to the men's room to find a stall that locks," came the reply.

Adam sucked in the cool desert air as the door banged shut behind him. He had the compound all to himself. As he headed toward the garage, all Adam could hear was the gravel crunching under his feet and the roar of the crowd imploring Tugg to get to work.

Chapter 54

Some tough guy. Adam had a tattoo and he'd ridden a few hundred miles on a motorcycle over the last few days, but what was he doing now? Hiding in the garage until it was safe to come out.

It was dark and quiet again. Adam had heard the crowd a couple of times over the last twenty minutes, but nothing for a long stretch. Then he heard a collective shout, followed by the clubhouse door opening and shutting, but no one was out in the compound yet. There was no music. No party. Was it still going on?

Adam heard a rustling over by the garage door. He remained still. Adam didn't want any part of this place anymore. Tugg would have to find him. Or maybe Tugg would find a way to talk to Wanda, get what they needed, and they could get the hell out of here once and for all.

"Adam?"

Had anybody else even used his name in the last week? It had to be Tugg.

"Over here," Adam said. "In back."

Tugg negotiated around a few tool cribs and assorted junk until he finally flicked his lighter.

"Over here," Adam said. "Ten steps forward."

Tugg walked over and snapped his lighter shut. Some conversations were best had in the dark.

Adam turned in the direction where he thought Tugg was standing and put his hand out until they bumped.

"Okay, so what happened?"

"Why did you leave?"

"I couldn't stand there and watch that," Adam replied. "Maybe I've been married too long, but it made me sick. They looked so helpless."

"It wasn't my idea of straight-up respect for women either, Adam, believe me. But what could I do?"

Adam took a breath. "So what happened? Did you lose it?"

"No, it didn't work."

Adam hesitated. "You mean you couldn't get it up?"

Tugg's chuckle was as welcome as a candle. "No, believe me, that wasn't the problem. I got hard the minute I came into the room. Have you ever even *imagined* some shit like that?"

"Not really, no," Adam said. "Maybe when I was fifteen. So you came, then? You screwed up the test? I thought you might. Probably the easiest way to keep from getting patched. Plus, I'll bet you couldn't last."

Tugg's voice was strong and low in the dark. "No, they couldn't."

"Huh?"

"The club called it off. They disqualified me."

"So you were hard and you didn't come, but they disqualified you? Did you actually screw anyone?"

"Yeah."

"Then what the hell happened?"

They both heard the noise up the path as the clubhouse door opened and shut. Someone would be looking for them soon.

"Tugg, tell me quick. Do we still have to stay and talk to Wanda or can we go now?"

"We don't have to. I didn't talk to her yet, but it's okay if we stick around. We're sort of in a holding pattern now."

Adam felt strangely relieved. "But you still haven't told me what happened."

"Keep your voice down," Tugg said. "I think I hear somebody."

They waited in silence.

"Hey, if you wanted to know, you should've stayed," said Tugg.

Chapter 55

"Okay, so just tell me."

A finger of light found them as the moon shone in the window, but other than that it was still dark and quiet.

"Well, I had to do something. It would've been easy to get disqualified the way they expected, I guess, but it wasn't fair to the women. What do you do? Dip into each one for ten seconds? I didn't know them. I didn't know how willing they were."

"Some of them looked pretty willing."

"Yeah, with a hundred guys standing there watching? Every girl's dream. Some of those girls are on the ragged edge. Candi was there. I'm sure this wasn't her idea. So I asked who wanted to go first and it was Crystal. Remember her? From Ashland."

Adam nodded, but he didn't know if Tugg could see him.

"I started in real slow. I read about a position once where a man can hold out for a long time, but it helps the woman along. So I asked Crystal to lie on her back and I entered her and got into this position and then I didn't move."

Adam couldn't help himself. "Someday when this is all over, you've got to tell me about this position."

"Yeah, well shit, Adam, *are* you fifteen? Anyway, the bikers are all standing around wondering when the show is going to start and the other women are starting to get a little pissed. I just keep sitting there not moving a muscle and pretty soon Crystal scrunches up her shoulders, throws her head back and has a sheet-ripping orgasm. Well, I guess that answered the question of how you know you're done with one girl and it's time to move on to the next. One of the bikers says 'You gotta be shittin' me,' and at this point three of the remaining girls have their hands in the air yelling 'Me next, me next!' It got a little weird.

Then another guy says 'Give *him* a hundred bucks!' but then a bunch of guys got pissed and started grabbing their girls out of there. I guess it's one thing to watch somebody fuck the club skank because you told her to, it's another thing to see her *want* it. So at this point they kick my ass out of there. The test is over. No patch, and no idea what happens next."

Adam just stood there.

"So you never — uh — finished?"

"No, I didn't want to pass. I guess I didn't, but it all happened so quick. They had me off her and everything was over."

"So you're sort of in the clear then, right?"

"Maybe, but who knows what happens next?" Tugg said. "You think that Jed's going to let me next to Wanda now, even with a bodyguard?"

"I don't know," Adam said. "But for the time being, I think *I* know what happens next."

"What's that?"

"Why don't you go look for a cold shower?"

Chapter 56

"Adam, where are you?" Kate's voice was as welcome as the morning sun, which had just peeked over the white pine trees and was angling into the windshield of the 1978 Plymouth Duster where Adam had spent the night behind the garage.

"I borrowed someone's cell phone. Everything's okay. I just had to hear your voice."

"I couldn't get ahold of you. I didn't know if you were dead or alive."

"Why were you trying to reach me?" Adam sat up in the back seat and snaked his foot down toward his boots that were caught in the wheel well.

Kate's voice was stressed. When she got stressed, her mobility deteriorated. Adam wanted to ask about her health. About the baby. About whether she was actually real or just a figment of his imagination.

"Steve Carnap called three days ago. He said Emma's in trouble."

"Trouble? Is she hurt?" Adam lived a lifetime in the next two seconds.

"No, but he wouldn't say anything more specific than that she needs to get out of there. Physically she's fine, but there seems to be some sort of issue coming up. I begged and pleaded, but all he'd say was that things are moving faster than he'd like and we need to get Emma out of her current placement."

Adam sat bolt upright. The temperature had dropped overnight and he could see the faint outline of his breath in the air.

"Kate, I'm working as fast as I can. Tugg and I are doing everything possible to find her." "Any luck so far?"

Adam hesitated. "No, but we're making progress. One more card to play."

"You'd better play it fast."

Adam didn't like the sound of that. "Or what?"

"Steve said that if we move quickly, there's still time. You can turn yourself in. He said that the minute you do that, he can petition for Emma to come back to me."

Adam waited. "It sounds like that's what you want me to do."

"No." Kate's voice had a catch. "That's not what I'm saying. It's just that it's complicated, and I'm worried sick about Emma."

Maybe they were right, Adam thought. If he went to jail, Emma could come home right away. Wasn't that the point of all this? Why not trade one for one? Was he being selfish?

They were quiet for a moment.

"I've been calling Lisa Castro nonstop," Kate said. "Finally she took one of my calls and said that she doesn't know what Steve's talking about. Emma's fine. She's in a stable placement and nothing has changed. Castro's concerned about you being on the loose, of course. And she confirmed that if you were in custody, it would be much easier to petition for Emma's release. But she said that there's no danger for Emma where she is. She's perfectly safe and there are no plans for her to go anyplace else."

"Then what's the problem? I wonder where Steve's getting his information."

"Maybe he has an inside source."

A better source than the placement director for CPS?

"This doesn't sound right," Adam said. "There's something wrong here."

"That's what I've been telling you."

A shadow drew across the trees. Adam glanced up to see Tugg standing by the car's rear window, just about to knock.

"Kate, I've got to go. We shouldn't have talked this long anyway."

"Adam, be careful!"

"You too."

Adam rolled down the window and Tugg leaned in. Adam didn't like the look on his face.

"Tugg, I just talked to Kate and she said —"

"No time for that now," Tugg said. "I was just in the clubhouse and heard something. The Forest Grove chapter is riding back to Portland this morning. In about an hour."

Adam grabbed his boots before Tugg could even finish his sentence.

"Wanda's leaving."

Chapter 57

By whatever complex turn of fate, an hour and a half later Adam found himself sitting on a motorcycle, next to Tugg, at the back of a pack of twenty riders getting ready to pull out of the gate of the Ontario club.

There'd be no way to talk to Tugg over the next several hours. Adam assumed that Tugg hadn't been able to get Wanda alone for a conversation, so this must be the next best plan. Tugg's status with the club was still unclear, but as a prospect with the Forest Grove chapter it probably made sense that he'd want to ride back with them. And of course that meant that Adam had to come.

God help us.

Tugg was still holding his helmet.

"This is going to go *fast*," Tugg said to Adam. "You'll get no slack if you fall behind. I can't stay with you or it's my ass too. Just do your best to keep up, but *don't* have an accident. We clear?"

Adam already had his helmet on and gave a thumbs-up.

"If we get separated, we'll meet at the club later. If we get stopped, just pull off, keep your hands visible and wait."

Adam took off his helmet. "That'd be a disaster, Tugg. I may have a motorcycle and a jacket, but I've still got Randall Oppenheim's driver's license. If the cops catch me, I'm toast."

A bike started up front and a swarm of noise blew up around them.

"You got a better plan?" Tugg shouted.

Adam shook his head.

"Then put your helmet back on. If you get taken into custody, I'll just stick with Wanda and get to the bottom of this. I'll get Emma out. Or you can stay here in Ontario if you want to let me go ahead?"

Adam put his helmet on again. He gave another thumbs-up, then started his own bike and watched Tugg do the same.

The big steel gates swung open.

As the leaders revved their engines, Adam took one last look around. Doc and Spider gave a back-slapping farewell to the leader of the Forest Grove chapter, then pumped their fists in the air and hooted.

Thirty-eight tires simultaneously bit into gravel as they pulled ahead.

Out of the corner of his eye Adam saw Kurt, standing off to the side like a proud father, cupping his hands under his legs in a pantomime of a prodigious male endowment.

"Kick some ass, teacher!" Kurt shouted. "You've got balls like a mountain lion now!"

Adam couldn't help but smile as he twisted the throttle.

Chapter 58

Adam was so far out front he wondered if he should back off a bit. Not bloody likely. After that first miserable 150 miles lagging behind, the club had put the hammer down. Adam could ride with the club only if he promised to skip all future breaks and get out ahead of them, while they stopped for a two-hour lunch and beer break just outside Pendleton. If they passed him after that, he was on his own.

Just as Tugg had predicted, he was on the hook too.

"He's your friend, Prospect. You keep an eye on him. He's on our gear, so someone from the club has to stay with him and make sure he gets back to us."

Pity they had no chase truck this time. Adam would have welcomed four wheels.

The sun was bright, but Adam felt a bit cold since the highway had turned down the Gorge, wind whipping them toward The Dalles at what seemed like light speed, but was actually probably closer to 55 mph. Tugg was about twenty feet behind him–slowly going crazy again–but Adam dared not look back to see if the club was within sight yet. All he could do was ride as fast as he could and hope that no one got pissed. Or that the cops didn't stop him again. There'd be no more hometown sheriffs this close to Portland.

The traffic had picked up a bit, but the visibility was perfect.

If Adam could stop worrying for a minute, the ride was gorgeous. Brilliant blue sky. Tangy river air. Nothing but smooth, swiveling curves up ahead, with the Columbia River on his right and Mt. Hood on his left.

In another hour or so, he'd be at Multnomah Falls, where he'd heard the club say they were going to take their next break. He and Tugg could wait for them there. After that, it would be an easy ride into Portland. He was sure he could keep up for the last fifty miles. And he'd need the cover.

Whatever lay ahead, heading back to Portland was a necessary part of the plan. If they wanted to talk to Wanda, this was the only way to do it. If that didn't work, Adam could always turn himself in and allow Emma to go home. Adam had caught a glance at a newspaper when the club stopped in Pendleton. There it was, on page three of the metro section. A suspected murderer and child-abusing father was "still at large."

Adam had to admit that he'd made damned little progress in determining Emma's whereabouts over the last few weeks. Plan Z so far was a failure. They had no realistic hope of getting some miracle information out of Wanda anymore, though they still had to try. After that, they were out of options.

At first Adam thought that Tugg had just changed gears. Then the whine behind him became a roar, and Adam knew what was happening. How fast were those guys going? Eighteen motorcycles shot past on his left at a speed great enough to make Adam feel like he was standing still. But the worst part was the razzing. Yelling and cat-calling — someone would have shown their ass if they could have figured out how to do it on two wheels. Jed brought up the rear, with his middle finger in the air and Wanda laughing on the back.

If it wasn't over yet, it was damned close. If they didn't catch up before the club left Multnomah Falls, he and Tugg could still ride to the clubhouse. But would Wanda even be there when they arrived? And after Tugg's sexual fiasco in Ontario, would they even let him near her? This was all assuming that Wanda even knew anything that was useful.

As Adam drew closer to Portland, he had a growing sense that his life was ending. That the problems he faced were bigger than the ones he'd left behind only a few weeks back. In a way, they were the culmination of a set of events he'd started long ago. Bad deeds had to be paid for. After twenty-three years, the long arc of karma was about to find him. Emma was just an innocent victim. It was time to let her off the hook. You couldn't outrun it when things came full circle.

Chapter 59

Tugg was riding alongside him. What was the point?

Adam saw no sign of the club up ahead. Just empty highway and a few passing cars. Two Harleys in the slow lane. *Some badass.*

The Oregon State Police car rocketed past, with the roof lit up. No siren.

Tugg looked over at Adam, then back at the road as another cruiser whipped by.

Even though they couldn't talk, it didn't require telepathy to know what was happening up ahead.

Just stay calm, stay in the slow lane, and try to get by without being noticed.

After a few minutes, Adam saw them all lined up on the right side of the road. Sitting on their motorcycles. Licenses held out in their left hands. No sudden movements. One squad car out front and one in the rear, with two officers walking up and down the line.

Easy does it.

Tugg sped up a bit and tucked in close in front of Adam. If they saw Tugg in front, no matter, but if they saw him from behind, better to have Adam blocking the view of his jacket. Thank God Adam wasn't wearing any insignia.

They were just two peaceful, law-abiding bikers out for a ride. Not like those outlaw one-percenters.

Thank you, officer. You've done a great public service today.

Now they'd see who'd make it first to Multnomah Falls.

Chapter 60

"Maybe we should've just gone on to the clubhouse," Adam said. "We were out front for once."

They were standing on the bridge at Multnomah Falls, looking at the tremendous splash as 500 feet of falling water met the streambed only 70 yards in front of them.

"No, we said we'd meet them here. This is actually our best chance to talk to Wanda."

Adam scanned the crowd for cops. On Tugg's recommendation they hadn't stayed with their bikes in the parking lot, figuring that after the traffic stop they'd be a cop magnet. They were much safer up here, trying to blend in as much as possible.

All around them fathers smiled, moms held ice cream cones, school groups swarmed, and tourists snapped pictures. *What's the best place to disappear? In a crowd. Go someplace where everyone is looking at something else.*

"So what happens when they get here?" Adam said.

"You know they'll be pissed. A stop like that happens about once a month, but the bikers will be talking about it for years. It's pure harassment. The cops can't stand to see anyone having fun. Usually they don't find anything. They hold 'em for about an hour, then let everyone go. Most I've ever seen is a citation for a burned out headlight or a muffler violation."

"Maybe speeding?"

Tugg smiled. "It may have looked that way to you, but they weren't actually speeding. Didn't you notice when we got passed by the minivan?"

"Okay, so I'm not so badass," Adam said. "That's why I thought maybe we should just go straight to the club. If we wait here and all leave together, we'll be behind again after the first mile."

Tugg looked down at the pool of water hitting the rocks and shook his head. "That's why I want to try to grab Wanda now. If we go to the clubhouse, anything could happen. They could give me my patch. They could kick me out. We're here now and she'll be here in a minute. Let's give it a chance."

Adam nodded, then looked at Tugg. "What makes you so sure they'll want to stay here long enough for you to talk to her?"

Tugg smirked. "You ever seen hippies in water?"

Adam had no reaction.

"Well, they look like a bunch of Bible salesmen compared to bikers."

Adam nodded again and turned back to the water.

The falls were beautiful, but his stomach was in knots. What a contrast from the last time he'd been here. Kate could walk then, with the canes, and Adam had rashly suggested that they walk up the mile of trail so they could watch the falls spill over the edge. He was surprised when Kate said that's exactly what they should do. He'd ended up carrying Emma, then 18 months old, most of the way, but Kate had turned back after a few hundred yards.

He'd found her sitting on a bench, smiling beatifically at the inner-city school group of kids who were splashing in the streambed, the falls a curtain of water in front of them. Adam had done the same thing as a kid once and made the mistake of putting his neck too far out into the downpour. He still remembered the panic as he disappeared under the water, fighting to know which way was up, as he bobbed to the surface and heard a woman screaming.

The unmistakable sound of motorcycle engines competed for a moment with the hissing water. Then it was silent.

What were a couple of "This Area Closed" signs to a group of outlaw bikers? As the band of merry cutthroats bush-whacked down the slope and headed toward the pool, Adam could feel the tension rise in the crowd on the bridge. When the jackets and bandanas started to come off — along with the first pair of pants — the civilians began to disappear.

"Let's go," Tugg said. "That's our cue."

Chapter 61

Wanda wasn't naked, but she was damned close. Her cherry-red nipples sat like topping on two of the loveliest ice-cream sundae boobs Adam had ever seen. Good thing the water was 60 degrees.

Tugg had made the strategic decision to keep his T-shirt on as he waded into the water. No sense making it a contest. Jed was about 60 feet away, swimming, laughing, and goofing off with the rest of the bikers. Adam and Tugg stood hip deep in the water, watching them.

Wanda paddled over. "Can you hand me my blouse?"

Tugg walked back to shore and grabbed it, as Wanda emerged from the water to reveal thirty inches of ass covered only minimally by a pair of wet panties. Tramp stamp on display, just where Tugg had said it was. She buttoned the blouse and sat down on the bank, as she waved to Jed.

"I know who you are," she said to Adam, and smiled at Tugg. "And of course I'm already familiar with *your* work."

Jed seemed to be chilling in the water, floating on his back in a pair of mirrored sunglasses. Did it still count as a dead man's float if you were on your back? The rest of the bikers were hooting and dunking one another in the water. The bridge above was empty.

"Don't worry," Wanda said. "Jed's not the type."

"He almost castrated a man with a hunting knife," Adam said, "just for putting his hands on you."

Wanda smiled. "Jed's a complex guy. A lot of what he does is an act for the other guys. When you get to know him, he's a real sweetheart. It actually gets him off to see another man want me. As long as he doesn't touch."

"I'll remember that," Tugg said.

Wanda rubbed the goose pimples on her arm and squeezed her long hair out in a loose ponytail. "You look like you don't believe me," she said. "I don't blame you. It's pretty clear you're not welcome back in Ontario or Ashland anytime soon, but they'll get over it. The guys from Forest Grove were actually pretty amused. Proud of their stud prospect, I think."

Tugg didn't smile.

"And I talked to Crystal," Wanda said. "Once she's off life support, I think she wants your number."

Although the nipples were now covered, they made a brief reappearance through the thin cotton fabric, then faded again.

Jed still looked like he was dead.

Tugg paused and gave a quick thumbs-up to one of the bikers who was walking along the rocks behind the falls, about to disappear behind the watery curtain.

"So," Wanda said. "What did you guys learn at the reservation?"

Chapter 62

"But we still can't figure out how Emma fits into it," Tugg said. "How is the governor making money off the suburban kids? And how is he getting CPS to do his bidding? Do you suppose Lisa Castro is in on it?"

Wanda's cheeks flared pink. She put her hand on Tugg's arm. "Now just hold the fuck on," she said. "Lisa is one of the sweetest people you've ever met in your life. She's tough in her job, but that's because she's *protecting* the kids, not exploiting them."

Adam's eyes betrayed him — *Lisa sweet?* — but he didn't say a word.

"If she's guilty, then so am I," Wanda continued. "There's been a lot of pressure on our office for the last few years. The governor's office has taken a special interest in the Native American kids. They're always pushing for more placements. Now maybe we know why."

"Four times the money is a pretty good incentive, especially when some of it's coming your way," Adam said.

"Yeah, that's pretty damning," Wanda said. "I'd never heard that before. I guess we've always had our suspicions, but no one wanted to say anything. Especially Lisa. She's such a straight arrow I think sometimes she has trouble imagining that other people aren't. But it all makes sense now. Why the governor's office was micromanaging things. Actually, most of the calls came from the governor's Chief of Staff, Peter Beauchamp."

The gears were turning in Adam's head.

"But we still don't know why the suburban kids," Adam said. "You told us last time that there was a lot of pressure coming down now about finding child abuse in rich neighborhoods. Maybe that's where my daughter fits in."

"Yeah, well, Lisa is all over that," Wanda said. "But she doesn't need any special motivation for that, given her — well, given her interest in justice."

The words hung in the air.

"I'm sorry for what might have happened to her, but I didn't hurt my daughter," Adam said. "There must be a reason Emma was taken. Someone set me up."

"Someone set up *all* the rich kids? That doesn't make any sense," Wanda said.

"Maybe that's the point," Adam replied.

Wanda picked up a hairbrush and promptly dropped it, then watched it roll down the bank and skitter into the water. Tugg jumped up and handed it back to Wanda, who smiled and touched his arm again.

A commotion was happening over in the pool. Someone had slipped on the rocks and was cursing a blue streak. Jed looked over.

"Maybe the rich kids are being used to cover up what's happening with the Indian kids," Adam continued. "Maybe someone in the governor's office got worried that they'd left too big a trail, so they needed a distraction."

"A distraction?" Tugg said. "How could more scrutiny on CPS bring anything but more publicity?"

Adam frowned. "Sometimes publicity is good."

Tugg looked puzzled.

"Look, what's the easiest place to hide?" Adam said.

"In a cave?" Tugg said.

"In a crowd. If you don't want the Indian placements to stand out, then you cover them over with a bigger story. One with lots of juice. It's publicity 101."

"I think I see where this is going," Wanda said. "The pressure changed from the Indian kids to the white kids because they *needed* the publicity. They *wanted* the attention. It shows that child abuse is everywhere, so it doesn't look like they're picking on the Indians."

"Even if they are," Adam said. "You've got to admit that having a story in the papers about a murderous, child-abusing Lake Oswego dad on the run for the last few weeks has been a great way to deflect attention from the Indian story."

Tugg jumped in. "Meanwhile, the governor is making a fortune. He puts the Indian kids in his old foster home and covers it up by feeding us a story about abuse in rich white families."

"Except that I didn't actually hurt anyone," Adam said.

"Yeah, except for that," Tugg said.

Adam looked back and forth between Tugg and Wanda. "So where can we get more answers?"

Things looked like they had settled down over at the falls. The cursing was over and it was back to fun and games.

"We should probably speak to Lisa Castro." Tugg touched Wanda's hand.

Jed stirred in the water.

"She won't tell you where Emma is. She can't."

Jed stood up and started walking over.

Tugg pulled his hand back. *"It's okay, we're just going to get on the road so we can get a good head start."*

Jed kept walking.

Tugg stood and turned to Wanda. "We don't need Lisa to help us find Emma. We need her to help us find the governor."

Jed was up to his knees in the water, steadily moving toward shore.

Adam stood up next to Tugg.

Jed emerged from the water, cold and bloated. "Hey, Prospect," he said. "Get over here for a minute."

Adam saw the look of concern on Wanda's face as it crested, then fell.

Jed took off his sunglasses. "So me and Wanda was talking on the bike. Out of earshot of the guys — how did you do that pussy trick on Crystal?"

Chapter 63

Lisa Castro couldn't concentrate anymore. Her headache was so bad that she'd done the unthinkable: packed up and gone home early for the weekend. Not that she'd let herself goof off. She planned to work straight through till Monday, as usual. But not now. Not till her head cleared.

The sun was on the other side of the sky and the light in Lisa's home office was growing dim. With Wanda still away on vacation, Lisa would have preferred to work at home anyway. What was the point of going into the office if she was going to be alone at her desk all day? Twice the space, but half the fun. She couldn't wait to hear some of Wanda's wild stories when she got back next week. Did Wanda live with a CIA operative? A jewel thief? Maybe he was an actor? Wanda would never say.

Lisa switched on the light, but immediately turned it off again. She closed her eyes, then realized it was futile. If she wasn't going to work, why stay at her desk? The Grammaticus case wouldn't leave her. The father was still a fugitive and the mother wouldn't stop calling. Foolishly, Lisa had answered one of those calls. What was this business from Steve Carnap? Was he crazy? Emma was safe in a foster home out in Troutdale. Kate Grammaticus must have gotten it wrong.

It was after five. Carnap might still be at his desk. But why bother? Lisa could check everything just as well on her computer. She switched on the light and logged on, passed the firewall, and entered Emma's name.

Case file terminated.

What?

Lisa backed up several screens and found the encrypted, password-protected page for protective custody placements and entered Emma's file number. No names on this screen; a rare compromise with the Information Technology people so that case workers wouldn't have to drive all the way into the office to use the database, but things would still be secure.

Placement terminated; transfer pending.

What? Wasn't this the right file number?

Lisa looked at the clock again and grabbed the phone.

"Fulop, Mars, and Carnap. May I help you?"

"Yes, this is Lisa Castro. I work for Child Protective Services in Multnomah County. I'm trying to reach Steve Carnap. It's urgent."

"I'm sorry, he's out of town this evening for a charity event."

"Can I have his cell number? Is there another way to reach him?"

A pause this time. "No, I'm sorry. You can leave a message and I'll send him an email."

Lisa left the message and hung up.

She shut her eyes and felt the headache radiate toward her neck.

"The hell with this," she said aloud.

Maybe there was a bug in the system. Maybe if she could get to the protective custody page at the office and enter Emma's name she could bypass all the security gobbledygook.

It had to be a mistake.

Emma was fine.

Lisa grabbed her keys and hurried out the door.

Chapter 64

After three mistakes at the security keypad outside the building, Lisa Castro just stood there on Sandy Boulevard, the last remnants of rush hour traffic whizzing by on a Friday night.

What was with her today?

She called the security company and gave the password, *Rosebud,* then reentered the passcode. This time the door opened.

As predicted, the place was empty.

This wouldn't take long. She'd bet that she did the same thing on the keyboard at home as she'd just done on the keypad. Why hadn't she tried a second time on the computer?

Lisa plopped down at her desk and logged into her account. She confirmed the Grammaticus case file number, then tried entering both that and the name in the protective custody database.

There it was again. *Placement terminated; transfer pending.*

What did that even mean? She was the director of placement, for God's sake, and she'd never seen that exact wording on a case file before.

Lisa scrolled over to her emergency contact information for the protective custody placements. Troutdale was a drive. It would be better just to call.

The sound might have been a car door slamming in the parking lot. But it sounded more like a bump against the building. Had she heard an engine? The traffic was still pretty heavy on Sandy. Probably she was imagining things.

She heard it again.

Bump.....ssshhhhh.....bump.

What the hell was that?

Then she knew what it was. After she'd called the security company, she'd forgotten to lock the front door.

The two men weren't wearing uniforms, but they weren't vagrants off the street, either. She knew them.

Oh, God. She knew them.

Chapter 65

"Put the phone down, please. No one's here to hurt you." Adam was trying to be reassuring, but the situation was every woman's nightmare.

But what could they do? They couldn't have called ahead. They couldn't have knocked. She would've turned them in to the cops in a fraction of a second. Hell, she looked like she was still trying to do that, with the phone in a death grip.

"I promise we aren't here for that," Adam said. "We just saw Wanda."

Lisa Castro drew a sharp breath.

"She's fine," Adam said. "We talked to her and she gave us some information that you'll probably want to know. We're almost at the bottom of the conspiracy behind why I got set up."

Lisa sat frozen in her chair.

"You don't believe us? It was the governor," Adam said.

Adam could see the smallest trace of recognition pass over her face, but Lisa Castro still didn't move.

Tugg held his empty hands out in front of him. "Look, I've never hurt a woman in my life and I'm not going to start now. If you don't believe him, don't put the phone down, okay? Let's call Wanda. You tell me the number and I'll dial it on my cell phone."

Lisa still didn't move.

"Tugg, she needs to drop that phone," Adam said.

Lisa's eyes flicked over to Adam. A badass biker and a deranged father. Who was more dangerous?

"Just give her a minute," Tugg said. "She's deciding. What she doesn't know is that if anything were going to happen, it already would have. I killed the landline outside before we came in. That's why we've got to call Wanda on my cell phone. See?" Tugg held up his cell phone.

It seemed to snap Lisa awake. She held the receiver for the landline up to her ear, then dropped it in horror.

"Or we can use your cell phone, if you prefer," Tugg said. "I'll bet you've got Wanda on your contact list in there somewhere already. Can I see it?"

As if in slow motion, Lisa reached into her bag and retrieved the cell phone, never taking her eyes off Tugg and Adam.

"Hey, I know how this looks," Tugg said. He took the phone gratefully. "I lost my wife to a bunch of shitbag men. I'd rather die than hurt you. We're just here for information." Tugg scrolled through the screens, then pushed one final button. "There you go. It's ringing. She's probably going 70 miles an hour."

Lisa took the phone warily and held it up to her ear.

"Adam, why don't you sit down," Tugg said. "This will take as long as it takes."

Lisa finally spoke. "Hello, Wanda?"

Chapter 66

Lisa was still shaken up, but she looked better when she put the phone down on the desk.

"What'd I tell you?" Tugg said.

Lisa rubbed her forehead with the tip of her fingers and looked up at Tugg, who was still standing. "How do I know you don't have someone holding her hostage? How do I know you didn't threaten her?"

"Did she sound worried?"

"No."

"Well, that's because she's not. She out riding with her boyfriend Jed on the back of his motorcycle and they're with a dozen other bikers. She's safer than if she were surrounded by a ring of cops."

Lisa had a quizzical look on her face.

"Oh, so you didn't know her old man was a biker, same as me?"

That did the trick. Adam could see something fall into place.

"Wanda said this is all connected to the Indian tribe," Lisa said. "I can't believe that, but I guess it makes sense. There's been a lot of pressure from the governor's office about this. Then recently there was pressure about the suburban families."

"From where?" Adam said.

"Same place. The governor's office. Actually his Chief of Staff. He seems to be taking a personal interest in CPS placements these days."

"And why do you think *that* is?" Adam said.

Lisa looked down. "I guess it always seemed weird that the Governor had such close connections with The Longlane Home. Then all those placements started coming. But I still don't see how the two populations of kids are connected."

"Neither did we," Adam said. "But maybe it's some kind of cover-up. A distraction for the real money-maker."

All three looked at one another until Tugg spoke. "Look, we think we know why all this happened, but we still aren't sure how. We don't have any proof. And until we get that, we can't get his daughter back."

"Unless you tell us where she is," Adam said.

Tugg glared at Adam and shook his head.

"I can't do that," Lisa said.

"You mean you won't."

"Adam!" Tugg said, then swiveled his attention back to Lisa. "So do you know anything about how this might have been done? Can you get us in the same place as the Governor?"

"Oh, God."

"What is it?"

"Oh God, I just realized something." Lisa looked shaken again. "A few weeks ago the governor pardoned someone named Richard Norwood."

Tugg looked lost until Adam clarified.

"Same last name as Rachel."

Chapter 67

They were all sitting down now, in swivel desk chairs facing one another.

"So I must have been targeted specifically," Adam said. "This wasn't about the other suburban families."

"Maybe," Lisa said. "We had a couple of other abuse reports from suburban nannies in the last few months. It seems weird, but when you think about it, it makes sense. Rich people don't use daycare."

"What happened to the other families?" Adam said.

"They all got their kids back," Lisa answered. "There wasn't anything to the claims."

"Until they got to me. Why?"

"Think about it," Tugg said. "How many rich guys are there in Lake Oswego with a prior abuse allegation — even if it was false — who turned out to have a twenty-year-old criminal complaint pending? They were looking for a zebra. They only needed one."

"So when Rachel died and I took off, they had their story," Adam said.

Even Lisa Castro nodded.

Adam looked at Tugg. "So you didn't kill Rachel, then. They did."

Tugg's eyes narrowed and he leaned in close to Adam. "That's what I've been trying to tell you."

Lisa looked awful. "I played a role in this."

"You were set up," Adam said. "Same as me."

"I should have seen it coming. All those calls from the Governor's office. I knew it, but I didn't see it."

Adam rolled his chair over to Lisa and put his hand out. Miraculously, she took it.

"All you can do now is try to make this right," Adam said. "Help us find the governor."

Lisa held Adam's hand a little longer. "How can I do that?"

"You said he calls you?"

"His chief of staff calls me. He texts me. He emails. Here, look." Lisa picked up her cell phone and hit a few buttons. "He just sent me this message yesterday. It's even got a picture of him with the governor at some sort of ribbon-cutting." She held it out so they could see it.

"Can I see your cell phone, please?" Adam said.

She handed it over and stared at him.

"I am so sorry for what happened to you."

Adam fiddled with the screen, without looking up.

"Where is my daughter? Is she safe?"

Adam was lost in a bevy of code.

"I don't know."

He looked up.

"What do you mean, *you don't know*? You don't know if she's safe, or you don't know where she is?"

The phone sat forgotten in his hand.

"I'm sorry, I mean I don't know *anything* anymore. The computer showed something screwy. That's why I came back to the office. I was just about to call her placement when you guys came in."

"Check now!"

Lisa reached for the landline, then remembered it was dead.

"Tugg," Adam said, suddenly remembering the cell phone. "Look at this. It looks like the Governor's chief of staff is up at Timberline Lodge right now."

"How in the world do you know that?" Tugg said.

"The picture he sent has a microtag on it. It's right there in the frame, if you know how to find it. Once you put that in GPS it can tell you the location of the person who sent the picture, if his cell phone is on."

"You mean where he was when he *sent* the picture?" Lisa said.

"No, where he is now."

Lisa looked like she was thinking the same thing as Tugg.

All those pictures on Facebook.

"If Peter's there, then the governor is probably with him," Lisa said.

Adam punched a few more buttons on the cell phone. "I just checked the Governor's website and it says he's got a fundraiser tonight. That must be up at Timberline Lodge."

"We can be there in 90 minutes," Tugg said. "If you think you can find third gear this time."

"Why aren't you calling about my daughter?"

"This phone is dead. Remember? You killed it?"

Adam handed Lisa back her cell phone and stood.

Then he stopped.

"You think I'm going to call the cops, after what I just heard?" Lisa's eyes were soft. "Go. I'll find Emma. And I'll call your wife too."

"Scratch that last part," Tugg said, heading for the door. "I guarantee they've got the line bugged."

Lisa looked puzzled. "The Governor?"

"The cops," Tugg said, turning back. "We may have convinced you, but this guy is still a wanted man."

Adam hadn't moved. He was staring at Lisa. "Call about Emma first."

Lisa punched in the numbers. "Sorry, it's busy."

"Busy? Who gets a busy signal anymore?"

Lisa put the cell phone up to his ear. "Listen."

"Adam, we've got to go," Tugg said.

Adam finally stood. He took a few steps toward the door, then stopped. "Call again."

Lisa nodded and grabbed the receiver on the landline.

Adam shook his head and pointed to the cell phone.

"Sorry," she said. "I keep forgetting. That line is dead."

Chapter 68

Cold air cut into the seams of Adam's leather jacket as they passed Government Camp and approached the final turnoff. It smelled like Christmas.

Timberline Lodge, five miles.

Headlights on, Tugg was out front as usual, but Adam kept the throttle open as his motorcycle hugged the serpentine road. Sheer dropoffs appeared without warning every few feet, and he could see the tops of 70-foot Douglas fir trees peeking over the rim. No guardrail. *Wasn't this where they'd filmed* The Shining*?*

Only one way up or down. They hadn't passed anyone yet. They'd run into security eventually. Timberline Lodge was a turkey shoot.

As Adam remembered, the Lodge had three parking lots. Long ones, stretching all the way up the last part of the hill as you approached the main building. Hordes of tourists normally filled them up in the daytime, but tonight a sign hung above the lower lot.

Closed for Private Event.

Up ahead Adam could see the security barrier at the upper lot, with a couple of cops checking IDs and waving people through. Lincoln Navigators, Mercedes, BMWs, and Lexuses scattered the parking lot. By the looks of things, the event hadn't started yet.

"Turn around," Tugg said. "Let's leave the bikes at the bottom of the lower lot."

Adam made a loop and followed Tugg down the hill, as the lights from the security perimeter winked out behind them. They pulled up side by side in the last parking spaces.

"So do we have a plan for what to do once we get up there?" Adam said.

"We find the Governor and we make him talk."

"Bullshit," Adam said. "That's not a plan."

Tugg looked annoyed. "Haven't you learned anything yet? Too much planning gets you locked in. We'll see our opportunities and we'll grab 'em."

Adam hesitated. "That sounds pretty half-baked."

"You got a better plan?"

"Yeah, as a matter of fact I do. We've not only got to find the Governor, we've got to get him alone, so —"

Tugg held his hand out flat. "Let's just think about how to get in first. That's my wheelhouse. After that, you're on."

"Okay," Adam said. He got off his bike and took a few steps up the asphalt.

"Hold on there, my man," Tugg said. "We should probably go up top, then drop down."

"You mean up the mountain?"

"Yeah, you're lucky it ain't winter." Tugg was in his ditty bag now, tossing out some gear. "And you'll need this." Tugg handed Adam the Glock 27 and put the Glock 23 in his own waistband.

Adam looked at the weapon in his hands. "Back to Plan Z?"

"No, we're past that. This is Plan S. Survival. You're one of the most wanted men in Oregon right now, and those cops up there *will* shoot you on sight. You need something to protect yourself, if things go hinky."

"It's so small."

"Bullshit. It's a 40 caliber, same as mine. Adam, do not underestimate this gun. Full frame or subcompact, it's still a Glock."

Adam felt the grip against his palm and aimed the barrel up the mountain while he looked down the sight.

"You know how to shoot that?"

"Yeah, sure," Adam replied.

"It ain't a revolver. It's loaded and a round is already chambered. That means it's cocked. And remember there's no external safety on a Glock. There are three internal ones, but you won't even feel 'em, so don't put your finger on the trigger until you're ready to fire."

Adam nodded and tucked the gun into the interior pocket of his jacket. Tugg took off his biker vest and put on a black leather jacket to match his black jeans, backpack, and boots.

"No one will catch us if we're quiet," Tugg said, stepping onto the pumice stone just off the asphalt. "Follow me straight up, then we'll cut over and drop behind the lodge. If we're lucky, they won't see us coming. After that, we'll need to improvise."

Adam blew in his hands and zipped up his jacket. "We definitely aren't dressed for the guest list," he said.

"This'll either work or it won't."

"What if it doesn't?" Adam said, as he followed Tugg's footsteps up the crunching slope.

"Why do you think I gave you the Glock?"

Chapter 69

The door handle gave way and Tugg motioned for Adam to follow.

"Just a second, Tugg. Shit."

They were standing at the ski entrance at the back of the building, in the shadow of a brilliant cone of light that was pouring from the Great Hall windows two stories above, bright enough to make the grey stones on the mountain appear white.

"What's the problem?"

"It can't be that easy."

"We aren't inside yet."

Adam hesitated.

"Look, Adam, this ain't exactly the Secret Service we're dealing with here. And this isn't Camp David. The Governor usually travels with a single police escort. They aren't expecting a terrorist attack."

"Then why all those cops outside?"

"You ever hear of overtime? The police union? They've probably got some state regulation about how many cops they need at a public gathering. And look at all those cars. I saw four limos. VIPs like to get a little special treatment before they give their money away. Trust me, the security is mostly for show."

Adam felt sick to his stomach. The cops still had guns and badges, didn't they? And he was still on their wanted list.

"Trust me Adam. This is my thing. I know you're all bad ass now, but I'm back okay? I know law enforcement. I'm not gonna let you down."

Tugg slipped in the door.

Chapter 70

"Where's our goddamned shrimp?"

They were standing in a dimly lit industrial kitchen, empty except for the tall maître d', who was standing on the back stairway glaring at them.

"And who, might I ask, are you two?"

Tugg stood there like he owned the place. "They told us we could get some shrimp. It's cold outside. I ain't gonna wait out there all night. I know I can't come in the front door, but the Penningtons said we could get some food once things got started. These things always have shrimp, don't they? I want some fucking shrimp."

Adam's breath was gone, but he noticed that the maître d' suddenly seemed a little winded himself.

"Well, there is some shrimp upstairs. Who did you say you were with?"

"The Penningtons," Tugg continued. "The big Lexus limo outside? You don't think they drove up here alone, do you?"

"You're the limo driver?"

"Do I *look* like a limo driver?"

Tugg was playing it perfectly. They might not find the governor, but Adam would bet his ass they were going to get some shrimp.

"We're the motorcycle escort," Tugg said.

"Where are your badges and sidearms?" the maître d' asked.

"We're not *cops*," Adam managed.

"Look, ain't you ever heard of a private detail?" Tugg said. He walked over to the giant refrigerator and opened it.

"Wait, don't do that." The maître d' rushed down three steps, then froze. "We aren't using this kitchen tonight anyway. The caterers are in the serving kitchen, just off the ballroom upstairs. I can get you some shrimp."

Tugg closed the refrigerator and spun around. "Okay, but we ain't gonna eat it outside."

"Or here," Adam added.

Tugg looked at him and nodded. Pity they didn't give an Academy Award for bullshit.

"Okay, follow me. I can put you in one of the offices upstairs. I'll bring you some plates, but then you've got to stay put, all right? I can't have you wandering around upstairs."

"You feed me and I'm golden," Tugg said. "I'm used to pulling my dick for three hours waiting on people, but I gotta eat something. I got a blood sugar problem. You want to see me get upset?"

The maître d' held out his hands. "Please, just come with me. I'll put you in one of the small offices, so we don't have to walk past the ballroom. I'll bring you your shrimp. But after that, I'm frightfully busy until this thing is done. You'll have to stay put."

"Said we would, didn't I?"

As the maître d' started up the stairs, Tugg looked over his shoulder and gave Adam a neat grin.

After Tugg had sucked down his fifteenth shrimp, he stood up and put his boots back on. "He's gone. Let's roll."

Adam set his untouched plate on the corner of the desk. "Okay the good news is I've been here before. Last Christmas."

"Great, so you know where the ballroom is?"

"Too easy. What we need is to find the room where the governor's *gonna* be." Adam saw that Tugg looked confused. "Before the event."

Tugg shook his head, thinking.

"His tux," Adam said. "He needs a place to change, right? This is a fundraiser. He'll need a room to get dressed before and to schmooze with some of his high rollers afterward."

"Like where?"

"The manager's office."

"Lead the way."

Chapter 71

The room smelled rank, but with the lights off Adam couldn't identify the source of the odor. Maybe it was the 50-year-old moose head on the wall above the huge mahogany desk that stood in front of the stone fireplace. Maybe it was the three-cigar-a-day habit of the hotel manager, who sat in this office eight hours a day, when the Governor's staff wasn't commandeering it as a secure location for His Honor.

Adam crouched behind the desk, waiting for the sliver of light under the door to break, indicating footsteps in the hallway. Although Adam couldn't see him, he knew that Tugg was standing right beside that door, ready to disarm anyone who came in unannounced or, Adam hoped, grab the Governor when he walked in looking for his tux, which Adam had found hanging on the back of the door.

Adam felt the reassuring bulge of the Glock in his pocket and admitted that Tugg had been right. This was the big leagues. If they were caught or killed, what would happen to Emma? But if Castro was right and Emma was missing, they had no time to be cautious. Was Emma safe? Had someone moved her? They had to get the Governor to talk, and worry about picking up the pieces later.

After Adam had led them to the manager's office, they'd only had time for a few quick whispers.

"He should be alone while he's dressing," Tugg said. "But whichever way this goes, getting in was a piece of cake compared to getting out. Once we hear what we need, we've gotta get back to the bikes." Tugg took one last look at Adam before he killed the lights. "What?"

"We've also got to keep him quiet while we escape."

"You let me worry about that."

All they could do now was wait.

* * *

Adam couldn't hear a sound from the hallway. The 80-year-old lodge was famous for its solid construction. Stone foundation. Old growth Douglas fir beams. Mortar in every crack. During the Depression, the out-of-work Civilian Conservation Corps men had nothing better to do than build it right.

It was getting late. Surely the Governor wouldn't be able to start the event without coming here first.

A light flickered under the doorway.

Was it finally him? Or maybe the maître d' had missed his wayward shrimp lovers.

The door swung open and light flooded the room.

Peter Beauchamp went down hard.

Chapter 72

The Chief of Staff rolled over in agony and looked up at two Glocks pointed directly at his face.

"Where the hell is my daughter?" Adam said, taking charge.

"What daughter? Who are you guys?" Peter Beauchamp was in obvious pain, but his attention was riveted.

Tugg rushed over and shut the door, then turned back to Adam. "Keep him on his back and make it quick. He knows or he doesn't."

Adam held the cool barrel against Beauchamp's eye.

The barking, imperious Chief of Staff was gone, replaced by a 30-year-old kid. "What do you want from me?" Tears rolled down his scarlet cheeks.

"Emma Grammaticus. I'm her dad. You tell me where she is, or I'll end you right here."

"How should I know?"

"Keep your voice down," Tugg said. "And hurry."

Adam pulled the gun back and leaned down. "We know everything about the Indian kids and the cover-up. And the money. You guys are toast once it hits the papers. Impeachment. Prison. But right now you've got bigger worries."

A shadow crossed the kid's face. The Chief of Staff was back. "You shoot that gun and a dozen cops will be here in ten seconds."

"Well shit," Tugg said. He rushed over and put a knee on Beauchamp's chest. "Adam, get over by the door. Lock it. Son, you just pissed me off."

Even though he was bound and gagged, Peter Beauchamp made no attempt to scream. He didn't dare.

Beauchamp's pants were in a bundle around his ankles as Tugg held the Ka-Bar tight against the base of his penis.

"I don't give a shit now whether you know or not," Tugg growled. He angled the knife as if he were getting ready to saw the drumstick off a Thanksgiving turkey, when Beauchamp started to nod violently.

"Yes?" Tugg removed the gag and a rivulet of spit spilled from Beauchamp's mouth.

"I swear to *God,* I don't know about any conspiracy. I just did what they told me."

"Wrong answer."

"I swear it!"

"You got balls, kid. Unfortunately, those are next."

"No! Don't you think I'd tell you? I always felt like there was something going on, but I had *nothing* to do with it! I don't know where his daughter is. They wouldn't tell me *anything.*"

What does he mean,"they?" Adam thought.

"What the fuck?" Tugg said. He pulled his hand back quickly and glared down at Beauchamp. "So who does know? The Governor?"

Beauchamp nodded. At least it looked like a nod. He was trembling all over.

"Where is the Governor right now?"

"Upstairs, with the First Lady. He sent me down to get his tux."

"He's lying," Adam said from the door.

"I don't think so," Tugg said, standing.

"How do you know?"

Tugg reached down and wiped his hand on the carpet. "Because it's very hard to lie to someone when you're pissing yourself."

Chapter 73

The lights were off again. Peter Beauchamp lay behind the desk, quietly whimpering beside the stone fireplace. Tugg had pulled his pants back up, but the gag was back in place too, joined by a black hood tied around the Chief of Staff's neck.

Adam and Tugg both waited by the door, which Adam had unlocked.

Beauchamp's cell phone buzzed in his pocket across the room.

"50/50 that the next person through that door is the Governor," Adam said. "And I'll bet he's pissed."

The faint sound of voices caught Adam's attention, then grew louder. When they stopped, Adam thought he heard soft steps shuffling on the carpet outside.

The door opened. "Peter? What the hell? Are you in here?"

Tugg practically lifted the man out of his shoes and snatched him into the room, while Adam shut the door.

"Lock it again," Tugg said, pushing the man face down onto the carpet.

Adam secured the bolt and turned on the lights.

Tugg rolled the man over. "Governor, your day just went to shit."

The backpack was open again.

"This time I'm doing it," Adam said.

The zip ties were easy, but the gag wasn't yet in place.

"Now wait. Wait!"

Adam hit the man's face so hard he wondered if he'd knocked him unconscious. He stood over the Governor and put a foot on his throat. "You've got two minutes. You know who we are, right?"

A blood vessel had burst in his right eye, but the Governor turned his head carefully and nodded.

"You took my daughter," Adam said. "You put her in foster care on a trumped-up abuse charge from my nanny. You remember her? The same one whose brother you just let out of prison? Quid pro quo, I guess. But I'm way past 'why.' I just want my kid."

The Governor let out a groan and rolled onto his stomach.

Peter Beauchamp gave a muffled cry from behind the desk.

The Governor sat up. "What did you do to him?"

"Not nearly enough," Tugg said.

"Cut the shit," Adam broke in. "We know about the Indian money. And we know you snatched my daughter to distract people from that. But Lisa Castro says Emma isn't in protective custody anymore. What've you done with her?"

The Governor lay there like a wounded elk. "I haven't *done* anything with her," he said. "If CPS doesn't know where she is, why should I?"

Adam smashed his fist into the Governor's jaw again. He rolled over and spit blood.

"Take it easy," Tugg said.

The Governor was breathing hard. His words came in a slur. "Look, my money's in a blind trust. How should I know *anything*?"

"Who said anything about your *money*?" Adam asked.

The Governor tightened his jaw.

"Okay, we're gonna have to do this the hard way again," Tugg said. He stepped over to the door and reached for his backpack.

"So who's the trustee?" Adam said.

The doorknob turned, but the bolt held it tight. "Governor, are you all right in there?"

Adam looked at Tugg, who simultaneously released the bolt and snatched the door open, then yanked the tall, astonished man into the room.

"That's it. No more visitors," Tugg said. He slid the bolt home, then slammed the intruder onto his back next to the Governor.

The man gave a confused look at Tugg, then recoiled in horror when he saw Adam. It was Steve Carnap.

Chapter 74

"I can get your daughter back," the Governor pleaded, looking at Adam.

"I thought you said you didn't know where she was." Adam was almost done lashing the Governor's feet to the legs of a hard wooden chair. His hands were already zip-tied behind him, but Adam cinched more nylon cord around his chest and down through his hands, just for good measure. No gag this time. They wanted him to talk.

"You almost done over there?" Tugg said.

Tugg already had Steve Carnap completely trussed like a prize steer, in a chair a few feet away.

Peter Beauchamp still lay on the floor behind the desk and seemed to be unconscious.

Adam walked over to the lawyer. "Okay talk."

Steve Carnap started crying like a baby. "I have no idea what's going on! I'm just here for the event!"

The Governor's voice was acid. "You were the goddamned mastermind, Steve. Don't deny it."

Carnap sat shaking his head, still blubbering.

"Does *he* know where my daughter is?" Adam said.

The Governor flushed red and glared at Carnap. "Ask him."

"I thought you just said *you* knew."

"I did not." The Governor held his mouth firm. "I said I could help you get her back. But we'll need *his* help."

Tugg stepped in close to Adam and cupped his hand next to his mouth. If he didn't want them to overhear, why was Tugg speaking in such a stage whisper? "You know, in an ideal situation we could start taking shots at the knee, go back and forth between them, until one of them talks. But with a 40 caliber, there wouldn't be much knee left. Plus we can't afford the noise."

What was Tugg doing? If he didn't know what to do, why was he working it out in front of them?

Finally, the penny dropped.

"But in this situation I think we need something quicker." Tugg's eyes were bright.

"Like what?" Adam whispered back loudly.

Carnap eyed them nervously. Apparently he wasn't so out of the loop that he didn't care what happened next.

"Well, I see two lamps on two different wall switches over there. I can cut the cords with my knife. And I'd bet my ass there are some paper clips over in the desk drawer."

The Governor sat up. "Look, I'll talk. I'll tell you anything you want to know. In fact, there *was* a conspiracy."

A dark river of hate poured into Adam's soul. *Now* he admits it?

Tugg raised his voice. "Shut the hell up. We already know that. Now we need to know where his daughter is."

Adam burned to hear the whole story from the Governor, but Tugg was right. *Keep it simple. Get the information about Emma and get the hell out of there.* This was already taking too long.

"So what's the paper clip for?" Adam said, egging him on.

"Oh, you don't know this one?" Tugg was back to his stage whisper. "You leave the lamp cord plugged in and attach it to a paper clip. Then you shove it in his urethra. You can hit the wall switch whenever you like."

Carnap looked over in horror. "That's torture!"

Tugg turned toward him. "In Turkey, they just call it damn good police work."

"Okay I'll talk," Carnap said.

"Adam, go get the paper clips."

"I said I'll *talk*!" Something had broken loose in Carnap. He was stamping his feet and bucking back and forth in his chair. He looked seconds away from pissing himself.

Adam walked over to Carnap and leaned in close. "Do you know where my daughter is?"

Carnap nodded. "She's on her way home to her mother."

Adam whipped around and felt his sinuses clear. "You fucking liar." He reached into his jacket and took out the Glock. "I will kill you right now."

Tugg took a step toward Adam and put a hand on his arm. *Cool down,* he mouthed.

Adam lowered the gun.

"It's the truth," Carnap said.

Tugg kept his body between them, then turned back to Carnap. "Why should we believe that?" he asked. "How would *that* help your plan?"

"It wasn't *my* plan to look for a cover-up. It was *his*!"

Tugg and Adam looked over at the Governor, while Carnap kept talking.

"All I've been doing this whole time is trying to help you and Kate get Emma back," Carnap whimpered. "I swear it."

The sound of his wife and daughter's names in this pig's mouth made Adam's eyes flash. Maybe he *should* kill him.

"Oh, come on!" the Governor broke in. "You were the one who set up the whole Indian thing, Steve. Your hands aren't clean." The Governor turned back to Tugg and Adam. "He tried to blackmail me. Once I made him my trustee, he started to funnel all the money from the Indian placements into my investment accounts. By the time I found out, it was too late. He said if I didn't go along, he'd go to the media. I'd be finished."

"Go along with what?" Tugg said.

The Governor squirmed helplessly in his seat. "He wanted me to appoint him Lieutenant Governor, then resign. I was going to have the press conference next week. I had to do what he said."

"Including kidnap my daughter?" Adam yelled.

"That was *his* idea," Carnap broke in. "He was trying to do everything he could to cover up the Indian money."

"*You* were the one who put all that goddamned money in my account, so I *needed* to cover it up. Christ, Steve, it was about to blow up whether you went to the media or not. All that money! Why in the world did you have to designate all those Indian kids special needs?"

"Well *you* were the one who found out about the nanny's brother," Carnap said.

"So I *was* set up," Adam said. "How?" Blood rushed up his neck. The gun seemed to weigh fifty pounds.

"Must have been the state database," Tugg said. "It wouldn't be hard."

"But how did they know about killing those skinheads all those years ago?" Adam said.

"That was just serendipity," said Carnap. "It fell into our lap. *His* lap."

Tugg looked at his watch. Their chances of escape were rapidly evaporating. If Emma was really safe, maybe it didn't matter.

"So you didn't know about that till after Rachel died? Till after you killed her?" Adam said.

"Nobody killed anybody!" the Governor said.

"That's true," Carnap agreed. "We didn't do that."

Adam lifted the Glock. "Fucking liars. I say we waste 'em both."

"Whoa, calm down." Tugg held his hand out and pressed on Adam's arm. "Be careful how you hold that."

Adam took a breath and lowered the gun again. "Look, Tugg, I know we were fucked since about ten minutes ago."

"Yeah, just about."

"So, what happens next? We shoot it out with the cops? I don't think so."

Tugg was silent for a minute. "Yeah, you're right. I don't see us leaving here under our own power. But first, there's one more piece of information I need from the lawyer. In private."

Tugg broke away, grabbed the Governor's chair and dragged it to the far corner of the room where he turned it toward the wall. As he walked back toward Adam and Carnap, Tugg took out his Glock.

"My friend is right," Tugg said as he approached Carnap. "We're cooked anyway, so to hell with the noise. I'm gonna put a couple of shots in your knee till you tell us what we want to know. After that, I don't care what happens."

Carnap's whole body tensed, as Tugg approached. Now he *was* pissing himself.

When Tugg got to the chair, he lifted his foot and kicked Carnap in the shin. The tall man cried out and doubled over.

"You don't strike me as a man who's used to much pain. Let's see if we can change that." Tugg gave a quick nod to Adam, who lifted his gun to Carnap's chest.

Tugg put his gun to Carnap's knee and leaned in. His mouth was practically on Carnap's ear. "Where is his daughter?"

Adam could just make out the words. He repositioned his gun at Carnap's head.

"I *told* you, she's on her way home."

Rivulets of sweat were coursing down the lawyer's face.

"Why would you do that? Why now?" Tugg had put his finger on the trigger, so Adam did as well.

Carnap's eyes were bulging. His mouth formed a circle, but no words came.

"If you don't tell me, I'm gonna take the shot."

"No, please! I'm begging you."

Adam's shoulders felt like a crossbow.

Suddenly Tugg stood upright and spoke in a full voice. "Okay, you asked for this."

"State police! Open up now!"

Adam gave Tugg a look of sheer terror as his whole body tensed.

"Don't shoot me!" the Governor screamed from the corner. "I'm in here too! They have guns!"

"Shut up!" Adam shouted.

His gun was digging into Carnap's temple.

"Adam, get your finger off the trigger." Tugg's voice was low and urgent.

"You're the one who made them take my daughter," Adam screamed across the room.

"Adam, stop squeezing the gun!"

Two shots rang out as the brass erupted onto the carpet.

"Don't shoot me! Don't shoot me!" The Governor was wailing as his chair tipped over and dumped him against the wall.

Carnap's body slumped forward.

His face was gone.

"Put your weapons down! We're coming in!" The door leapt on its hinges.

Tugg aimed his Glock across the room.

The Governor squirmed on the floor, kicking his feet as if he were trying to tread water on dry land. "No! No!"

Tugg squeezed the trigger. Two bullets ripped into the moose head on the opposite wall.

As the door burst open, Tugg dropped his weapon, then reached over and knocked the gun out of Adam's hand.

Chapter 75

Peter Beauchamp's head hurt like a motherfucker.

"Hey, here's another body. No, he's moving!"

Bright lights assaulted his eyes.

His ears were ringing.

"Don't move him. He's in shock."

The air smelled heavy. Like fireworks.

"Watch the brass. Forensics."

Had he been shot?

"Don't we already know who the shooter was?"

"Can't tell. Both guns were discharged."

Peter's head felt full of broken glass.

"How many casings?"

"Four."

"How many slugs?"

"Two so far. Both in the victim."

"Keep looking."

They were rolling him somewhere. He was on a bed with wheels.

If the Governor didn't hurry, he was going to miss his speech.

Chapter 76

Adam swore that his feet hadn't touched the ground since the cops had cuffed him and dragged him from the room.

It was cold in the parking lot. They'd taken his jacket before they left the Lodge. They had Tugg duck walking in front of him wearing both cuffs and leg irons. Four cops were on him; Adam had only three.

"I killed him," he heard Tugg say.

"We already read you your rights, so just keep talkin', pal," said one of the state troopers.

"I also killed Rachel Norwood. And those skinheads when we were kids. My friend is completely innocent. He didn't kill anybody. I compelled him to come here. I threatened his life."

What the fuck was Tugg doing? Going for an insanity defense?

They pushed Tugg into the nearest squad car and slammed the door.

"Somebody find my daughter," Adam said to the cop on his left shoulder.

"Was she in there?"

"No, she's with CPS."

The cop squeezed Adam's arm and hustled him hard down the hill toward another squad car. Looked like they had separate rides.

In the distance, down by the lower parking lot, Adam heard a familiar sound.

The cop cradled his head and shoved him into the back seat.

When Adam turned around he saw it. Eighteen motorcycles were lined up like a gauntlet in the lower parking lot.

And every one of the bikers was holding up a patch.

Chapter 77

Denial.

Anger.

Bargaining.

Depression.

Someone had forgotten to tell him about boredom. Or isolation.

It had been two weeks.

Is Emma out yet?

Are they ever *going to let me talk to Kate?*

Adam listened to the passing traffic on the street below his cell on the sixth floor of the Portland Justice Center. If he bothered to get off his bunk, he could look out the window and play his game of counting motorcycles on 4th Avenue. But what was the point?

The arraignment had gone by in a blur and Adam had just tuned out after that. One thing about being taken into custody, he'd finally gotten that criminal lawyer. Just a public defender though. What was the point of spending all that money on a fancy lawyer if they'd caught him red-handed? Better to leave Kate as much as he could in their anemic savings account. His attorney told him that due to the complexity of the charges, the next several months would probably be taken up with squabbling over preliminary issues that had to be settled before they could even set a date for trial. The attorney also told him that Tektel had fired him. Duh. You get arrested on four counts of murder and it tends to hurt your employment record.

One good thing about being accused of a quadruple homicide though: they gave you your own cell. He would have preferred to be with Tugg, to talk it out. Tugg always had a way of making Adam feel better, not to mention the obvious security advantages. If they ever opened that cell door, this was Jefferson High

School all over again, this time with murderers. Adam supposed he wasn't in any physical danger until after the trial, but what would happen after he was sentenced? When he went to the State Penitentiary in Salem?

There was some irony for you.

Maybe if he was lucky, Kate could get an apartment in "Death Row" and wheel down the street past The Longlane Home to see him every day. If he was *very* lucky, maybe he could get a cell with Tugg.

He'd bet the Governor would get a private cell.

Adam heard a metallic sound out in the hallway. Keys turned in his door. It was Caswell. The good guard. The one whose sister had a kid in the system.

"Hey, G. You got ten minutes."

Adam sat up on the bed. "Ten minutes for what?"

Caswell held a cell phone. "She's already on the line. Keep your voice down. I'll be back."

"Which hospital did you say you were in?"

"OHSU."

"And the baby's gone? Just like that?"

Adam sucked in a shuddery breath. He could feel the prickles like cat's claws working their way up his neck.

"That's not what I said. I've got cervical incompetence."

"What's that?"

"Just what it sounds like."

"Can they treat it?

"Yes, they gave me a cerclage."

"What's that?"

"You don't want to know."

Adam caught his breath and tried to steady his voice. "You're only four months pregnant!"

"Yeah, I know. But don't panic, all right? They've got me on strict bed rest right here in the hospital for the rest of the pregnancy."

"For five months? You'll never walk again. Your muscles will be shot."

"Adam, what choice do I have? I'll probably never walk again anyway. But I can do physical therapy. Keep the muscles supple. Remember Christopher Reeve?"

"Yeah. He's dead."

"Well, I'm not going to die. I'm going to have this baby, and I'm going to walk again, too. In the meantime, it'll give me a chance to lie here and think. Oh, Adam, this was all my fault."

Adam's stomach was still tense from the adrenalin, but at least his peripheral vision was back. He sat on his bunk. "What do you mean your fault? How could this be anyone's fault?"

"You don't understand. I brought this on myself."

"Stop talking that way! These things can happen to anyone. You can't help it that you've been under so much stress, not to mention the MS, but for now just lie there and rest. Stop blaming yourself. Try to think positive thoughts."

Adam had yearned for this conversation so many times over the last few weeks, but this wasn't the way he'd imagined it. Why were they being so sharp with one another? There was so much to say, why couldn't he say it? Kate sniffled through the phone. The guard would be back soon. He'd better get to it.

"So have you heard anything about —?"

Kate broke in. "I've been so worried about you being in jail. Have they hurt you? Are you safe?"

He'd better deal with this first. "I'm fine. They've still got me at the Justice Center and I'm in some sort of protective custody, all alone. My lawyer says there's some sort of issue about jurisdiction for the trial. It could be a while. They won't send me to Salem until after sentencing."

A cell door slammed in the hallway.

"Have you seen Tugg?" Kate said.

"No, they're keeping us separated."

"I heard he confessed to everything."

"Yeah, he did."

"So why don't they let you out?"

"Because it doesn't work quite like that."

Finally both of their minds went to the same place.

"Emma's not out yet," Kate said.

"What? Why not? We handed this thing to them on a silver platter. What more do they need?"

"I know. I know. I got so upset that they sent me to the doctor, and that's when they found the cervical incompetence."

"What's their reason for keeping her? Do they know where she is?"

"Yes. Castro said she's where she was all along. But there was some sort of paperwork snafu about her status that delayed things. Someone at CPS said she'd already been released, if you can believe that. That's when I lost it. Now they're saying that since one of her parents is in jail and the other is in the hospital, she needs to stay in place. The judge wrote an order to keep her in foster care until I get out of the hospital."

"Son of a bitch!"

"Believe me, I could kill someone. The only good thing is that Lisa Castro came to the hospital and apologized for everything. She said she's going to work as hard as she can to make this right. She said that Emma's in a very good placement. She personally vouched for her safety. And she said that now Emma can come for some visits. Castro said she'll bring her to the hospital herself. That's something, anyway."

"God, I wish I could see Emma," Adam said. "And you, too. But what? Maybe in twenty years to life?"

"Adam, don't say that."

"Kate, they've investigating me for four homicides. Even with Tugg's confession, there's a lot to sort out. And I'll be here till they do." There was a pause on the line. Adam's voice was husky when he continued. "I'm in a very dark place right now. We all are."

"Yes, we are." Kate's voice was steady. "But we are going to get through this. And, if it's any consolation, have you heard what happened to the Governor?"

"Yeah, he got off too easy."

"Impeached and arrested! Thrown out of office and jailed on a sealed indictment."

"What do you mean sealed?"

"Just what I said. Nobody really knows what happened other than that it had to do with kickbacks of some kind. I always knew he was dirty."

"Didn't the Indian thing come out?"

"What Indian thing?"

Bastards!

"It's too complicated to explain now. I'll talk to my lawyer and make sure it comes out at my trial. But hey, did they get him on Rachel's murder yet? My lawyer says that Tugg's confession will probably get me off for the skinheads, and that those were arguably self-defense anyway. And he said that Tugg probably saved me from the one about Rachel too, but obviously it would be better if they could hang that one on the Governor or Carnap. But they caught me red-handed up at Timberline Lodge, even though it was an accident. My lawyer says that doesn't matter. It's still felony murder—for both of us—because we were in the process of kidnapping them. That one'll stick."

The keys jingled in the lock and the door swung open.

"Time's up G."

"Damned Governor will probably try to pardon himself!" Adam shouted desperately, as the guard reached for the phone.

"Bet he would if he could," Kate said. "But there's a new Governor now."

"That I did not know. Who?"

Caswell retrieved the phone as Kate's voice trailed off into empty space.

"You wouldn't believe me if I told you."

Chapter 78

"Your move Caswell. I haven't got all day."

"Yes you do. For another couple of months now. Then maybe longer."

The guard advanced his rook and captured Adam's queen.

"Ouch! I taught you too well." Adam smiled. "Forfeit."

"Told you I was a fast learner."

For the thousandth time in the past few months, Adam looked where his watch should have been.

"You got a bus to catch, G?"

Adam shook his head. "Guess we don't have time for another game. Your break's almost over."

"Yeah, I guess I should be gettin' back to the idiots."

Caswell stood up and stretched, then took a few shambling steps toward the door. What was it with prison guards? This guy was twenty-five and he moved like an old man. Lots of time probably. No one was going anywhere.

"Hey Caswell?"

"Yeah?"

"Come back tomorrow? Isolation sucks. You're all that's kept me sane."

"I do what I can, Mr. G. I do what I can."

Adam reached down and swept the contraband pieces into a plastic bowl.

"Say hi to your sister for me."

Caswell stopped by the door.

"Yeah, she's always tellin' me to say hi back to you."

"She ever get her kid back?"

"Naw, probably won't. You get her on your jury and you're a free man."

Adam felt his cheeks flush.

"Instead I'll probably get the death penalty."

"G, I keep tellin' you, there ain't been no executions in Oregon since 1997."

"But it's still legal. They've got death row in Oregon."

"Yeah but the Governor stopped it."

Adam smiled. "You forget who I kidnapped."

"He ain't Governor no more!"

"Guess again. New Governor isn't going to help me either."

"Oh, that's right. You may be screwed. You and your friend."

"Thanks." Adam stood and carried the bowl over to the toilet, where he lodged it behind the rim. "My lawyer says this is a death qualified set of charges. They're pushing pretty hard."

Caswell looked down.

"Still lots of time on death row," Caswell finally said. "A man can last years there. 'specially if he's got somethin' he cares about. Somethin' to live for while he's inside."

"That I'll probably have," Adam said.

Caswell shook his head slowly from side to side. "That's not what I mean, man. Even if your friend's there, you'll still need somethin' to do. Somethin' to live for day to day."

Adam imagined a life waiting for the axe to fall. A life without family. Even with Tugg in the next cell, what would he have to look forward to?

"Like what?" Adam said.

Caswell raised his hand and knocked on the tiny window. The door buzzed and he held it open with his palm.

"Well it sure as shit ain't gonna be chess," Caswell grinned. "I'm already beatin' you."

Adam returned the smile. "Yeah, I guess that one's out."

"So what else you interested in from before? I mean before you got here?"

"Revenge?"

"You'll last two weeks."

Adam sat on his bunk and watched the guard casually holding the door open. That small act of freedom had never seemed like much till this moment.

"Yeah, you're probably right," Adam said. "I guess what I really want is justice."

Caswell nodded. "That's better. Justice for you and your friend then. And maybe for your little girl too?"

Adam frowned. "Not just for us though. For all of 'em. All of the people who got caught up in this mess. The other families. Especially the kids."

Caswell swung the door wide and stepped through it. "That's great G. Make it about somethin' bigger than yourself. That's how my sister's makin' it. But can I ask you a question then?"

"Go ahead."

"In the time that you've been here, right up till this very moment, what have you done about that so far?"

Chapter 79

Adam's heart was beating like a trip hammer as he mashed his nose against the tiny window. Where was Caswell? Wasn't it today?

Adam sat back on his bunk and listened for the courthouse clock in the distance. After the fifth month he'd broken the habit of looking down at his left wrist. The angle of the sun through the window was a pretty reliable hour hand and the chimes supplied the minutes, more or less.

Caswell was definitely late.

Which meant that dinner wouldn't be far behind and the whole thing would have to wait until tomorrow. Or next week. Or never.

Adam thought he heard the dinner cart in the hallway, then suddenly the keys were in the lock and there was Caswell.

He stepped in and bounced the cell phone onto the bunk.

"That one's a burner," Caswell said. "Can't use my phone no more. They check it and I'm dead. But you didn't get that one from me, hear? They find it and I don't know you."

Adam instinctively swept his hand across the mattress and cupped the precious contraband behind him.

Caswell looked over his shoulder at the door.

"Gotta go. If this thing is as big as you say it's gonna be, I can't hang around here so much now. They'll investigate. And they'll find that phone, trust me. So better make the call today. Get it done. Her number's already programmed in. You got about an hour till supper. Make it count."

Adam held the phone up between his palms in front of him, a prayer of gratitude.

"Thank you my friend."

"Yeah well, this *is* the Justice Center, I guess," Caswell smirked. "So go get you some."

"Veronica Styles. *Oregonian*."

"Ronnie? It's Adam. From Tektel."

"Yes, I know who you are Adam. Everyone does now. Damn, aren't you still in jail? What did they finally give you your phone call?"

"Ronnie, I've got limited time here. Do you still want to get out of the business section? Maybe win a Pulitzer while you're at it?"

Adam could hear some shuffling in the background, then keys clicking.

"Go."

"So the Governor was arrested five months ago, but I'm betting no one really knows the full backstory yet."

The keys were clicking furiously.

"Just rumors. Some sort of mismanagement over at CPS. The charge was public corruption, but there's a gag order till his trial. Everyone's going crazy here."

Adam could picture the scene. A five foot tall, frizzy-haired woman who'd started thirty years ago with visions of Woodward and Bernstein, only to become a galley slave writing stories about local mergers and the chamber of commerce.

"Indians, Ronnie. Native American kids. All those kids on the reservation who were taken by CPS and ended up in foster care. There was federal money attached to them and it all got funneled to The Longlane Home. Which used to be managed by you-know-who."

Adam could hear a couple of guttural noises, punctuated by more clicking.

"And you know this because....?"

"Steve Carnap set it all up. He and the Governor were in on it together. But those kids have to go *home* Ronnie. Do you understand me? Those Indian kids were basically kidnapped and every day this story doesn't get out is a day they're separated from their families."

There was a pause on the line.

"Ronnie, you still there?"

"They're going to crucify you for telling me this you know. Did you talk to your lawyer? How can this be good for you?"

Adam swallowed dryly.

"I appreciate your concern Ronnie, but I don't give a shit. I'm baked here anyway. Promise me you'll use this. And get those kids free."

Adam heard a cell door slam somewhere down the hallway. Could it be dinner already? Was Caswell coming back?

"You understand that I'll have to verify all this with other sources. But fill in some details first, okay? How long can you talk?"

"Until they take the phone away. I don't know. I was going to call Kate if I had some time left…."

"No, just keep talking."

Adam saw the sunbeam creeping up the doorway and heard a couple of horns honking on 4th Avenue far below. Rush hour.

"Okay I've got about another twenty minutes."

"A lifetime," Ronnie said. "I've been waiting my whole life for this story."

"Okay then." Adam scooted back in his bunk and leaned his head against the wall. "What do you wanna know?"

Chapter 80

Adam was running down the steps of the Multnomah County Courthouse.

Again.

For the second time in seven months, he'd been let out of a jail cell and was moving toward his family. To make things right. To protect them.

Was this a dream? The feeling was delicious.

"Mr. Grammaticus, would you like to make a statement?"

The cops were doing their best to keep the press back, but of course he could still hear their questions.

"Do you feel that you got away with murder?"

Adam hurried toward the taxi. "OHSU Hospital, please. Hurry!"

The taxi leapt away from the curb and the driver banged out a left, so he could get off 4th Avenue and head up toward Pill Hill.

Adam still couldn't believe it.

Everyone knew that Timberline Lodge was on Indian land, but it had never occurred to him that this might have an effect on his own life. Was this really happening?

"Just go," Tugg had said. "One of us had to get lucky."

"Tugg, I can't really leave you here to –"

"Yes you can. Your family needs you. Better go now."

Tugg was still hooked on the charges for Rachel's death and the skinheads, and it was pretty clear that after today's jurisdiction fiasco about Timberline Lodge, the district attorney would be in no mood to look the other way on Tugg's confession.

Technically, Adam wasn't off the hook either. Just a day? Maybe two? The tribe's attorney had argued that the kidnappings and Carnap's death had occurred on Indian land, so they needed to take Adam and Tugg into custody and try them in *their* courts. Of course, whether they refiled the charges might be another matter. But Adam couldn't wait around for that, today of all days.

"Say, you're the guy, right?"

Adam looked up at the eyes regarding him in the rear view mirror. "Yeah, I guess I am."

The road snaked up the hill and Adam slid from one end of the back seat to the other.

"So I was listening on the radio before. Are you an Indian or something?"

"No, not really," Adam said.

The driver took a hairpin turn, then looked at him again in the mirror. "Then you're one lucky guy."

"Yeah, I guess so."

The driver pulled up to the curb. "Too bad about your friend."

No reporters were in the lobby, thank God. Adam hurried down the corridor toward the nurses' station on 6 North.

Was she going to be all right?

Was she in pain?

After court, he'd had time for only a quick word to Tugg before the guards hurried him out a side door, and Adam found himself standing there, a free man, unsure of what would happen next.

His lawyer had slipped him a cell phone. Two minutes later he got a text message from Mrs. Nguyen: *Univ Hospit, hurry!*

He hoped it wasn't too late.

Chapter 81

Adam arrived at the nurses' station and looked in every direction.

All the halls looked alike.

"Excuse me, I'm looking for the maternity —"

"Daddy!"

The sound came to him like an angel. Adam wheeled around and saw her standing at the end of the hallway.

He'd heard that Emma could come home, but the reality of her presence was almost too much for him. Was this another dream?

As Emma bolted toward him, Adam's eyes flooded with tears. All the troubles in the world dissolved as he knelt down and held his arms wide open.

Emma ran into him so hard that Adam collapsed back like a punching-bag clown. They both fell to the hard linoleum floor, crying and laughing at the same time.

As Adam lay on his back, he held Emma's face in his hands and looked at her. "Baby! Sweetie! Are you all right?"

"Daddy! I missed you!"

Adam pulled Emma toward him and hugged her so hard he thought she might break. Then he rolled up into a sitting position and she scrambled into his lap.

"I've been looking for you," Emma said.

She'd been looking for *him*?

"I was looking for you too," Adam said. "A *lot*."

Adam reveled in the smell of her hair. In her bony little arms. She squirmed around and refused to let him get off the floor.

"When can I see my baby brother?"

"I don't think he's born yet. Honey, are you okay?"

"Yes. My hair is longer."

Adam felt like jumper cables had been attached to his heart.

Emma frowned. "Why does everybody keep asking if I'm okay? Mommy's the one who's been in the hospital."

"I don't know, sweetie. But how did you get here? Where's your Mom?"

"They've been letting me see her sometimes. I cried a lot. Then today they said I didn't have to go back to the other house anymore and I could just stay with Mommy till the baby was born."

"Are you here alone?"

Emma held up the sleeve on Adam's polo shirt. "What's this?" She ran her fingers across the tattoo. "That's my name! When did you get it?"

"When I was out looking for *you*. It helped to remind me. Do you like it?"

"Yes."

"Do you think your mom will like it?"

"No."

Adam looked up and saw a figure approaching down the hallway.

"Don't worry, Dad. We're friends now. She's the one who's been bringing me to see Mommy. She's not going to take me back now that you're here, is she?"

Adam lifted his hands to his daughter's face and smoothed away the worry.

"No, never again," Lisa said. She towered over the two of them. "But we'd better get your father off the floor and over to the maternity ward. He still hasn't seen your mother. I can stay with you while he's in there, if you like."

Emma took Lisa's hand, then her father's, and lifted her feet as she swung on their arms while they walked down the hallway.

"It's a high-risk delivery and they've already started," the nurse said.

"But I haven't seen my wife in seven months," Adam pleaded.

The nurse motioned with her eyes and Lisa took the hint. "Emma, let's walk down the hall and look at the babies through the glass."

The nurse turned back to Adam. "You know she has to have a Caesarean."

"I was there when she had the other one."

"But this time you can't. She's already on the table. You'll have to wait here."

Adam sat on the couch and watched Emma push some colored beads along a curved wire. Then she plopped down in front of the fish tank and started naming the fish.

Lisa got up from her seat and joined Adam on the sofa.

"She seems fine," Adam said, marveling at the small miracle before him.

"She *is* fine," Lisa replied. "She's glad to be back, of course, but she shouldn't have any long-term problems. Kids are more resilient than people think. And we had her in a good placement."

Adam nodded and looked down.

"You wife's going to be fine too," Lisa said.

"She's in there alone."

"I asked them to give her a message that you were here. That seemed to calm her."

"She's awake?"

"I think so, but you still can't go in."

Adam sat forward in his seat. "What am I supposed to do? I can't think about anything else."

Lisa put a hand on his arm. "Are *you* okay? You've been through a lot. Do you want to talk about something else?"

Adam looked at her and let a few seconds pass. "How did CPS let you come here today? With me here?"

Lisa hesitated, then gave him a smile. "I quit. I've had enough."

Adam looked at her, uncomprehending.

"Wanda turns out to be quite the rebel. She's down in the lobby. She said I needed closure."

Adam couldn't bring himself to say the words yet, but he hoped his eyes said enough. "So you've been talking to Wanda?"

Now Lisa was smiling for real. "Yes. We've been talking every day. She's been a real help at filling in some missing pieces."

Adam saw his chance and decided to ask his real question. "So what happened to Emma after she left protective custody? How did *that* happen?"

Lisa shook her head. "It looks like Steve Carnap got someone in the Governor's office to override the system. He was in the process of having Emma transferred back to your wife. It was right there on the page, but we were too scared to see it. *Placement terminated: transfer pending.* But the transfer was back to your wife."

Adam's jaw tensed.

So Carnap *had* been telling the truth. Right after he'd completely screwed over Adam's life.

"A regular humanitarian."

Emma was done with the fish. She walked over to a little desk with colored markers and began to draw pictures of the fish.

"Can I ask *you* something?" Lisa said.

"Sure." Adam looked up.

"How in the world did you get Steve Carnap for a lawyer?"

Adam's cheeks burned, but it was a legitimate question.

"My wife's college friend. She's a lawyer back in Boston. Turns out she went to law school with someone on the Governor's staff. When she asked for the name of a good family lawyer in Oregon, guess whose name they gave her?"

"Coincidence?"

Adam shook his head. "Couldn't be. They knew who I was by that point. They were reeling me in. Carnap worked the whole goddamned time to frame me."

Lisa shifted in her seat for a moment, like she was working up to her *real* question. "Frame you for some things, but what about now? I was shocked when I heard what had happened up at Timberline Lodge, but I was even more shocked when I heard this morning that they'd let you go. How did *that* happen?"

Adam studied his hands. "Well, they didn't really have any eyewitnesses."

Lisa gave him an incredulous look.

"Beauchamp was in shock and the Governor has been so discredited that I don't think anybody will ever believe a word he says again. Plus, I don't think he saw what happened to Carnap. Hell, he may even be glad he's dead."

Lisa looked like she'd just bitten into a bad peach.

"And you heard about the jurisdiction issue from today right?" Adam said.

"Yes, it's been all over the news. I guess it's not over with the tribal courts yet, but I gathered that what happened today was pretty extraordinary. Maybe this helped."

Lisa lay a copy of yesterday's *Oregonian* newspaper on Adam's lap and the headline screamed up at him:

STATE VOWS ACTION ON TRIBAL CUSTODY: "Every child will go home."

Adam looked down.

"This is the first newspaper I've seen in months. Did the *Oregonian* already print the Indian – ?"

"It's been full of it. For two weeks now. No one can talk about anything else."

Adam tensed.

"Which must be partially why you had to leave your job –"

Castro looked away for a moment, then shook her head, "It was time for me to go anyway. I don't blame you for that. But I do assume that this was you." Lisa pointed to the paper that was still in his lap. "The reporter hasn't given up her source yet and says she won't, but who else could it be? Only a few people know what really happened: Wanda, a couple of bikers, and maybe a whole lot of Indians."

Adam flashed on what it might look like to see Edward White Robe smiling.

"So you think that might've been what helped me today?" Adam said.

"Probably more than a bit. But there must've been something else too. I heard that Tugg confessed to killing Carnap, but why did they believe him?"

Adam could tell by the question that Lisa believed she was sitting next to the killer. He owed her the truth, but did he owe her a confession?

"A twist of fate and a damn good friend."

Adam saw the look in Lisa's eyes and decided he could risk it.

"It turns out that a Glock is unique. With a standard handgun there are nicks on the bullet from the rifling in the barrel, which is there so the gas can escape when it's fired. The police use those for ballistics. But Glocks use a hexagonal barrel to solve the gas problem instead of rifling. Which means that if you get two Glocks with identical calibers, you can't tell which slug came out of which gun."

"Oh," Lisa said. "It sounds like you're some sort of firearms expert."

"Not me, Tugg."

"I see."

"What?"

Lisa fixed her gaze. "It sounds like the twist of fate and the damn good friend might be the same thing."

Chapter 82

Adam looked down at the beautiful sight before him.

Just as he'd dreamed, his family was back together again — plus one.

Adam sat on the corner of Kate's hospital bed while she tried to nurse the baby. Lisa Castro had left hours ago, as Adam and Kate finally had their tearful reunion in the recovery room. Then they'd gone off to Kate's room, where Emma now slept in an oversized chair in the corner.

They had so much to say, but was now the right time to say it?

"He's beautiful."

"He's you," Kate replied. She tried to push her nipple into his mouth again, but he was still rejecting it. His little stocking cap had slipped down over his eyes. Kate adjusted it.

"I haven't seen you stand yet," Adam said.

"Duh."

"No, I mean how were you during the pregnancy? It must have been terrible."

Kate smiled and looked up at him. "All I did was lie there and think about you and Emma. And I made them work on my leg muscles every day. I'm going to fight this. After all we've been through —"

Adam smiled and brushed a lock of hair from Kate's face. "You are my life."

Kate beamed up at him and snuggled her chin into the palm of his hand.

The little guy looked like he had fallen asleep.

"I'm just so damn relieved that we've got everyone back together again," Adam said. "We'll make it somehow. We came up from nothing once, we can do it again. As long as we're together."

"But for how long?"

"Yeah, I don't know," Adam said. "The tribal court thing will go like it's going to go. But I don't think they're going to come after me for the other stuff now. Tugg's confession put the kibosh on all that. He confessed about Rachel *and* the skinheads, even though I don't think he did either of them."

Kate seemed to get the hint about the skinheads. She'd hadn't asked him about what had happened at the Lodge, so maybe twenty-three years ago didn't matter. It was so long ago.

"So you think Steve Carnap or the Governor killed Rachel?" Kate said.

Adam shook his head. "I don't know. They denied it, but so did Tugg, initially. Then he confessed."

"So you think Tugg did it?" Kate said.

"No, I don't believe that. I don't know what happened but that wasn't it."

The baby gave a grimace and put all four limbs out at once. Then he settled down and went back to sleep. What in the world could he have to dream about?

"So do *you* think Tugg did it?" Adam asked.

"No I'm pretty sure he didn't." Kate looked over at Emma, then down at the baby. "Because I think I did."

Chapter 83

An electric shock passed through Adam's spinal cord. He looked down at Kate, who was fussily rearranging the baby's blanket. He looked toward the door, but it was closed tight. It was just the four of them.

"Kate, how could you do it?"

Kate looked up and stopped smiling. "She threatened my family and lied about my husband."

"No, I mean *how* did you do it? Good God, did Tugg help you?"

"No." Kate was smiling at the baby again. "I said he didn't do it."

Was she really going to make him ask?

Kate wouldn't look at him. "Families in Transition, remember? You're not the only one with loyalties. Or connections to some tough guys."

Kate had a shattered look on her face, but her voice was still strong. A wind over reeds.

"I asked a client whose family I helped out while he was in prison. I won't say his name, but he owed me. He was always asking if there was anything he could do for me. Finally I had something. *I didn't ask him to kill her.* I asked him to go talk to her. Try to get her to confess that she'd made up the whole abuse charge. But I guess things got out of hand."

Adam had the sensation that his body was floating upward.

Kate kept talking. "Anyway, then things got pretty bad. I couldn't tell you because I knew you'd confess to protect me. But I also knew that you'd be the main suspect. The one silver lining was when I remembered that case they dropped when the main witness recanted after the initial abuse allegation. I hoped that maybe the same thing would happen if Rachel was dead and couldn't testify. But I never figured on Steve Carnap. Setting us up the whole time and trying to make you the scapegoat. I hope he suffered."

Adam looked down at the stranger who was wearing his wife's face. Then something occurred to him. "Does Tugg know?"

Kate's eyes were vacant for a moment. "Maybe. But if he does he'll keep quiet. Tugg would never do anything to hurt us. Maybe I should turn myself in."

Was she serious? Adam had had enough sacrifice for a lifetime. But then he saw that the court's judgment wasn't the one she really cared about.

"No, you can't do that." His voice was soft. "Think of Emma and the baby. Think of all we've been through. I would've done the same thing as you. You aren't responsible for how things turned out. There's no going back now. Tugg confessed to four murders that he didn't do, but as long as they're not going to execute him, we can't ever speak of this again. It's too dangerous."

This thing dies with both of us.

Adam was still sitting on the edge of the bed, but the world had shifted. Things had come full circle, but this time the debt had been paid.

"It's like we're throwing him to the wolves." Kate's eyes were glistening.

"No, there's got to be a better way than that," Adam said. "Tugg will be okay. He's been to prison before. And Tugg would say that this was what he wanted. He did what he thought was right – for all of us – and he knew the consequences."

"But that doesn't make it right." Kate's eyes were like crushed grapes now.

They were both silent for a moment before Kate continued.

"We owe Tugg our lives."

"Yes we do," Adam said. "And I'll make sure this comes out right somehow."

Emma shifted in her sleep. Somehow she'd turned four while Adam had been in jail.

"What do you mean?"

Adam gave a cryptic smile. "Trust me. Tugg's a survivor. He'll make it. I'll make sure of it. Tugg will be set for life."

Kate crinkled her eyes. "Adam, that makes no sense. He's hasn't even had a trial yet, let alone been sentenced to life."

"That's not what I mean."

Kate's confusion was palpable, but Adam just let it lie, as he stared off into the mid-distance.

"Life and the next life too, I guess. That's what Kurt always said. Remember, Tugg's one of the Immortals now."

Chapter 84

She looked out the window of the pickup truck and saw the high mesas in the distance. A rooster tail of dust had kicked up behind, but the road ahead was clear and the sky was bottle blue. The wind tousled her hair as it blew through the cab.

Suddenly, she saw a dust cloud up ahead.

What the hell was that? Was it even on the road?

She slowed to a crawl, then realized it was a pack of wild mustangs thundering across the high desert.

Lisa pulled off the road and jumped out of the cab. "Ahhhhhhhh, go go go!" she screamed joyously.

Orange and white. Dappled and grey. She spotted pure black, tan, white, and a couple that were lost in the cloud of dust.

She heard a spurting noise and turned around to see wisps of white smoke coming from her radiator.

Damn.

It had been a long journey. Three hundred miles and about fifteen years, but finally she had made it. Even if she had to walk the rest of the way, she could do it. But which way was town?

Governor Beauchamp had told her that he'd give her his highest recommendation for the new job, for what it was worth. Under the circumstances, she said, it would probably hurt her.

She suspected that Peter Beauchamp was in love with her, but with a five-year age gap and all that had happened, how in the world could she stay? So she'd called in the favor. Played it smart for once. Even if it was tilting at windmills.

"You know he was only 14 when the skinheads were killed, Peter, so that was a juvenile offense anyway."

"Yes, I know it," the Governor replied.

"And there must be enough of a trail between Governor Halliday and Steve Carnap to show that they brought Rachel into it. They were leveraging her by offering a pardon for her brother. They got what they wanted from her once she'd accused Adam. They're probably the ones who killed her, too. Can't you get the police to dig a little? See if there's any evidence?"

"It doesn't matter," Governor Beauchamp said. "They found Morgan's old cell phone in the desert in Arizona. There were calls from the local cell towers five hours before the murder. I'll write the pardon myself. But you know I've got no jurisdiction over the tribal courts. They've got him now. He's locked away tight as a drum from what I hear. And they *are* going to prosecute."

"That's what I heard too," Lisa said.

The horses were gone now, disappeared toward the horizon.

Lisa took out her handkerchief and opened the hood.

A plume of white smoke rose up toward the sky.

Smoke signals, Lisa laughed. Another culturally inappropriate reference that she'd have to scrub from her vocabulary.

It'd be a steep learning curve, but she was committed. How much more good could she do by helping to strengthen the tribal foster care system than she'd done in fifteen years of work for the county? All those Indian kids coming back would need places to go. Most could go straight back to their families, but some had been the victims of real abuse or neglect. She could help with that. After all, placement was her specialty.

Did she really want to walk? Maybe she should call for help. But who did you call for a tow truck on an Indian reservation?

Lisa remembered that she had Tulie Price's number in her cell phone history. Tulie would tease her, of course, but then she'd come. Even if Lisa couldn't describe where she was.

This was Tulie's land. She wouldn't need a milepost to find her.

Lisa spied another dust cloud on the horizon. Damned if she wouldn't learn to ride a horse, now that she was here. But today it was hopeless.

Lisa held her hands up against the bright sun and stared at the approaching cloud. Then she heard the whine of an engine.

She'd be damned if she'd be rescued. Who wanted to start out like that?

Lisa turned around and pretended to work on the radiator.

* * *

"Do you need some help?"

Lisa smiled at the impertinent wall of muscle that was facing her.

No helmet. No leather jacket. No shirt at all. Just black jeans, boots, and a pair of Ray-Bans.

"I thought you biker guys always had to wear your vests."

Lisa could feel his sly smile all the way down to her boots.

"Are you gonna rat me out? Biker clubs usually steer clear of the reservation. They won't see me unless you turn me in."

Lisa squinted into the sunshine. "And I see you're on a brand new bike. Where's your Harley? I thought you guys always rode a Harley?"

"I lost mine. Got a new bike from the tribe, though. Said they owed a debt to a friend of mine. You like it?"

"It's red." Lisa smiled. "But where's your license plate? What kind of motorcycle is that?"

"Don't laugh."

"Why would I laugh?"

"It's called an Indian."

"Oh, that is funny," Lisa said.

"Hey, it's American."

Lisa put her handkerchief back in her pocket and closed the hood.

"And what do I need a license for?" He was tall in his seat. "I don't need no stinking license!"

"Oh, you are a rebel."

"I've got the world right here. A hundred thousand acres." He held his hand out toward the mesas in the distance. "As long as I stay on the reservation, I'm golden."

What did she know? What did anybody know? If he said it, it must be true. Or maybe she knew it from a previous life.

"So do you need a lift?"

Lisa grinned. "It'd be my first time on a motorcycle. And I'm not sure where I'm going."

"That's okay," he said. "I kind of like the sound of that."

Lake Oswego, Oregon
Six Months Later

Kate Grammaticus pulled herself up off the floor and used her canes to walk over to the front door to get the mail.

"Hold him up," she chirped to her daughter Emma. "Jack can't sit up by himself yet."

"Okay, but when *will* he?" Emma said.

"Soon," Kate smiled. "You'll see."

Adam Grammaticus pretended to focus on the stack of papers before him as he sat cross-legged at the coffee table, but he was actually just eavesdropping, reveling in the bliss of domestic life that percolated all around him.

"Adam the benefits package came," Kate said.

"Well, there goes the rest of the afternoon. Let me see it."

"It does weigh a ton."

Kate made her way slowly over to the coffee table and dropped the envelope with a thud.

"If there's a check in there, please fish it out," she said. "I know it's just a start up, but when are they going to send you your first paycheck?"

"Patience my sweet. Patience. Just remember your mantra."

"*Stock options. Stock options.*"

"That's a good girl."

Jack made a funny spitting sound with his tongue and Emma dissolved into laughter.

"I don't think Jackie likes 'sock options'," Emma said, as her parents smiled.

"Oh look," Kate said, rifling the rest of the envelopes, "we got a postcard."

As she turned it over to read, Adam spied a photo of a buxom woman on a red motorcycle on the front: *Come Ride the New Indian.*

"There's no message," Kate said. "Just a postmark from Bridal Veil, Oregon, and some initials."

"What are they," Adam asked.

"IIWII....what's that?"

Adam smiled. "It is what it is. It's a biker thing. It's one of Tugg's stock phrases."

Kate's eyes lit up with possibilities.

"It means you have to accept what you can't change. They've even got a patch for it."

"Is Uncle Tugg coming?" Emma said.

"No, I don't *think* so," Kate answered, handing the postcard to Adam. "He's just saying hello. I *think*."

Adam flipped the postcard over and back several times, then noticed that there was another imprint superimposed next to the postmark. It looked like the faint outline of a lipstick kiss.

Well, I'll be damned, Adam said to himself. *I guess something HAS changed.*

"Adam," Kate called to him, breaking the reverie.

"What?"

"We got something *else* in the mail too. This is even weirder."

Adam pushed himself up and walked over to Kate.

"What is it?"

He put his arms around her slender waist and laid his chin on her tiny shoulder.

"Is this some kind of a joke?" She held out the glossy magazine with a photo of a nearly naked woman in black chaps straddling a motorcycle on the cover. "How in the world did you end up with a subscription to *Easyriders*?"

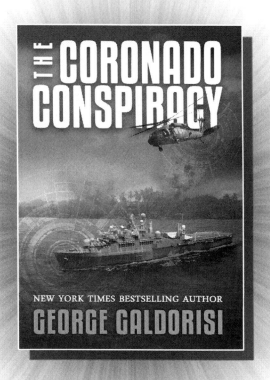

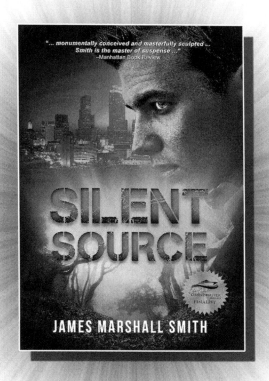

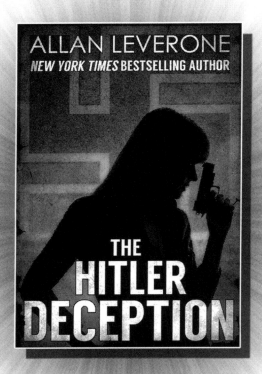

Printed in Great
Britain
by Amazon

31325853R00163